The Landscape of Death

A Yorkshire Murder Mystery

Tom Raven Book 1

M S MORRIS

This book is a work of fiction and, except in the case of historical fact, any resemblance to actual persons, living or dead, is purely coincidental.

M S Morris have asserted their right under the Copyright, Designs and Patents Act 1988 to be identified as the author of this work.

Published by Landmark Media, a division of Landmark Internet Ltd.

msmorrisbooks.com

ISBN-13: 978-1-914537-22-6

CHAPTER 1

It was scarcely eight o'clock on a Monday morning, but already a man had lost his life. Detective Sergeant Becca Shawcross made her sure-footed way across the rocky beach in the direction indicated by the uniformed officer who had met her by the sea wall. Her junior partner, Detective Constable Dan Bennett, stumbled in her wake, panting and muttering. In his sharp suit and polished leather shoes he looked completely out of place in this watery environment. He swore loudly every time he slipped on wet seaweed or stuck his foot ankle-deep into a pool of seawater. Becca sighed at his clumsiness. No doubt his shoes were ruined already.

Becca was Scarborough born and bred and had spent her childhood exploring every inch of this coastline with her brother, always on the hunt for treasure. You never knew what the sea might wash up. Driftwood mostly, which in their childish imaginations had come from wrecked pirate ships or Viking longboats.

This morning the sea had washed up a body.

'Could be a drowning accident, sarge. A fisherman perhaps?' Dan's voice sounded distant, his words whipped away by the gusting wind. Gulls circled overhead, their cries urgent and shrill.

'Hmm.' Becca wasn't willing to speculate until she'd taken a closer look. In her experience it was best to garner the facts first. There had been no overnight calls to the coastguard to report anyone falling overboard or getting into difficulties at sea. There was no telling where the body might have come from.

She lifted a hand to acknowledge a second uniformed officer, who was standing by the body, his fluorescent jacket billowing in the wind. It was a blustery morning in late October and the weak sun was only just scrabbling to climb above the flat horizon of the sea. It had been hard for Becca to drag herself from the comfort of her warm bed when the call came in, but now that she was here, she felt fully awake and energised. Detective work was more than just a job for her. It was what gave her the strength to keep going each day.

'Or maybe he slipped and fell in after too much to drink?' suggested Dan.

This time Becca turned to stare at him, hands on hips. 'You think?' They were at the far end of the North Bay, up near the Sea Life centre, a long way from the bars and amusement arcades that crowded the South Bay. The only nearby drinking establishment was the Old Scalby Mills pub. In any case, it was stretching credulity to think that the man might have slipped and fallen accidentally over the sea wall.

'Or it could be a suicide,' offered Dan.

Becca squelched the last few yards across the hard, wet sand to where the officer was standing, hands clasped behind his back, his big booted feet planted firmly apart to withstand the buffeting of the wind. Only his reddened cheeks betrayed the cold and the salt spray in the air.

'Morning,' said Becca. 'Bit of a stiff north-easterly today.'

'Aye, it is that.' The sea was the dull grey of gunmetal, the sky not much brighter. It would probably rain later. In

October in Scarborough, it always rained later. Unless it was raining already.

'Let's see what we've got then,' she said, snapping on a pair of blue, latex gloves.

The body was wedged between some low rocks, surrounded by seaweed, plastic bottles and other detritus deposited by the sea. At high tide the water came right up to the sea wall, but now it was lapping ten feet or more below where the body lay.

Becca leaned over the man, getting her first impressions. He was lying on his back, one arm twisted sharply behind him, the other outstretched, his sightless eyes turned towards the sky. Young, early to mid-twenties at a guess. Blond, shoulder-length hair. Dressed in jeans and a T-shirt. Not sensible outdoor clothing for this time of year.

'Any ID on him?' she asked.

'Not that I could see,' said the officer. 'No phone, no wallet. Nothing.'

'What are your thoughts now?' she asked, turning to Dan. The DC had fallen strangely silent when faced with an actual body rather than the kind of training exercises they ran at police college.

'Not sure,' said Dan, fidgeting nervously with his cufflinks. 'Had we better move him before the tide comes in?'

'It's already been in. That's how he washed up here.'

Dan glanced at her uncertainly. 'How do you know that?'

'Because the sand and rocks are all wet. So are his clothes.' Becca caught the eye of the uniformed officer, who treated her to a wry grin.

There were signs that the body had been in the water for some time. The man's skin was pale and waterlogged, his lips tinged with blue, his body bloated and entangled with seaweed.

'A drowning accident, then,' concluded Dan.

'Or it could have been the bullet that killed him.'

'What? But there's no blood.' Dan sounded defensive, as if he thought he was being teased.

'Washed away by the sea.' Becca knelt down, smoothed out the wrinkled T-shirt and pointed to a hole in the fabric, close to the man's heart. She lifted the shirt to expose the wound in the man's chest. Definitely a bullet hole.

Dan swallowed and took a step back. His skin had turned almost as pale as the corpse.

A man shot and thrown into the sea. Not a pleasant way for Becca to begin her working day. And not the first such murder to come to her attention.

But where had he come from? There were strong currents in the sea off Scarborough. In the summer a surfer had been caught in a rip tide down in Cayton Bay, and a boy had been dragged under near the spa. The current moved in a southerly direction, so if he'd washed up here he could well have entered the water further north, an uninhabited stretch of coastline. Once they'd done the post-mortem and got an idea how long he'd been in the sea, they could speak to the coastguard and try to narrow it down. But it would be an approximate location at best.

Becca tilted her head towards a woman who was perched on a rock a little distance away. 'Is she the one who found him?'

'Aye, that's her,' said the officer. 'A dogwalker.'

'I'll have a quick word with her.'

The woman rose to her feet as Becca approached. She was late fifties – about the same age as Becca's mum – and dressed for beach walking in a pair of polka dot Wellington boots and a long, waxed coat. A bedraggled cocker spaniel was sniffing around the rock pools nearby. The dog trotted over to Becca and she bent down to rub its ears. Dan kept his distance from the animal.

'Morning,' said Becca, extending a hand. 'I'm Detective Sergeant Becca Shawcross and this is my colleague Detective Constable Dan Bennett. We're with North Yorkshire Police, based here in Scarborough.'

'Barbara Smith,' said the woman, shaking Becca's

hand. Strands of grey hair were escaping from beneath a hand-knitted beanie.

'You've had a nasty shock this morning,' said Becca. She wished she'd thought to bring a thermos of tea with her. The woman looked like she could do with warming up and her hand had been icy. 'Can you talk me through what happened?' She mimed note-taking to Dan and after a moment he got the hint, retrieving a notepad and pencil from his jacket pocket.

'I was taking Charlie for his walk.' At the sound of his name the dog looked up expectantly. 'He likes to run on the beach and examine the rock pools. But this morning when I called him he wouldn't come back, which isn't like him. He's a good dog really.'

'I'm sure he is.' Becca had always wanted a dog but it wasn't practical in her parents' house which doubled as a bed & breakfast.

'Anyway, once I'd caught up with him,' continued the woman, 'I saw what he'd found.' She glanced warily in the direction of the body. The CSI team had arrived and were now making their way over the rocks with all their equipment. The woman shifted her attention back to Becca. 'That poor boy – well, I suppose he's a young man really – just lying there. He was obviously dead, there was nothing I could do except call the police. There's not much more to say, really. Except that I didn't touch the body, because I know you're not supposed to tamper with the evidence. Although Charlie poked his nose in before I could stop him.'

'That's all right,' said Becca, looking fondly at the dog. 'I'm sure he won't have done any harm. What time was this?'

'Seven fifteen. I remember seeing the time on my phone when I called the police.'

'And was there anyone else around then?'

'Not a soul. It was still quite dark. That's why I like it here. Charlie and I usually have the place to ourselves.'

'Do you come here often?'

'Most mornings, at least if it's not bucketing down or blowing a gale.'

'You live nearby?'

'Scholes Park Road in Scalby.'

'I know it,' said Becca. Her maternal grandparents lived in a bungalow on Scalby Mills Road overlooking the golf course. Quite possibly her Nana and Grandad were passing acquaintances of Barbara Smith and her dog Charlie, but now wasn't the time to get into local gossip. 'Okay,' said Becca, 'if you could give DC Bennett here your contact details then once he's written up your report, he can pop round and get you to sign it. Will that be all right?'

Barbara Smith nodded her head vigorously. 'Of course, anything I can do to help.'

Becca rubbed Charlie's ears once again and was rewarded with a lick of his pink tongue. She waited until she was sure that Dan knew what he was doing, then she went to meet the CSI team who were struggling to erect a tent against the wind.

'Sod it,' said a woman's voice from beneath a sheet of billowing white polyester. 'Forget the tent. We're not going to be here long enough to make it worth our while. We'll manage perfectly well without it.'

The CSI team leader disentangled herself, her coveralls already caked in wet sand, leaving her young assistant to continue battling with the disobedient tent. In her early forties, Holly Chang was second-generation Hong Kong Chinese and diminutive in stature, but she was as fierce and stubborn a Yorkshire-woman as any Becca knew. Holly had risen through the ranks to become one of the most respected crime scene investigators in North Yorkshire Police. She had a reputation for thoroughness and was as tenacious as a Yorkshire Terrier. She also had the ability to remain cheerful and totally unflustered in the face of even the most brutal crimes.

'Morning,' said Holly brightly as if they were meeting by the coffee machine in a warm office. 'They got you out here early then?'

'I live nearby,' said Becca. It was only a five-minute drive from her parents' B&B on North Marine Road to the Sea Life centre where she'd parked her car.

'Single gunshot wound to the chest,' said Holly with a nod to the victim. 'But I guess you'd already worked that out.'

'But no ID on him by the looks of it.'

Holly shook her head. 'No phone, no wallet, but I did remove this from the body.' She held out a clear-plastic evidence bag. A gold ring nestled at the bottom.

Becca held it up to the grey light, but couldn't see anything special about the ring. She sensed that the CSI team leader was waiting for her to notice something.

'Take a closer look,' said Holly. 'On the inside.'

Becca peered through the plastic bag. Sure enough, two names were engraved on the inside of the ring in fancy lettering. *'Tristan & Iseult,'* she read aloud. She raised her eyebrows at Holly.

Holly shrugged. 'Don't ask me what it means. I just collect the evidence. It's up to you what you do with it.'

Becca nodded. 'I'll wait until you finish searching the area.'

'Don't hold your breath,' said Holly. 'The sea's probably washed everything away.'

Becca thrust her hands in her pockets, wishing again for a hot mug of tea. Overhead the gulls cackled, and on the headland the ruins of the castle looked down, its empty windows like watchful eyes over the bay. But whatever those eyes had witnessed, they were keeping it to themselves.

CHAPTER 2

It was the landscape that told him he was home. Not the people, nor the weather – though both were very different here to the place he had left behind – but the crests and folds of the land itself. In London, the sky was glimpsed only in the narrow spaces held between concrete and glass. Here, it was everywhere. Big, bright, and always in motion, just like the sea that rose to meet it at the far-off line of the horizon.

Tom Raven stood at the top of Woodlands Cemetery, contemplating the distant headland, his overcoat buttoned up against the biting north-easterly that was blowing all the way from Scandinavia.

His father's funeral had been a perfunctory affair, the first of the day at the crematorium, and the celebrant leading it had given the impression of wanting to get it over and done with before moving on to better attended ceremonies. Raven didn't blame him. He'd wanted it to be over too. He didn't know the two old men who'd wheezed and coughed their way through the proceedings. Probably drinking cronies from the Golden Ball on Sandside or wherever Alan Raven had drunk away the remaining years of his life. Raven wouldn't know. He hadn't seen his father in nearly thirty years. And now he would never see him again.

It was the solicitor, a Mr Harker from a small local firm in York Place, who had tracked him down in London and informed him by phone of his father's death. 'A sudden cardiac arrest on his way back from the pub,' Harker had explained in the sort of voice used to convey bad news while avoiding upset. 'It would have been very quick, I'm sure. Passers-by called for an ambulance but there was nothing they or the paramedics could do. I'm very sorry.' Raven had thanked the solicitor for getting in touch and had then gone straight back to work, putting together the case for the Crown Prosecution Service against a man charged with aggravated burglary and grievous bodily harm. The man's sadistic assault of an elderly woman in her own home hadn't been nearly as quick as Alan Raven's heart attack, nor had there been any helpful passers-by to come to her assistance. Now the best Raven could hope for was that the perpetrator would get a few years behind bars. His victim would get nothing. It was the kind of case that made Raven wonder if his work really made any difference to people's lives. Suffering and misery were his bread and butter these days.

The news of his father's death had taken a while to sink in. If he was honest with himself, he was surprised that the old man had lasted this long. *Not dead yet* was probably a fitting description of his dad's final years. His liver must have resembled a pickled herring. Well he was dead now. And Raven wasn't sure how he felt about it. Weren't you supposed to feel guilty for not having patched up a relationship that had foundered decades ago? Well, it took two to mend a broken bridge, and Alan Raven had never shown the slightest desire to reach out to his son.

He lifted his gaze to the heavy clouds streaming low overhead. His father had never believed in God, and it was hard to imagine him up in Heaven now, unless Heaven was stocked with enough bottles of whisky to drown out an eternity's worth of regrets and self-pity. As for himself, he yearned to believe in a world better than this one, but his trust had been broken too many times for him to have any faith in promises of an afterlife.

After learning of his father's death, he'd spoken to his boss at the Met and requested a fortnight's leave. Not so much on compassionate grounds, but on practical ones. As his father's only living relative, the burden of sorting out his worldly affairs fell on him.

'Take as long as you need, Tom,' the Chief Super had said, glancing up briefly from his desk. 'I'm very sorry for your loss.' Mechanical words, that Raven himself had used professionally so many times and that meant as little as *hello* or *good morning*.

'Two weeks will be plenty,' Raven had assured him. With his father's meagre possessions and solitary existence, he expected to be done within the week.

The following day he'd driven up to Scarborough, intending to stay in one of the town's many hotels – he could easily have found somewhere nice at short notice during the off-season, but had somehow ended up back in his dad's house – his own childhood home – on Quay Street near the harbour. It was as convenient a place as any.

He rubbed his hands together and thrust them into his coat pockets as the wind whipped the grass between the headstones. He should have thought to bring gloves. And a scarf. The temperature on the North Yorkshire coast was always well below that of London, and the windspeed several miles an hour faster. Perhaps he'd grown soft, living in the south for so long. If so, the weather seemed determined to punish him for his lack of fortitude. Icy gusts ruffled his hair, carrying the salty tang of the sea. It was invigorating, for sure. He inhaled the sharp air and let out his breath in a long sigh. That was something you couldn't do in London – breathe deeply. Not unless you fancied a lungful of carbon monoxide and diesel particulates.

With the funeral done and dusted, he still had a week

before he was due back at his desk in London. All that remained now was to clear out his dad's old house and put the property up for sale. He didn't expect to get much for it, not considering the state of the place. An optimistic estate agent had described it as a "great opportunity for a buyer willing to do a bit of work". In fact, the place needed gutting. New bathroom, new kitchen, total refurbishment throughout. The plumbing was shot, the wiring a deathtrap. He should get rid of the place as quickly as possible. Make it someone else's problem.

So, why hadn't he told the estate agent to put it on the market?

Standing here on the raised ground of the cemetery, looking out at the headland and the steel-grey sea beyond, he began to understand why he was dragging his feet over the house. He felt a connection to this rugged coastline in a way that surprised him. It was as if the landscape itself was stirring something deep inside, awakening a sense of belonging he never knew existed. Or had chosen to forget. He'd been gone for thirty years, having left at the age of sixteen to join the army, vowing never to return. But now, gazing out at the distant line of the shore, the wind doing its best to flatten him, he felt alive in a way he hadn't done for a long time. Maybe not since his teenage years.

He'd promised the Chief Super he'd be back at his desk as soon as he could, but already his London life – the one-bedroom flat in Clapham, the grind of the daily commute, the faces of his colleagues – seemed distant and remote, as if he'd only dreamt them. His first evening back in Scarborough, he'd walked past a fish and chip shop and the smell of salt and vinegar on freshly-fried batter had transported him straight back to his youth. The next thing he knew he was walking along the sea front eating fat, juicy chips out of paper and sinking his teeth into the best battered haddock he'd tasted in decades. London chippies did their best, but they weren't a patch on those in Scarborough.

In his mind, a radical idea was taking shape. A

dangerous idea. Could he just stay here? Not return after two weeks as planned? Not return… at all?

All that was keeping him in London was his job as a detective chief inspector with the Met. A job he was good at, and that he'd made sacrifices for. But London was an impersonal place and it was sometimes hard to push aside the feeling that he was trying in vain to hold back a tide of crime that would one day overwhelm him. The pace of life in the capital was exhausting, and while he didn't care to admit it, he wasn't getting any younger. As for Lisa, his wife of twenty-three years, she was one of the sacrifices he'd made along the way. Lisa certainly wasn't keeping him at home anymore. She had left him and moved in with Graham, an accountant, whose main attraction seemed to be that he worked regular hours and drove a sensible car. Lisa's justification for leaving Raven had been that she saw so little of him she might as well have been single. And what about the most important person in his world, his daughter Hannah? As much as he still imagined her as his little girl, he had to face facts. She was twenty years old and in her final year of a degree in Law at Exeter University. She was talking about travelling and doing voluntary work overseas. She didn't need him anymore.

Well, he couldn't stand here in the wind all day mulling it over. His right leg was already starting to throb in the cold – a legacy of the old injury that had caused him to quit the army and join the police force. With one final look at the view, he started back down the hill, wrapping his coat around him and promising himself that by the time he got back to Quay Street, he'd have made up his mind.

CHAPTER 3

'You should have seen him,' Dan Bennett was saying to DC Tony Bairstow, his hands busily miming the lurid scene he had witnessed on the beach that morning. 'His face was all bloated and there was seaweed stuck to his...'

Now that they were back at the station, Dan had overcome his earlier squeamishness and was gleefully giving anyone who would listen all the gory details of the morning's discovery, contorting his bland but good-looking features into a hideous mask, and embellishing freely for effect. Anyone would think he'd single-handedly pulled the body from the waves instead of just trailing around uselessly in Becca's wake. She wished he'd get on with the job of checking the missing persons' register, which was what she'd asked him to do. They were still no nearer to getting an ID for the victim.

She cleared her throat and Dan jumped, his sensational account of the discovery of the body coming to an abrupt end.

Tony gave her a grateful look and went back to checking the tide times on his computer screen. A man of few words, Tony would give her an answer when he was good and ready. But it would be an answer she could rely on.

Becca had stayed with Holly and the CSI team until they'd finished scouring the beach for evidence, but they'd found nothing more. She had returned to base, expecting the place to be all action stations. But while people were keen to get going – a murder made a change from break-ins at amusement arcades, drunken revellers on the Foreshore, and nightclub brawls – the investigation had barely got off the ground and it was already mid-afternoon. Becca hated wasting time. The first twenty-four hours in a murder enquiry were crucial. Everyone knew that.

She'd phoned her mum at lunchtime to say she'd be back late and not to bother cooking an evening meal for her. Sue Shawcross had expressed her usual motherly concern, reminding Becca to eat properly, while digging brazenly for information. 'Was it an accident? The tides can be treacherous. Was it anyone you know?' They had already had a journalist on the phone and no doubt the story would be all over *The Scarborough News* before long. You couldn't keep a dead body quiet in a place the size of Scarborough, especially not one that had washed up on the beach. But there was nothing that Becca could tell her mother, not just because details of the case were confidential, but because no one had any idea who the victim was or how he had come to be found at the top of the North Bay. What the investigation needed was someone to give it clear direction.

Instead, they'd been lumbered with Detective Inspector Derek Dinsdale.

Becca had groaned on hearing that Dinsdale had been assigned the role of Senior Investigating Officer. Couldn't the Super have found someone more inspiring, someone capable of rallying the troops and getting things done? It was common knowledge in the station that Dinsdale was cruising until his retirement, his feet quite often literally to be found on his desk. He'd already bought himself an apartment in Bridlington with a sea view. When Becca had reported to him that morning, he'd had a golfing magazine open in front of him. Right now, he was on the phone and had been for the last half hour. She wouldn't have been surprised if he was checking his pension fund or booking his summer holiday for the coming year. He hadn't even visited the location where the body had been found. If Becca had been running this investigation, she'd have wanted to see the beach for herself before the sea washed it clean. But as a detective sergeant, she was too far down in the pecking order to be considered as SIO for a murder investigation.

'How are you getting on with missing persons?' she asked Dan. She noticed that he'd taken the time to brush the sand from his shoes, even though he showed little urgency to get any real work done.

'There's no one on the system who might be a match.'

'No one?' She blinked in disbelief. Somebody was reported missing in the UK every ninety seconds.

'Not by the name of Tristan,' said Dan.

Becca looked at him blankly. 'Sorry?'

'Well, the guy had his name engraved on his ring, didn't he? So I've been looking through the lists for a Tristan, but–'

'That's not his real name,' interrupted Becca, failing to keep the impatience out of her voice.

'It isn't?' said Dan. 'But I thought the name on the ring…' His voice trailed off under her stare.

Becca almost felt sorry for him when he gazed up at her with those puppy-dog eyes, but her sympathy didn't last long. 'Tristan and Iseult are fictional characters from an old story,' she explained as patiently as she could. 'Tristan is a knight and Iseult is a princess. They have a doomed, adulterous affair and it all ends in tragedy.' She'd googled the details on her phone and found that the story originated in the twelfth century. It was linked to Arthurian legend and had been turned into an opera by Wagner. A love potion was involved, apparently. 'Tristan and Iseult are probably just nicknames.'

'Oh,' said Dan, looking deflated.

Becca noticed that Tony was suppressing a smile.

'Keep checking through the lists,' she said in what she hoped was an encouraging tone of voice, 'and keep an open mind. Remember, we're looking for an IC1 male, aged early to mid-twenties, blond hair, five foot eleven.'

She glanced across at Dinsdale's office, separated from the main room by a glass partition. He was still on the phone. That gave her time to do some digging of her own.

The morning's discovery bore a marked similarity to a case she had worked on three years earlier as a newly appointed DC: a body with a bullet wound to the chest washed up on the beach. Come to think of it, Dinsdale had been in charge of that case too. Becca's role had been confined mainly to taking witness statements. She hadn't been privy to the big picture, and it wouldn't hurt to refresh her memory of the case. They'd put a man behind bars for that murder, but given what she'd seen this morning, she had to wonder if they'd got the right man. She had just logged on to the police database when DC Jess Barraclough burst into the room in her usual whirl of energy.

'I'm dying for a cuppa,' said Jess, shrugging off her parka and blowing on her wind-reddened hands. 'Anyone else in need of a brew?'

'I'll give you a hand,' said Dan, jumping to his feet.

Becca and Jess exchanged a look. The fact that Dan was besotted with the sassy, young constable was no secret. The fact that he didn't stand a chance was common knowledge to everyone except him.

Jess and Dan returned a few minutes later with a tray of steaming mugs and a plate of chocolate Hobnobs that Jess had conjured up from somewhere. *Bless her*, thought Becca. She was just the sort of person you needed on your team. Becca took a mug of tea and helped herself to a couple of biscuits. Despite her mother's exhortations to take care of herself, it was hours since she'd eaten or drunk anything.

'How did the door-to-door go?' she asked.

'Zilch,' said Jess, dunking her biscuit in her tea and taking a bite. 'We knocked on every door in Scalby, but no one knew a thing. They were no help at the Sea Life centre either. I spoke to the landlord at the Old Scalby Mills but he couldn't recall seeing anyone matching the victim's description. A couple of old sea dogs having a lunchtime drink said he must have gone into the water further up the coast to have washed up where he did.'

Further up the coast. Becca had deduced that much already. It didn't give them much to go on. *Further up the coast* could mean anywhere between Scarborough and the north of Scotland. She looked once again in Dinsdale's direction. He'd finally put the phone down and it was about time something happened. Taking the initiative, she marched over to his office, knocked twice, and poked her head around the door without waiting for a response.

'Sir, shall I gather everyone together for a briefing? The door-to-door team just got back.' Not that they had anything to report, but that wasn't the point. It was time Dinsdale gave the team a clear lead. She was fed up of doing his job for him and not getting the credit.

'What's that?' He was shuffling papers around his desk and barely glanced in her direction. Did he even know who she was?

'I just thought it would be good for team morale if we could pool our knowledge so far.' Did she have to spell it out for him?

He looked up then. 'Yes, yes, all right. Just give me a minute.'

'Thank you, sir. I'll make sure everyone is ready.' She left the room, leaving the door open behind her. 'Team meeting,' she announced, loud enough for Dinsdale to hear.

Five minutes later, the DI finally emerged from his lair. Dressed in a brown suit with a dusting of dandruff on his shoulders, Dinsdale's appearance did nothing to inspire confidence. His tie was askew and his shirt buttons were straining against his paunch. None of that would have mattered if under the shambling exterior there had been a charismatic personality or a sharp mind. Becca's grandmother was a big fan of the seventies TV show *Columbo* with the eponymous detective in his crumpled raincoat. But while Dinsdale could give Columbo a run for his money in the clothing department, he lacked the TV detective's charm and insight. The team hardly paid him any attention as he ambled to the whiteboard.

'All right,' called out Becca, clapping her hands together for attention. 'Quiet, please.'

A hush fell and everyone looked expectantly at their boss. He was studying the photographs on the whiteboard as if seeing them for the first time. Eventually he turned to face the room. 'All right,' he said. 'This is our victim. White male, found washed up on the beach with a bullet in his chest. Do we have an ID yet? His name is Tristan, is that right?' Dinsdale cast a glance around his team, waiting for a response.

'Sir.' Becca raised her hand. 'We're searching missing persons for an ID. The victim was wearing a ring engraved with the names Tristan and Iseult, but' – she wondered how to frame her response tactfully – 'these may well be nicknames. However, as I'm sure you're aware, this case bears a marked similarity to–'

The door opened and Detective Superintendent Gillian Ellis entered the room. Everyone jumped immediately to their feet and Becca noticed Dan quickly tucking his shirt front into his trousers. Dinsdale straightened his tie and ran a hand through his thinning hair.

'As you were,' said the Super, with the graciousness of one who knew she commanded respect, fear even, and could afford to be magnanimous to her subordinates. A broad woman in her early fifties, Ellis had not risen to the top of Scarborough's CID by being weak or submissive. She could be abrasive at times, but in Becca's opinion she was worth a hundred Dinsdales.

Everyone sat down again but with straighter backs than before. No one ever slouched in the presence of the Detective Superintendent.

'I was just–' Dinsdale began.

Ellis cut him off. 'DI Dinsdale, my office now if you wouldn't mind.' Whether he minded or not was clearly irrelevant. The Super didn't wait for a response but left as abruptly as she'd arrived. Dinsdale followed her with a look of annoyance.

Well, that's the end of the team meeting, thought Becca. It had barely started. She checked her watch. It was already nearly six. Probably too late to phone the pathology lab and see when they were likely to do the post-mortem. She sensed a restlessness in the team – having stopped what they were doing for the sake of the meeting, there was now little enthusiasm for returning to their computer screens. She didn't blame them. It had already been a long day, especially for herself and Dan. She considered giving her mum a call and saying she'd be home in time for the evening meal after all, when the door opened again and Dinsdale reappeared, red-faced. Meetings with the Super weren't usually over so quickly.

Instead of resuming his position in front of the whiteboard, he went straight to his office and slammed the door behind him. Becca caught Jess's surprised look. What was going on? Maybe the Super had told him to get his act together. Through the glass wall, Dinsdale appeared to be stuffing objects into his briefcase.

A minute later his office door flew open and he stormed out. Without a word of explanation or a backward glance at the team, he kicked open the door of the incident room and disappeared down the corridor. The team sat in stunned silence.

'Did he just get the boot?' Dan was the first to speak. For once, it looked as if his conjecture might not be wrong.

Before the speculation could start in earnest, the Detective Superintendent reappeared, followed by a tall man in a dark suit and black tie. He looked as if he'd just come from a funeral and had an expression to match, his heavy brows knitted together in a brooding, saturnine manner. They all rose to their feet again, but Ellis bade them sit back down with a hand motion.

As if she were controlling a pack of dogs.

The Super took up Dinsdale's former position in front of the whiteboard, hands clasped together, back ramrod straight, like a headmistress about to lead a school assembly. Or a military leader announcing the overthrow of the government.

'This' – she indicated the stranger to her right – 'is Detective Chief Inspector Tom Raven. He's transferring to this department from London and will be taking over the case from DI Dinsdale who has been reassigned to other duties. DCI Raven is to begin immediately, and I'm sure that everyone here will do their best to make him feel welcome. Any questions?'

They were all too shocked to say a word.

CHAPTER 4

The gulls woke him with their raucous cries. Tourists and visitors to Scarborough called them seagulls, but being a local, Raven knew they were herring gulls. Big and belligerent, they were not to be confused with the smaller kittiwakes that only stayed during the spring and summer months to nest and raise their young. The herring gulls were the bully boys of the beach, strutting around like gang members, screeching like banshees and stealing chips from unsuspecting holidaymakers. Raven hated them.

But they were a part of him too.

Lying in his childhood bed at the top of the three-storey house, the wailing of the vociferous rulers of the sky took him back forty years or more. He vividly remembered the time when, as a little kid of no more than six or seven, a gull had snatched an ice-cream cone out of his hand just as he was about to take that first, mouth-watering lick. The brazen robbery had brought tears to his eyes, but his father had shown no sympathy. 'What's a big boy like you blubbering for?' he'd said. 'You should've eaten it quicker. You'll know next time.' His mother had looked at him kindly, but hadn't dared to contradict his father. Neither of them had bought him a replacement ice-cream.

His first experience of loss, but not his last.

He pushed back the layers of sheets, blankets and eiderdown that covered the bed, made up the old-fashioned way his mother had always insisted upon. Raven felt trapped under the tucked-in bedding. He couldn't remember the last time he'd slept under a blanket or an eiderdown. But it was cold enough here to appreciate their warmth.

He rubbed his legs into life and swung his feet onto the bedside rug. His father, like a lot of old people, seemed to have acquired a great many rugs over the years. They were everywhere in the house – beside the beds, in front of the fireplaces, in the hallway, even in the bathroom. On the upstairs landing they were shoehorned in so tightly they overlapped. It was a wonder the old man hadn't tripped and broken his neck in a drunken stupor.

They would all have to go.

Raven opened the curtains and peered through the salt-encrusted window. Another overcast day, the sky a dull grey, promising rain. He stretched, yawned, and made his way down the creaking stairs to the bathroom on the ground floor.

The house was tall and narrow with a winding staircase running through the middle. His childhood bedroom and a box room occupied the top floor. On the middle floor were his parents' old room and a guest room. Not that Raven could recall any guests ever coming to stay. The ground floor boasted a living room that was so outdated it was almost retro chic, a kitchen with a lethal-looking gas cooker and an under-the-counter fridge, and a tiny bathroom tacked on to the back of the house in place of the old outhouse in the yard. There was an attic in the roof, accessed via a trap door on the top landing, but he'd never ventured up there and had no idea what it might contain.

There were no photos of his father in the house, thankfully, and there were certainly none of himself. But a silver-gilt frame on the mantelpiece contained a faded print showing his mum sitting on the beach in front of the pier. She must have been about forty when it was taken, and she was wearing a simple cotton dress and a sunny smile. It was how he remembered her. It was how he would always remember her.

There was no proper shower in the bathroom, just a rubber shower hose attached to the bath taps so you could rinse your hair. The bath itself was not big enough for him to lie in at full stretch. The sink was tiny and missing a plug, and the toilet had a chain-flush cistern fixed high on the wall. The water heater was temperamental and made its own rules about whether or not it would work. Raven ran enough lukewarm water to wash himself in the tub and then, wiping the mirror with a damp towel, prepared to shave. Looking at his face in the mildew-spotted glass – black stubble, heavy brow, premature wrinkles around his mouth and eyes – he wondered what Detective Superintendent Gillian Ellis had seen in him that had made her take such extraordinary action yesterday.

He still couldn't quite believe the speed at which events had moved. In the morning he'd bid his final farewells to his father. In the afternoon, his request for a transfer had been accepted and he'd been put in charge of a murder enquiry. Well, there had been a few steps in between.

After leaving the cemetery, he'd gone to the police station on Northway and asked to speak to the person in charge. He hadn't really expected to be admitted. If no one had been available, he would have gone straight round to the estate agent's and put the house on the market and that would have been that. The decision about whether to stay in Scarborough or return to London would have been made for him. A sliding doors moment. Instead, he'd been shown into the office of Detective Superintendent Gillian Ellis. A big woman, who filled her chair and seemed to fill the whole office with her presence. She'd gripped his hand like a wrestler, peered at him over the top of her reading glasses and listened to what he had to say, her expression giving nothing away. But eventually her face had broken into a sudden smile and she'd told him something he hadn't expected to hear.

'DCI Raven, I don't believe in miracles, but you might just be the answer to my prayers.'

Raven had assumed that a transfer or even a temporary secondment to Scarborough CID would take weeks if not months to arrange. He hadn't even discussed the matter with his superiors in London yet. But it seemed that once Gillian Ellis made a decision, she didn't hang around or allow petty bureaucracy to slow her down. A phone call to his boss at the Met, another to the Assistant Chief Constable of North Yorkshire Police, and a secondment had been arranged in less time than it took to process a detainee and put them into custody.

'You should understand that you're here on a trial basis,' Gillian told him, some of the grit returning to her voice. 'But a case has just come in and, well, suffice to say that it wouldn't hurt for a fresh pair of hands to be in charge. Someone with no preconceptions.'

Maybe he should have asked more questions. Preconceptions about what? And what kind of case? But it wasn't every day that someone told him he was the answer to their prayers. He'd been flattered. And what the hell. If it didn't work out, he could always return to London. This was a temporary secondment, Gillian had made that clear enough. It would do him good to get away from the capital. Put some distance between himself and Lisa. If he was up here, there was no chance he might be tempted to go round and punch her new boyfriend in the face or kick out the headlights of his Volvo. It was safer for everyone.

Dinsdale, the DI he'd replaced, hadn't looked too kindly on him. He'd been summoned into Gillian's office and promptly dismissed from the investigation. *A sideways transfer*, Gillian had called it, though it was obvious that Dinsdale didn't see it that way. But it wasn't Raven's fault that the Super didn't think the man was up to the job.

It was a surprise to learn that the case he was going to

be heading up was a murder enquiry. He didn't suppose there were a lot of those in Scarborough. But it would give him a chance to demonstrate his experience and expertise to Gillian.

He dressed once more in his funeral attire – the dark suit, black tie and somewhat creased shirt were the only smart clothes he'd brought with him from London – and grabbed his car keys. There was nothing in the house for breakfast. His father didn't appear to have had any food, and Raven still hadn't found the time to go shopping. There'd been a half-finished bottle of whisky on the kitchen worktop, and he had poured its contents down the sink and put the empty bottle out with the recycling.

He'd pick up a coffee at the station – unless he passed anything better on the way. In the Scarborough of his youth there had been nowhere to drink except tea houses and pubs, but surely Starbucks and their ilk had made it this far north by now.

He smiled to himself when he saw his car waiting for him like a faithful friend. Quay Street was far too narrow to accommodate his BMW M6, and in any case had double yellow lines painted down both sides, so he'd left it in the tiny car park at the end of the road, more than filling the bay.

Long, wide and low, the gleaming silver coupé was his pride and joy. Lisa would have preferred to own a bland five-door SUV like all the other families they knew. A box on wheels, in other words. She complained that with only two doors and such cramped rear seating it was far too impractical for a family car. Well, okay, he'd never seen it as the *family* car. It was *his* car.

He had let her choose their kitchen, their bathroom, their dining-room furniture, their soft furnishings, and just about everything else in their home, and had never once complained. Let Lisa moan all she liked. The M6 devoured miles like a hungry surfer tucking in to a large portion of fish and chips. And it drank petrol like, well, like an alcoholic on a bender. But the chassis would have to fall to pieces before he'd consider getting rid of it. Especially now.

Now that he'd made the move from London, the BMW was all he had left of his former life. The reality of that dramatic break hadn't quite hit him yet. Perhaps the magnitude of his decision would rise up and kick him in the gut in the days to come. Or perhaps, like so many of his life choices, he would bury it firmly in the past.

He realised then, that by choosing to stay in Scarborough he was giving up on Lisa. Well, so be it. She was the one who had dumped him and his fast car for an accountant with a family hatchback. When exactly had she lost her taste for excitement? He wondered if it had somehow been his fault that she'd grown so staid over the years, or if that was just what happened under the weight of adult responsibility. Perhaps that burden had been what truly drove them apart in the end. It should have been a shared burden, yet each had chosen to shoulder it alone.

He sank into the driver's seat and breathed in the familiar smell of worn leather. The V10 engine roared to life when he started the ignition. Seventeen years old, and still going strong. Were car years like dog years? That would make the M6 a hundred and nineteen in human terms. For such an old lady, she was in remarkably good shape. He tapped the steering wheel. 'Welcome to Scarborough, old girl.'

CHAPTER 5

Raven could tell they'd been talking about him from the way they all fell silent when he entered the incident room. Their eyes followed him as he crossed the room into Dinsdale's hastily-vacated office. He glanced around. A small room, screened off from the rest of the space behind a glass partition, with a desk and some shelving. Not quite the swish modern surroundings Raven had enjoyed in the Met, but he didn't care for status symbols. It was people who mattered, not fixtures and fittings.

He propped the door open with a chair – he didn't believe the senior investigating officer should be cut off from the rest of the team – and re-entered the main room bearing an armful of paper bags, which he deposited on a spare desk. He could feel all eyes on him.

Turning around, he took in his team. They were all at their desks, a mix of ages and sexes, but no one of rank higher than detective sergeant. It was a smaller team than he was used to working with, but Gillian had assured him they were competent. Well, he would find out for himself soon enough.

Gillian had run through their names with him the previous day, and Raven had a good memory for names and faces. Right now, all the faces were focussed on him. He supposed he must be an object of intense curiosity, this stranger who had come from nowhere and replaced the former SIO so suddenly.

He gestured at the paper bags. 'Breakfast is on me today,' he said. 'But don't get used to it. I'm not usually so generous.' He'd spotted a bakery near to the station and had stocked up on croissants and Danish pastries. It would take more than free carbohydrates to gain the respect of a new team, but he knew from experience that it was a good place to start.

'Thank you, sir.'

He recognised the speaker as DS Becca Shawcross. At Gillian's introductory briefing, Becca had stood out as someone who knew which way was up, and with Dinsdale gone she was the next most senior detective on the case.

'Would you like a tea or coffee?' she asked. 'How do you take it?'

'Coffee, please. Black, no sugar.'

He waited for everyone to help themselves to a pastry and for Becca to bring his drink. Then he removed his jacket, rolled up his sleeves and took up position in front of the whiteboard. He was already a day behind and needed to catch up quickly.

'Right,' he said, 'you already know who I am, and I know you all by name. We can get to know each other better as we go. For now, I want to find out how much progress has been made on the investigation.'

No one said a word. It was difficult to know what they were thinking. The pastries were going down well though.

He tapped the victim's photo on the board. 'A man was found on the North Bay yesterday morning, probably washed up by the tide. A gunshot wound to his chest. Do we have a name for him yet?'

A young man in a shiny suit hastily wiped crumbs from his mouth with the back of his hand. DC Dan Bennett.

'Sir? Becca – I mean DS Shawcross – asked me to search reports of missing persons.'

'Yes?'

'There's no one matching the victim's description.'

'And there was no ID on the body?'

'Well, there was a ring…' said Dan hesitantly.

'A ring?'

'Sir,' said Becca, 'the victim was wearing a gold ring with two names engraved on the inside. Tristan and Iseult.'

Raven frowned. Gillian hadn't mentioned a ring. 'They were lovers, right?'

'Yes, sir,' said Becca. 'We believe the names may refer to the characters from the legend of Tristan and Iseult. Presumably the names have some personal significance, like nicknames.'

'Okay, and what do we know about how long he spent in the water and where he might have come from?'

An older man sitting at the back rose to his feet. DC Tony Bairstow. Tony's hair was longer than in the photo Gillian had shown him, and streaked with grey, but it was clearly the same man. 'Sir, high tide was at 6:36 yesterday morning. The body was discovered shortly after seven o'clock, by which time the sea was on its way out. Once we have a time of death, I can speak to the coastguard and try to establish where the victim's body entered the water, based on the currents.'

'What?' said Raven. 'Hasn't the pathologist established a time of death yet?'

Tony looked to Becca for support.

'Sir,' said Becca, 'the post-mortem is still outstanding.'

Raven thumped his fist against the wall. 'What the hell was Dinsdale doing all day if not arranging the post-mortem?'

The room fell silent and he realised that he had scared them with his outburst of anger. He would have to watch that. He couldn't afford to alienate his team on day one. But perhaps this explained why Gillian had been so keen to take him on. He couldn't possibly do a worse job than someone who had failed to get even the basics sorted out.

Once again, it was Becca who spoke up for the rest of the team. 'We don't know what DI Dinsdale was doing yesterday. We had only just started a team meeting when the Super replaced him with you.'

'Well, we need the post-mortem carried out as soon as possible,' said Raven. 'DS Bairstow, can I ask you to arrange it, please?' The older constable had struck him as more competent than Dan Bennett, who had stumbled when questioned about the names engraved on the ring.

'Will do,' said Tony.

'What about witnesses?' asked Raven. 'How many statements do we have?'

'Sir.' A young woman with blonde hair tied back in a ponytail sprang to her feet. Raven recognised her as DC Jess Barraclough. With her high cheekbones and clear blue eyes, she was quite the beauty. 'I led a team of uniformed officers conducting house to house enquiries in the Scalby area yesterday, but nobody was able to help us. The only relevant witness statement we have is from the dogwalker who discovered the body, a Mrs Barbara Smith. She didn't recognise the victim though.'

'What about forensics?'

'The CSI team searched the beach,' said Jess, 'but they didn't find anything apart from the ring.'

'So is that all we've got?' asked Raven. An unidentified male with a single gunshot wound to the chest, washed clean by the sea and with no identification except a ring engraved with names from a medieval legend. It wasn't a lot to go on. He was starting to wonder if he'd been given an unsolvable case. In a few weeks he'd be heading back to London with his tail between his legs, a failure.

'Sir?' Becca raised a hand.

'What is it?'

'There are similarities between this murder and a previous case.'

Raven's ears pricked up. 'Go on.'

'Three years ago another body washed up in similar circumstances. It was further down the coast at Cayton Bay, but that victim also had a single gunshot wound to the chest. The man was a known drugs dealer in the area.'

'Was anyone charged with the murder?'

'Yes. A nightclub bouncer. He was found guilty and is currently serving life at Full Sutton near York.'

Raven picked up on a slight hesitation in her voice. 'Do you have any doubts about his conviction?'

'No,' said Becca hurriedly. 'There was solid forensic evidence, and he admitted his guilt.'

'What then?'

'Well,' said Becca, 'someone must have put him up to it. I mean, he was only a nightclub bouncer, not some big shot dealer.'

'Do you have any suspicions about who might have been behind it?'

Becca exchanged glances with Tony, who nodded encouragingly. 'Well, the obvious suspect would have been his employer, the owner of the nightclub. He's a local man with all kinds of business interests. But as far as I know, he was never questioned about the murder.'

Raven narrowed his eyes, thinking. There was more to this case than met the eye, and as an outsider he was at a distinct disadvantage. He needed inside knowledge, and the best route to that seemed to be via DS Becca Shawcross.

'Well, what are we waiting for?' he asked, grabbing his jacket. 'Let's go and see this nightclub owner and see what he has to say for himself.'

CHAPTER 6

'Would you like me to drive, sir?' Becca hurried to keep up with her new boss as he exited the building and strode towards the car park. While DI Dinsdale rarely got off his backside, DCI Raven hadn't sat down since he'd arrived. She didn't yet know what to make of the newcomer. The croissants and Danish pastries had been a nice touch, much appreciated by the team, but there was a restlessness about him that was disconcerting. She knew how to handle Dinsdale, even if you did need to put a bomb under him to get him moving. Raven, on the other hand, remained an enigma.

'Drive?' he said.

'Yes, sir.' As the senior officer, Dinsdale had always been happy to be chauffeured around. It gave him more time to make calls on his mobile. She indicated her Honda Jazz which was parked unobtrusively at the rear of the car park.

'In that?' The corners of Raven's mouth twitched. 'I don't think so.'

Becca bristled. 'It's a very good car, sir.' The Jazz was an ideal vehicle for navigating Scarborough's tight, narrow streets. She'd have preferred an all-electric model for the sake of the environment, but they were out of her price range, and the town wasn't flush with electric charging points. This hybrid was a good compromise.

But Raven wasn't listening. He was already clicking his remote at some monster of a car that was taking up more than its fair share of parking space. A BMW coupé, Becca noted, trying not to look impressed. You could tell a lot about a person from their car. This one was pretty ancient, judging from the registration plates, but it looked to be in good condition. And it was obviously a high-performance model. No doubt it guzzled far more petrol than her Jazz. But she could tell by the smile that had spread across Raven's face that he was smitten with it. *Boys and their toys.* She hurried to join him as he swung open the silver door.

'Wouldn't you like to get some background on the previous case before we go to interview the nightclub owner?' she asked.

'You can fill me in en route,' said Raven, sliding into the driver's seat.

Great, thought Becca. Now she'd have to rely on her memory rather than having her notes on the previous case to hand.

As she eased herself into the passenger seat, she noticed other clues to Raven's character. Despite the age of the car, its mahogany dashboard gleamed with polish, the carpets in the footwells had been freshly vacuumed, and the door pockets were devoid of chocolate wrappers, parking tickets and the usual detritus that normally accumulated in cars. Or at least in Becca's car. She made a mental note to give it a good clean when she got home.

'So where are we going?' asked Raven, starting up the engine, which growled loudly like a big cat.

'The address is Weaponness Park,' said Becca as Raven slid the car into gear and headed towards the exit. 'It's at the expensive end of town, up on Oliver's Mount overlooking the South Bay. Turn right at the end of the road and then–'

'I know where Weaponness Park is.'

'Oh, right. I just thought that being new to Scarborough–'

'I'm not new. I grew up here.'

That surprised her. She'd assumed he was a Londoner, or at least a southerner. There was barely any trace of Yorkshire accent in his speech, so she guessed he'd been gone a long time. 'So what brought you back, if you don't mind me asking?'

Apparently, he did mind because he ignored her question. Instead, he swung the car into a gap in the traffic and signalled a right turn. The wheels of the BMW spun as he accelerated round the corner just as the lights turned red. 'Tell me what you know about this previous murder,' he said.

Becca took a breath, trying not to notice the speed at which they were flying past the line of parked taxis just inches from her side of the car. 'I was a DC at the time,' she said, 'so I didn't have a full picture of the investigation.'

'That's all right, just tell me what you know.'

They were driving past the railway station, passing charity shops, nail bars, hairdressers, betting shops, takeaway pizza outlets and a dry cleaners where Becca had once had a Saturday job as a teenager. The leafy enclave of Oliver's Mount was just visible in the distance. She tried to focus on the case and not on Raven's driving.

'Okay, well it was almost three years ago. A body washed up on the beach at Cayton Bay. Single bullet wound to the chest, just like our guy. But in that case the victim was easy to identify. Max Hunt. A local drugs dealer.'

'What kind of drugs? How big a player was he?'

'He was very active in Scarborough, dealing in Class A drugs. Cocaine, ecstasy, heroin, LSD. He had convictions for a range of offences – assault, harassment, criminal damage, possession of an offensive weapon – a nasty piece of work all round.'

'I bet not too many people cried when Mr Hunt turned

up dead.'

'No,' said Becca, 'but there are still just as many drugs on the streets today.'

Raven nodded grimly. 'One dealer exits, another moves onto his patch. The problem never goes away.' His voice sounded weary, betraying his age. 'So you think the killing was the work of a rival trying to muscle in on Hunt's turf?'

'That's my guess.'

'And who was convicted of the murder?'

'A bouncer at a nightclub in town called Vertigo. His name is Lewis Briggs.'

'And you told me there were no doubts about his conviction.'

'I don't think so,' said Becca. 'The gun that fired the shot was found at his home, with his fingerprints all over it. When confronted with the evidence, he confessed.'

'So Lewis isn't the brightest spark. Any indications that he was involved in the drugs trade?'

'A conviction for low-level dealing, nothing major.'

'You think he was working on behalf of someone else.'

It wasn't a question, and Becca felt relief that Raven was taking her theory seriously. 'It seemed obvious to me that someone else had ordered the killing. But as far as I know nothing was ever done to follow up.'

'Hmm.' Raven fell silent, his eyes fixed on the road as they flew across the bridge that spanned the Valley Gardens below. The road began to climb as it left the town's commercial centre behind and entered a more affluent part of town. Up ahead, the green peak of Oliver's Mount rose clearly into view. Gone were the betting shops and nail bars – now the backdrop was of large Victorian houses, the street bordered by wide pavements and trees.

'So Lewis Briggs pulled the trigger,' said Raven after a break of a few minutes, 'but who gave the order?'

'I can't say, for sure,' said Becca. 'But I wondered about Lewis's employer, the owner of the nightclub.'

'Any reason for your suspicions, other than the fact that the two men knew each other?'

'Nothing concrete, but he's the criminal type. I know this isn't how police investigations are supposed to work,' she added hurriedly, 'but you'll understand what I mean when you meet him for yourself. He has his fingers in a lot of pies. He owns a number of businesses in town. Amusement arcades, a pub or two. Maybe more.'

'Cash businesses,' said Raven. 'Perfect for money laundering.'

'Exactly,' said Becca. 'Like I say, this is all just circumstantial.'

'But it's your hunch,' said Raven. 'That's okay. I can work with hunches. Especially when we have nothing else to go on.' She thought she detected the ghost of a smile on his lips.

He turned the car off the Filey Road and onto Weaponness Park. The gradient steepened, the tree-lined road winding uphill, its large, detached houses set back behind neatly trimmed hedges and shady conifers. The further they climbed, the quieter the road became, the more substantial and secluded the houses. Tennis courts and conservatories were glimpsed behind the hedges. The road narrowed to almost a single track, but Raven didn't ease his foot off the accelerator.

'Just here,' said Becca, pointing to a driveway flanked by stone pillars. She thought he was going to overshoot, but Raven braked sharply at the last possible moment, manoeuvring the car expertly through the open gates and bringing it to a standstill. He pulled on the handbrake and killed the engine. It was a relief to come to a halt at last, although Becca had to admit that she'd quite enjoyed the thrill of the ride.

Raven looked out of the window. The house was a sprawling mock Tudor property dating from the nineteen-twenties and nestled in the grounds of a well-tended garden. Mature shrubs bordered the driveway, and the trees were putting on a fiery autumnal display of red and gold. 'So, this nightclub owner. What's his name?'

'Darren Jubb.'

Raven jerked his head sharply to one side. 'Jubb,' he muttered to himself. 'Darren Jubb.'

'You know him?' asked Becca.

'I know him. Or at least I did. But that was a long time ago. His father, Frank, owned an amusement arcade down on the seafront.'

'Yes. Frank's retired now, but Darren still owns the arcade. He's added more businesses over the years. As you can see' – she indicated the house – 'Darren Jubb is doing very nicely for himself.'

'Darren always did.'

Becca waited for him to elaborate, but she was quickly learning that information sharing wasn't one of Raven's strengths, especially when it came to his personal life. She guessed that he and Jubb might have known each other when they were growing up. They were probably about the same age. Late forties. 'Sir,' she asked, 'is there something I should know?'

'Like what?'

'I don't know, sir. It's just that if you have a personal connection to a key suspect–'

'I don't have any personal connection to Darren Jubb,' snapped Raven. 'I haven't seen him in more than three decades.' He glared at her. 'And don't keep calling me "sir". It makes me sound like a schoolteacher.'

It was hard for Becca to keep the exasperation from her voice. 'What should I call you, then?' she demanded.

He said nothing for a second, then his face broke into a grin that made his dark eyes sparkle with mischief. 'Call me Raven. Everyone else does.'

CHAPTER 7

'And they say crime doesn't pay,' said Raven as they got out of the car.

Darren Jubb had done well for himself – very well. Big house, nice garden, a brand new Range Rover parked at the end of the drive. Raven took all this in at a glance. Was he surprised? Not really. Darren's father, Frank, had got his son off to a flying start with the amusement arcade. And Darren had always had that way about him, the natural confidence of someone who knew their stars were in alignment. A lucky bastard, in other words.

'He'll probably refuse to see us,' said Becca.

'I don't think so,' said Raven, crunching his feet on the gravel. 'He won't refuse to see me.' He pressed the bell, which chimed deep inside the house.

The door opened to reveal a man in his mid- to late twenties dressed in a leather jacket and black jeans. Raven studied his face closely. The family resemblance wasn't immediately obvious, but the more Raven looked, the more he thought he could detect traces of the father in the son. The hair colour was the same – dark brown, almost black – and yes, those piercing blue eyes that Darren had always used to such good effect in winning people over now stared at Raven out of the youthful face in front of him.

'Yes? What do you want?'

Raven couldn't help but smile. Even the hectoring way of talking was the same. He pulled out his warrant card. 'DCI Tom Raven, and this is Detective Sergeant Becca Shawcross. We'd like a word with Darren Jubb.'

'What about?'

'A police matter.'

'No way.' The young man planted himself firmly in the doorway, arms folded. 'You can't just come here with no warning and demand to see my dad.'

'No?' said Raven. 'I'm pretty sure that's what I just did. So is your father home?' He peered over the young man's shoulder.

'I don't have to tell you anything.' Jubb Junior was about to close the door when a figure appeared in the hallway behind him.

'Who is it, Ethan?'

He was greyer and stouter than when Raven had last seen him, but in essence Darren Jubb had aged well. His hair had receded at the temples but was otherwise still thick. It was gelled off to one side, giving him a raffish look that suited him. He wore an open necked shirt, tucked into expensive-looking jeans. It was easy to picture him in a nightclub, chatting up women half his age at the bar. He took one look at Raven and stopped in his tracks.

'Well, well. The Raven returns.'

Ethan looked decidedly put out by the turn of events. 'You know this policeman, Dad?'

'Policeman?' Jubb's gaze didn't leave Raven for a second. 'Who would have guessed that, Tom? And I take it this is your sergeant?' He turned to Becca, his azure eyes drinking her in.

Becca regarded him as if he were a cockroach. 'DS Shawcross,' she said defiantly.

'Nice to make your acquaintance,' said Darren with a sly smile.

'We're here on police business,' said Raven, cutting off any ideas Darren might have about sweet-talking Becca. Not that she seemed remotely open to his charms. 'Perhaps you'd like to invite us inside?'

'Of course,' said Darren, opening his arms wide. 'Do come in. You're most welcome to my humble abode. Although it's not so humble, is it? Even though I say so myself.'

'Humility never was your strong point,' said Raven, following him into a lounge that was trying way too hard to flaunt itself. Crystal chandeliers hung from the ceiling, the leaded windows were draped in an excessive quantity of salmon-pink silk, and the enormous carved wooden fire surround looked as if it been taken from a baronial mansion. And no way did Darren ever play the baby grand piano that stood conspicuously in one corner.

'Tasteful,' said Raven drily. 'Is that the right word?' He winked at Becca. 'Oh no. I remember now. The word is *vulgar*.'

'Tease me all you like, Tom,' said Darren with a thin smile. 'It shows how jealous you are. How much does a policeman earn these days? No, don't tell me. I don't want you to be embarrassed.'

Ethan followed them into the room and stood by the door like a sulky child, waiting to be admitted into the presence of the grown-ups.

'We'd like to speak to your father alone,' Raven told him. 'If you don't mind.'

'But Dad–'

Darren waved his son away. 'It's all right, Ethan. Tom and I go back a long way. We're old friends, isn't that right, Tom?'

Ethan withdrew grudgingly, closing the door behind him. Raven wondered if he might linger in the hallway to listen at the keyhole. Well, let him listen. He might learn a thing or two about his father.

'A drink?' asked Darren, making his way to a glass cabinet arranged with whisky and brandy decanters and a collection of crystal glasses. 'For old times' sake?'

'Not while I'm on duty.'

Darren looked piqued but quickly hid his disappointment. 'I suppose it is a bit early in the day, even for me.' He laughed, then became suddenly serious. 'My condolences, by the way. I heard about your old man. Heart attack, was it?'

Out of the corner of his eye, Raven caught Becca's surprise. 'Thank you,' he said to Darren in what he hoped was a tone of finality. He had no wish to discuss his father's death, especially in front of his sergeant. But Darren was clearly in the mood for catching up.

'Sit down, why don't you?' Their host waved them towards an enormous cream sofa. 'It must be, what, thirty years since you last graced these shores?'

'Thirty-one.'

Raven and Becca sat at opposite ends of the sofa, a good six feet apart. Darren settled himself into an armchair opposite, hands resting on the arms of the chair, the ankle of one foot balanced on the opposite knee. A relaxed, confident pose. Or one carefully contrived to give that impression.

'You've clearly done well for yourself,' said Raven. 'Business is good?'

A cocky smile came to Darren's lips. 'I won't lie to you, Tom. I've had some lucky breaks over the years. Starting with the property crash in the nineties. I persuaded my old man to pick up a couple of arcades that had gone bust. He was nervous about taking them on, but I was able to turn them around. I added a couple of pubs to my portfolio over the years. Then when the financial crisis came along I had the chance to get my hands on a nightclub. It was going for a song.' He whistled through his teeth.

'Lucky,' agreed Raven. *Though not for the former owner of the nightclub.* Darren had always landed on his feet and was no doubt capable of driving a hard bargain.

'What about the pandemic?' asked Becca. 'That must have been bad for business, particularly for pubs and clubs.'

Darren waved away the suggestion. 'Sometimes you've got to take the rough with the smooth. Every problem brings an opportunity. That's what I've tried to teach Ethan. He's a real chip off the old block, you know. He saw the potential in holiday rentals early on. Staycations have been booming these past couple of years.'

'Not everyone in hospitality fared so well,' said Becca pointedly.

Darren gave her one of his charming smiles. The kind that Raven recalled from the days when they'd both been chasing the same girl. 'Fortune favours the bold.'

'What about Frank?' asked Raven. 'Is he still involved in the family business?'

'Not so much. Dad takes it easy these days, although he still insists on dropping in to the arcades to check on business. I might think about retiring myself, once I'm sure that Ethan's up to speed. It's a young man's game, you know, Tom? You've got to be hungry to succeed. Old timers like you and me need to know when to step back.'

Raven knew that he was just being goaded. Darren Jubb was still as hungry as he'd ever been. 'Do you have any other kinds of business interests?' he asked.

'Like what?' Darren fixed him with those piercing blue eyes. For a moment Raven was thirteen years old again, pinned by that same stare. He heard Darren's teenage voice in his head. *Go on, I dare you.* The challenge. The dare. Himself, not wanting to appear weak, especially in front of the others. He hadn't understood then that turning his back on Darren Jubb would have been the strong thing to do. The right thing.

But Darren had always been so persuasive. That had been part of his charm. And his danger.

As a teenager, Darren had been the one urging the rest of the gang to cross the line. Mostly petty theft, like shoplifting CDs from Woolworth's or bars of chocolate from the corner shop. Skipping school. Breaking into empty houses. It was a miracle they'd never been caught. But that was Darren – always getting away with it somehow. Once, he'd got his hands on a stash of weed. They'd smoked it at the far end of the South Bay beyond the spa, oblivious to the incoming tide. They could have drowned. They almost did.

As if reading Raven's thoughts, Darren leaned towards Becca and said, 'I could tell you a thing or two about your boss from back in the day.' Then to Raven, 'Don't worry, Tom, your secrets are safe with me.'

'Where were you on Sunday?' asked Raven. It was the day before the discovery of the body. Raven was making a guess about when the man had been killed. But his guesses often hit the mark.

Darren leaned back in his chair and steepled his fingertips beneath his chin, a gesture that Raven recalled well. 'Is this about that dead body that washed up? News travels fast in a place the size of Scarborough.'

Does it? Raven wondered. The police hadn't yet issued a statement. But no doubt a man like Darren Jubb had eyes and ears on the streets. 'Where were you?' he repeated.

'I don't know why you're asking me,' said Darren, 'but if you must know, I was busy all day. Ethan and I had a meeting with our accountant in the morning.'

'On a Sunday?'

'I pay that man well enough,' said Darren. 'If I ask him to come and see me on a Sunday, then that's when he comes. Afterwards I took my wife and daughter out to lunch. What about you, Tom? Got anyone to take out to lunch?'

Raven said nothing.

Darren gave him a bloodless smile and carried on. 'After lunch, I played a round at the North Cliff Golf Club. You play golf, Tom?'

'Never,' said Raven.

Darren grinned broadly. 'And in the evening there was a charity fundraising event at the Grand Hotel. In aid of good causes. That's me, you see. Always willing to do what I can to help those less fortunate than myself.'

Becca was busy writing everything down in her notebook.

'I can give you full details if you want to check my alibis,' Darren told her.

'That would be helpful, Mr Jubb,' she said.

A business meeting, a family lunch, a round of golf and a charity event. *How respectable*, thought Raven. *And how convenient, to have every minute of the day accounted for.* And since when did Darren Jubb do charity? The Darren Jubb of old had always taken, never given.

'You mentioned a daughter,' said Raven. 'Is that her?' He pointed to a photograph on a side table of a young woman in dark glasses somewhere hot and sunny with a cloudless blue sky behind her. Not Scarborough.

A fond smile flickered across Darren's face. 'Yes, that's Scarlett. My princess.'

'Is she involved in the family business too?'

Darren laughed loudly at the suggestion. 'No, Scarlett has much grander ideas than that. She wants to be famous. In fact, from what she tells me, she already is. She's a social media influencer.' He held up his hands in a gesture of bewilderment. 'I don't pretend to know what that means, but she's got over ten million followers, would you believe it? Makes a small fortune from sponsorship and advertising. Perhaps if I was younger and better looking, I'd do the same.' He leaned in towards Raven once more. 'What about you, Tom? What would you do differently if you were young again?' When Raven didn't answer, he said, 'You ran away. It took you thirty years to summon the courage to return. The rest of the crowd stayed behind in Scarborough. Do you want to know what happened to them?'

'No,' said Raven. He took a printed photo from his jacket and passed it to Darren. 'Do you recognise this man?'

Darren sighed. He reached into his pocket for a pair of

reading glasses and plucked them out bashfully, saying, 'Age, eh, Tom? It's a cruel thing.' He put the glasses on to study the picture. For the first time in their encounter, the confident demeanour left him and suddenly Darren Jubb looked every one of his forty-seven years and more. He wasn't smiling now. His face was ashen. 'Is this the body on the beach?'

'Yes,' said Raven. 'You know him, don't you?'

Darren took off his reading glasses and returned the picture to Raven. 'I should do. He's engaged to marry my daughter.' He rose to his feet. 'I don't know about you, Tom, but I'm bloody well going to have that drink now.'

CHAPTER 8

There were tears and there were tissues. Then fresh tears. Becca made soothing noises to the weeping girl sitting next to her on the sofa while Raven left the room and returned a few minutes later with a new box of tissues. More tears followed. Eventually the crying ran its course, petering out into just a few hiccoughing sobs and the occasional shudder. Scarlett Jubb wiped her heavily made-up eyes and blew her nose with the latest wad of tissues before dropping them onto the sodden pile at her feet.

Raven had asked Becca to lead the interview with Scarlett, and she judged that now was as good a time as any to start asking some questions. Raven was sitting in the corner of the room observing, and Becca felt herself under scrutiny.

'I'm very sorry for your loss,' she said, genuinely meaning it. It was hard not to feel pity for a young woman whose life had just come crashing down in ruins. Scarlett had seemed supremely self-confident when they'd first met her. But that was before the news of her fiancé's death had been broken to her. Then the confident façade had slid from her face just as quickly as her eyeshadow and mascara. Becca didn't think that the rising internet star would be posting any photos for her online fans today.

Becca didn't bother much with social media herself. She still had a Facebook account that she'd set up in her teens when everyone else was doing it, but she hadn't posted anything in a long time and rarely bothered to check her newsfeed. What was there to say about her life that was interesting? She worked all day and still lived at home with her parents, although she and her boyfriend had once very nearly put down a deposit on a small but charming ground-floor flat in a converted Victorian house. The fact was, if Raven thought that as a woman in her twenties she was better placed than him to understand what Scarlett Jubb did for a living, then he was mistaken. *Internet influencer* didn't seem like a real job to Becca. DC Jess Barraclough would be the best person to ask.

But what Becca did understand was a young woman who had just received the worst news imaginable and had, quite understandably, fallen to pieces. It ought to be Scarlett's family consoling her right now. But the girl's mother was out and Darren Jubb had retreated into his office, trying to contact her. Ethan, the sulky brother, was nowhere to be seen. So much for a supportive family.

'Had you and Patrick been together for a long time?' she asked gently. Darren had given them the victim's name. Patrick Lofthouse, the son of a wealthy business owner. A good boy from a good family, according to Jubb.

Scarlett lifted her head and pushed back the veil of silky blonde hair that had fallen over her face. Her impossibly long fingernails were elaborately decorated, alternately in metallic blue and glittering turquoise.

'Since I was sixteen,' she said. 'Six whole years.'

'That's a long time,' said Becca. The whole of Scarlett's adult life, in fact. 'And you were engaged to be married?'

Scarlett twisted the ring on her left hand. A deep blue oval sapphire surrounded by tiny diamonds set on a platinum band. It had no doubt cost a bomb. 'Patrick proposed to me in the summer and I'd just started to check out wedding venues. I wanted everything to be super special. It was going to be the biggest day of our lives.' A fresh sob escaped her.

'How did the two of you first meet?' asked Becca.

'At school,' said Scarlett. 'Patrick was in the year above me. I'd noticed him around, he was so good looking, but we'd never really spoken. Then one day he asked me out on a date.' Her lower lip trembled. 'We've never been apart since.'

Becca reached automatically for more tissues. 'What did Patrick do for a living?'

Scarlett dabbed at her eyes with the tissues and they came away black with mascara. 'He worked for his father. His dad runs a car dealership on the road out of Scarborough.' She clapped a hand suddenly to her mouth, looking horrified. 'Oh my God, I'm such a selfish cow. Here am I going on about wedding venues, but what about Patrick's parents? Do they know what's happened?'

'A police car is on its way to Mr and Mrs Lofthouse now,' said Becca soothingly. 'Don't worry. They'll be well taken care of.'

The words seemed to calm Scarlett down a little. Becca pressed on. 'When did you last see Patrick?'

'Sunday morning,' said Scarlett. 'We went to a club on Saturday night and then came back here.'

'And then?'

'Mum and Dad took me out to lunch on Sunday. I arranged to see Patrick again that evening, but he messaged me to say he was going to Redcar to see his mate, Shane. He said Shane needed him and he'd be back in a couple of days.'

Becca ran the timeline through her head. It was now Tuesday and Patrick's body had been found on Monday morning. If he'd last been seen on Sunday morning, that left almost a full day unaccounted for.

'Do you still have his message?' she asked.

Scarlett picked up her iPhone and with a couple of deft

strokes produced the message. She showed it to Becca. It was short and to the point.

Got to go and see Shane. He needs me. Back in a couple of days. Love Px.

Becca noted the time the message had been sent. 6:05pm on Sunday. That narrowed things down somewhat. She passed the phone to Raven and turned back to Scarlett. 'Who is Shane?'

Scarlett pulled a face. 'Shane Denton. He's a mate of Patrick's.' Her tone was dismissive, even scornful.

'And he lives in Redcar?'

Scarlett sniffed. 'I suppose we should feel sorry for him.'

Becca knew the town of Redcar, located some forty-five miles north of Scarborough, well enough. When she had studied at Teesside University she had sometimes taken the bus there when she wanted to see the sea. But despite being a seaside town with a pretty decent stretch of beach, Redcar lacked the grandeur of its more famous neighbour or the charm of Whitby. An air of gloom hung permanently over the town, not helped by high unemployment rates following the closure of the nearby steelworks at Warrenby.

'What does Shane do?' she asked.

'Not a lot,' said Scarlett. 'I can't understand why Patrick bothers with him.'

Becca noted that Scarlett had lapsed into speaking about her dead boyfriend in the present tense. It was a common enough trait in people who had just learned about the death of a loved one. 'I'm afraid I have to ask this,' she said, bracing herself for a fresh round of crying, 'but can you think of any reason why someone would have wanted to kill Patrick?'

Scarlett shook her head, dissolving into more tears and Becca put a comforting arm around the girl's shoulders.

Raven rose to his feet. A black figure towering over them. 'Just one more question,' he said. 'Do the names *Tristan* and *Iseult* mean anything to you?'

Scarlett looked up at him uncomprehendingly. 'Tristan

and who?'

'Iseult,' said Becca. She spelled it out.

'I've never heard of them,' said Scarlett.

'Thank you, Scarlett,' said Becca. 'We'll leave you in peace now.' She glanced up at Raven who gave her the briefest of nods. She'd passed the test by the look of it.

*

'So what did you make of Darren Jubb's reaction to the photo?' Raven asked Becca. They were back in the car, returning the way they had come, down Oliver's Mount. Raven had been impressed by the calm and sympathetic way Becca had handled Scarlett. Now he was keen to find out what she had made of his erstwhile associate.

'He seemed genuinely shocked,' said Becca. 'Until that point, he'd been enjoying himself, showing off to you. But as soon as he saw the photo, his whole demeanour changed. The bluster went out of him. He already knew a body had been found on the beach, but when he realised it was his future son-in-law... well, I rather got the impression he'd been expecting it to be someone else.'

'Like who?'

'I don't know. Someone he wanted out of the way?'

'Maybe he wanted Patrick out of the way. Maybe he didn't think this Patrick Lofthouse was good enough for his precious daughter.'

'I didn't get that impression,' said Becca.

'Yes, well, Darren Jubb always was a good actor.' Raven touched the accelerator with his right foot and the BMW leapt forwards, hugging the curves of the hill like a well-tamed beast, its true power hidden for the time being. He longed to be out on the open road where he could really open the throttle.

'You two used to be friends?' queried Becca.

'Friends?' Raven turned the word over in his mind and found it wanting. His relationship with Darren Jubb had always been far more complex than that. 'Friendship is a slippery concept. Sometimes your best friend can be your worst enemy.'

He signalled left and turned onto the Filey Road, heading back into town. It felt strange to be driving around these once-familiar roads after a gap of so many years. It was like following grooves etched so deeply into his memory that he didn't even know they were still there. Almost as if he'd never been away at all. Not that he'd ever been inside one of the big houses on Oliver's Mount before. As teenagers they used to go to the mount to watch the motorcycle racing and drink cans of lager pilfered from the supermarket. 'What did you think of the daughter?'

Becca thought for a moment. 'It's hard to say when someone's in such an emotional state, but on the whole I thought she was articulate and likeable.'

'Not merely self-obsessed and vacuous?'

'I try not to have preconceptions regarding witnesses,' said Becca.

He shot her an amused glance. He'd asked her to lead the interview because in his experience female witnesses responded better to female detectives. And he'd been right. Scarlett had opened up under Becca's gentle probing, whereas she'd likely have been less forthcoming if he had grilled her himself. There were two kinds of detectives in his experience. Those who cajoled, and those who intimidated. Now he knew which kind Becca was.

'Fair enough.' He pulled up at a set of traffic lights and put the car into neutral, engaging the handbrake. 'You didn't think she was putting it on a bit?'

Becca twisted in her seat to face him. 'Not at all. The poor girl had just lost the man she was going to marry. Of course she was upset. She'll need a lot of support to get over something like this. And just because you and Darren Jubb have some kind of longstanding grudge, it doesn't mean you have to think the worst of everyone in the Jubb family. Perhaps you ought to consider whether you have preconceptions regarding witnesses yourself, Raven.'

Raven liked it when junior officers stood up to him. He

hated the timid compliance that often characterised his younger colleagues. Or worse, the world-weary cynicism that too many older officers wore as protective armour. Becca had spoken with a passion that demonstrated how much she cared about the job, and he let her words sink in for a moment, feeling that he'd been put in his place. Of course, she was right. Scarlett was just a young woman, barely out of her teens. Nothing in her privileged upbringing could have prepared her for a shock like this.

The lights changed and they drove on in silence.

After a short while, Becca said, 'I was sorry to hear about your father.'

She sounded as if she was trying to make amends for her momentary outburst. 'Thank you,' he said, acknowledging her sentiments with a nod. 'But we hadn't spoken in over thirty years, so no great loss.'

'Still,' she said. 'You only have one family.'

He dropped her outside the station with instructions to check Darren's alibis and to get hold of Patrick's call records from the phone network. And to find out all she could about the victim now they had a positive ID.

'I'll get onto it right away. And you?'

'Off to the mortuary. I'll meet the parents there when they're brought in to identify the body.'

She gave him a sympathetic look. Meeting bereaved parents was one of the most difficult aspects of the job. But as senior officer, Raven knew better than to dump the task on someone else. He signalled right and turned to join the traffic.

CHAPTER 9

Gordon and Janet Lofthouse looked to be in their early sixties. He was a broad, lumbering man with hands like hunks of cooked ham. A fringe of coarse grey hair circled the bald patch in the middle of his crown. His wife, neat and trim with auburn hair in a short, practical style, was a full head shorter than her husband even in heels. She clutched his arm with leathery fingers. Given their age, Raven deduced that Patrick must have been a late baby. Maybe the couple had married late, or perhaps Patrick had been a surprise after they had tried and given up hope of ever having a baby. A child like that could sometimes become the object of parental over-indulgence. Raven was reminded of the way Darren Jubb had referred to Scarlett as his "princess". Perhaps Patrick Lofthouse and Scarlett Jubb had made a good match for each other.

Raven stood discreetly off to one side as the mortuary assistant prepared to turn back the white sheet covering the body on the gurney. He had no desire to intrude on the moment when the parents would come face to face with the body of their son. The family liaison officer, a competent-looking woman who had introduced herself as PC Sharon Jarvis, was waiting in the corridor.

Patting his wife's hand, Gordon Lofthouse nodded to the mortuary assistant who turned back the white sheet and stepped aside. For a moment, time seemed suspended. And then the unmistakable wail of a bereaved mother filled the room. Raven turned away as Gordon Lofthouse tried in vain to comfort and restrain his wife. It was all the proof Raven needed, if there had been any doubt, that the body that had washed up on the beach was that of Patrick Lofthouse.

He let himself quietly out of the room and waited in the corridor with the family liaison officer. She reached into a pocket and offered him a packet of cigarettes. 'A smoke, sir?'

Raven shook his head. 'No thank you. I don't smoke.'

She slid the packet back into her jacket. 'Nor me. Or at least that's the story I keep telling myself.'

Raven smiled. That was another thing he hadn't done for a long, long time – smoke a cigarette. He'd smoked as a teenager, with Darren Jubb egging him on. And during his army years of course – who hadn't? But not since then. He'd given up when he joined the police force. Which made him something of an oddity. It was supposed to be the other way round.

The door opened and Gordon Lofthouse emerged, steering his wife before him. Her initial outpouring of grief had run its course and she was dabbing her eyes with a lace-trimmed handkerchief. Her eyes were still bloodshot however, and her shoulders shook gently as she allowed herself to be guided out of the room as meekly as a lamb. Behind them, the mortuary assistant was replacing the white sheet over the body.

Raven nodded his condolences to them. 'I know that this is a difficult time for you both, but if you feel up to it, it would assist the investigation greatly if you could answer a few questions.'

'Of course, Inspector,' said Gordon. 'We want to do

everything we can to help.'

'There's a room we can use along here,' said the family liaison officer in a kind but matter-of-fact way. She led them to a small room with mismatched orthopaedic chairs arranged around a low table. Raven tried not to get in the way while she fussed over the parents, making sure they were comfortable, and asking if there was anything they wanted.

'A cup of tea,' said Janet.

'I'll fetch some.'

Raven waited patiently until she'd returned with three paper cups filled with hot pale liquid, no doubt the best she'd been able to rustle up, courtesy of the NHS. She placed them on the table, giving one to each of the Lofthouses and one to Raven.

'Thank you, love,' said Janet, giving her hand a squeeze. 'You've been very kind.'

It was a gesture Raven had noticed many times before – the tendency of those in distress to be pathetically grateful for any small act of kindness.

'It would help me,' he said gently, 'if you could tell me a little about Patrick.'

'He was a good boy,' said Janet.

'I'm sure he was, Mrs Lofthouse. Could you tell me how old he was?'

'Twenty-three.'

'And was he your only child?'

'Yes,' said Janet through trembling lips. Raven could see that she was on the brink of breaking down again. He tried to imagine how he might feel if his own daughter was stretched out on the gurney in the adjacent room. Hannah. Just twenty years of age. Despite all the corpses he'd seen during the course of his career, his mind just couldn't picture her lying there cold and lifeless. No parent could. Until it happened.

'I understand that you own a car dealership in Scarborough?' he said to Gordon.

Gordon drew himself a little taller, puffing out his

chest. 'I own a *network* of dealerships, Inspector. Lofthouse Cars. We're one of the biggest in North Yorkshire.'

'I see. And did Patrick work with you in the business?'

'That's right. I was grooming him to take over from me when I retire.'

When Scarlett Jubb had talked about Patrick working at a car dealership on the road out of Scarborough, she had clearly been understating the extent of her future in-laws' business empire. Perhaps she had no interest in such matters. She was too focussed on building her own online career.

'The business is successful, then?' queried Raven.

Gordon's nostrils flared. 'Like I told you, Lofthouse Cars is one of the biggest dealerships in the county.'

'And Patrick was keen to take over?'

Gordon grunted. 'It was a great opportunity for him. A gift. Most sons would have jumped at the chance.'

'But not Patrick?'

'He was young,' said Janet, as much to her husband as to Raven. 'I always said, he's young, he'll come round to it when he's older, but well…' She heaved a great sigh as if imagining what might have been and now would never be.

Gordon's face was flinty. 'Patrick had his head in the clouds. He was too much of a dreamer. He was easily distracted. Like with that girlfriend of his.'

Girlfriend, noted Raven. 'You mean Scarlett Jubb, his fiancée?'

'Fiancée, yes. That's what I meant.' His scowl deepened. 'That *girl*… that *family*…'

Janet shook her head. 'Please, Gordon, not now…'

But Gordon Lofthouse had no intention of keeping his opinions to himself. 'I said they were bad for Patrick. I always knew that something like this would happen.'

Raven fixed him with a questioning stare. 'You knew that Patrick would be killed?'

'Not *killed*,' growled Gordon. 'But something… *bad*. They're a bad family, the whole lot of them. I don't know what Patrick saw in her. I told him to drop her. But he wouldn't. He could be pig-headed when he wanted to be.'

Raven didn't have to look far to determine where that particular character trait had come from. He waited for Gordon to simmer down before asking his next question. 'Did Patrick live at home?'

'Yes,' said Janet. 'At least, when he wasn't round at Scarlett's.'

'When was the last time you saw him?'

'He came home on Saturday morning, to pick up his clean laundry.'

Definitely over-indulged, thought Raven. 'And when were you expecting to see him again?'

'I don't know,' said Janet. 'Patrick didn't really tell us when he was coming and going.'

Gordon's face darkened again. 'He took my wife for granted, breezing in and out, expecting her to do his laundry for him.'

'Gordon, I didn't mind,' said Janet.

'Well, I did,' said Gordon. 'And he was the same at work. Unreliable. It was that *girl!* He was always in too much of a hurry to get back to *her!* He was obsessed.'

'Was there a particular reason you didn't want him to marry Scarlett Jubb?'

Gordon narrowed his eyes. 'The clue's in her name, don't you think? Do you know the Jubb family, Inspector?'

'I know their reputation,' said Raven guardedly.

Gordon nodded with satisfaction. 'Then enough said. They're a bad lot, and I told Patrick that no good would come of him getting involved with them. We tried to persuade him, but he just wouldn't be told. If you had a child, Inspector, would you want them marrying one of the Jubbs?'

Raven refrained from comment and decided to move the conversation on. 'Scarlett Jubb told us that on Sunday Patrick went to Redcar to see a friend of his called Shane Denton. Do you know Shane?'

'Humph,' said Gordon. 'Another bad influence. He worked for us some years back, but I had to let him go.'

'Why was that?'

'Drugs,' said Gordon, injecting the word with the full force of his disapproval. 'We couldn't have that sort of thing going on. We're a trusted family firm. We have a reputation in the community. And he was stealing cash too. I had no choice other than to get rid of him.'

'But Patrick and Shane became friends?'

'If Patrick had a fault, Inspector,' said Janet, 'it was that he was too trusting of other people. We tried to tell him that Shane wasn't good for him, but he wouldn't listen. He said that Shane was misunderstood.'

'Misunderstood!' snorted Gordon. 'He was understood all too well!' He turned on Raven. 'But if you think that Shane Denton had anything to do with my son's death, you're mistaken. Look at the Jubb family if you want to find out who's responsible! Look at the father!' His voice cracked and a single tear ran down his cheek. He brushed it away impatiently.

'Are you implying,' said Raven, 'that Darren Jubb was behind your son's murder?'

'I'm not implying it,' snapped Gordon. 'I know it. I just can't prove it.'

*

The pathologist's handshake was as cold and hard as the mortuary slab. A tall, angular woman dressed in surgical scrubs, she regarded Raven with the kind of look she might have given to one of her cadavers. 'Dr Felicity Wainwright, Senior Pathologist.'

'DCI Raven.'

She released him from her grip and returned to her work, examining a glass slide under a microscope. 'I'll be carrying out the PM on your murder victim this afternoon,' she told him. 'But I expect you've come here hoping to get all the answers already. Well, I'm afraid you've jumped the gun.'

'I just wanted to introduce myself while I was here,'

said Raven, feeling that he'd been wrong-footed. He knew it didn't pay to hassle pathologists for details until they were ready to tell you.

She turned to look at him again. 'Yes, you're new, aren't you?'

'I'm on a secondment from the Met. This is my first case in Scarborough.'

'Staying for long?' she enquired.

He wasn't certain whether she meant in Scarborough or in her lab. 'At least until this case is over,' he said.

'Hmm,' she murmured, returning to the lens. 'Well, don't let me keep you.'

Raven lingered at the door to her temperature-controlled environment. Fluorescent tubes cast a cold, uniform light over the white walls and stainless-steel benches, making a shiver run down his spine. He hated laboratories and morgues, but in his experience it always paid to be on friendly terms with the forensic and medical staff who worked there. They were often the people who made it possible for him to swoop in and catch the killer. He would get the glory, but they deserved more credit. Dr Wainwright was the first female pathologist he'd had the pleasure of working with. Although so far there had been very little pleasure.

'Look,' he said, 'I think we might have got off on the wrong foot.'

She looked up, clearly irritated by his continued presence. 'Do you think so?'

'I do, and I'd like to apologise for barging in here unannounced.'

'Well, I do have work to be getting on with…'

'And I don't want to take up any more of your time,' said Raven.

Dr Wainwright left her microscope and raised herself to her full height. 'But you have a few questions that you urgently want answers to?'

'Well… yes,' he said, grateful for her understanding. 'As a matter of fact, I do.'

'Time of death?' she suggested.

He offered a tentative smile. 'That would be a good start.'

'Don't have one,' she snapped. 'Next question?'

Raven gritted his teeth. 'Then perhaps you have an idea how long the victim spent in the water?'

'On initial inspection I'd say that he was in the water for a matter of hours, a day at the most.'

'That fits with what we already know,' said Raven.

'Then I wonder why you so desperately needed to ask me.' Dr Wainwright folded her arms against her narrow chest. 'It's traditional in these kinds of scenarios to be allowed to ask three questions, isn't it? Would you like to know if it was the bullet that killed him, or if the cause of death was something else?'

'That would be helpful.'

Dr Wainwright shook her head. 'I couldn't possibly say at this stage. Now, perhaps you'd like to come back for the post-mortem itself, when all will be revealed.'

'And what time will that be?'

'I'll be opening him up at two o'clock sharp.' She looked at him expectantly. 'Will I have the pleasure of your company?'

Raven sensed this was a test which she hoped he would fail. He looked at his watch. 'I'm afraid that I have to be somewhere else at that time.'

She regarded him with a look of triumph.

'I'll send my sergeant over instead,' he told her, hoping that Becca wouldn't mind. 'Her name is DS Shawcross.'

'Becca? Excellent. I look forward to seeing her. And now I really must ask you to be on your way.'

Raven didn't need asking again. He left the icy environment of the morgue and returned to the welcoming bosom of his car.

CHAPTER 10

The M6's five litre engine howled as Raven pushed his foot to the floor and the needle of the rev counter spun up the dial. A speed limit sign flashed past, little more than a blur in his side mirror. This would have been impossible back in London, where traffic cameras lurked around every bend. Raven wondered why it had taken him so long to make the move north out of the capital.

On a fine day the view across the North York Moors could be breath-taking, with mile after mile of rolling purple heather beneath clear blue skies. But such days were rare. Today a mist had crept in from the sea, obscuring the scenery behind a thin veil of grey. As he drove further up the coast the mist thickened and Raven slowed the car to a more modest fifty miles an hour. He recalled the saying by Oscar Wilde: "I don't desire to change anything in England except the weather." Or to put it another way: the weather could be really crap up north. Perhaps that was why he'd stayed in London.

He filled the miles by going over in his mind what he'd learnt so far about the victim. Patrick Lofthouse appeared to have gone out of his way to surround himself with people his parents disapproved of – like Scarlett Jubb and Shane Denton. He had also disappointed them by his lack of enthusiasm for joining the family business. But how many kids ever wanted to follow in their parents' footsteps? Ethan Jubb might be a chip off his old father's rotten old block, but Scarlett was forging her own unique path.

Patrick was a rebel, then, and Raven was starting to warm to him.

The weather didn't improve the further north he travelled. By the time he reached the outskirts of Redcar, the charms – or otherwise – of the post-industrial town were camouflaged behind a blanket of steady rain.

He turned up the volume on his music to drown out the drumbeat of the raindrops against the windscreen. Late eighties gothic rock. The soundtrack to his life. During happy moments and sad, the heavy bass guitars and gloom-filled droning lyrics had been there throughout. It had driven Lisa nuts. Hannah's voice echoed in his head. *You're a dinosaur, Dad. A total throwback.* He smiled. *Guilty as charged.* He had never tried to deny it.

The only address he'd been able to find for Shane Denton was a static mobile home on a caravan park on the town's north-eastern edge. Pulling in to the park, he was reminded of one of the few family holidays he'd had as a child: a fortnight with his maternal grandparents in a caravan in Berwick-upon-Tweed. His dad had never been much of a one for holidays, and in the summer his mum couldn't get time off from her job as a chambermaid at the Grand Hotel, so that particular year – he must have been, what, eleven, twelve? – he'd been packed off to Berwick with a holdall of freshly laundered clothes, courtesy of his mother, and a warning from his father to stay out of trouble or face the consequences. He hadn't had high hopes for the holiday, and had resented being farmed out to his grandparents, who had seemed old and decrepit to him. In the event, the holiday had turned out better than he could have hoped. While his grandparents sat on deckchairs outside their caravan, chatting to the passers-by who all seemed to be regulars at the park, Raven had been free to roam the rugged Northumberland coast. On one cloudless day he'd taken a bus south, then walked across the causeway to Holy Island, only just making it back to the mainland before the tide cut him off. He'd looked forward to going back the following summer, but by then his grandad had suffered a stroke and needed constant care. There had been no more holidays. Instead he'd stayed in Scarborough, bored. It was then he'd got to know Darren, hanging around the amusement arcades together. And look where that had got him.

He parked the BMW near the park entrance and turned up his coat collar before stepping out into the rain which was now lashing down in sheets. It was hard to imagine anyone coming on holiday here, even in high season. The park wasn't within sight of the sea, being situated just off a residential road with the old steelworks visible in the distance.

He trudged along the rows of mobile homes, looking for Shane's. Baskets of bedraggled flowers hung from one or two of the caravans in a futile effort to brighten the surroundings. Many of the homes even had satellite dishes. He wondered how many were permanent dwellings.

He found the one he was looking for at the end of a line overlooked by the back of a row of terraced houses. Rain drummed on the metal roof and churned the ground where he was standing. He knocked on the door. No response. He peered through the grimy window. The interior was a clutter of empty pizza boxes, unwashed clothes and scrunched up beer cans. No sign of the occupant.

He was about to knock on one of the neighbouring homes when a young lad in a denim jacket with hair flopping over his forehead rounded the corner, a Tesco carrier bag swinging breezily from each hand.

'Shane Denton?' Raven reached inside his breast pocket for his warrant card.

But Denton clearly had other ideas than hanging

around to inspect his credentials. He dropped both bags, spilling crisps, biscuits, chocolate bars and fizzy drinks over the grass, turned on his heel and ran.

Shit, thought Raven, setting off in pursuit. Denton didn't look like much of an athlete – his physique was what you might expect from a diet of processed convenience foods – but he had more than a twenty-year advantage on Raven and disappeared with astonishing speed into the maze of mobile homes.

Raven caught a glimpse of a rain-soaked denim jacket swerving round wooden decking and pushed himself to catch up. But the grass was worn down by the tramp of too many feet and the rain was fast turning the ground into a quagmire. It didn't help that he was wearing a suit and smart shoes. Skidding on the slippery mud, he felt his old injury protest at the unaccustomed exertion and a sharp pain shot through his right thigh. *Not now*, he thought, gritting his teeth. He pressed on.

Denton was gaining ground, now more than fifty yards ahead of him. He was making straight for the edge of the caravan park. With surprising agility for one carrying so much excess weight around his middle, he leapt over a low concrete wall and disappeared from view. Reaching the wall moments later, Raven peered over and saw that Denton was now sprinting down a grassy bank, heading straight for the Tees Valley railway line. An approaching train rumbled along the tracks.

Raven heaved himself over the wall. 'Stop!' he yelled.

But Denton didn't even pause for breath. Instead he launched himself in front of the oncoming train.

Pain jolted through Raven's leg as he landed on the other side of the wall, but he forced himself on.

The two-carriage Northern Line train let out a blast of its horn, but Denton jumped across the tracks just before it clattered past. Raven caught the look of alarm on the face of the driver, who must have been wondering what this crazy guy was doing. Raven wondered the same. Why was Denton acting so recklessly unless he had something serious to hide?

When the train had gone, Raven crossed the tracks with care, then looked around for Denton. His quarry had vanished.

Then he spotted him, crouching down in the lee of a blasted tree. Denton's eyes met his and he was on the move again. Raven lumbered after him, the wind and rain plastering wet hair against his face. But soon the youth found himself trapped in front of a long, narrow strip of water, undecided which way to go. Left or right, he was basically out of options.

'I just want to talk to you,' shouted Raven through the deluge, but Denton had other ideas. He dashed off to the left, and Raven cursed, stomping after the youth, his shoes caked in squelching mud.

Denton was still ahead, but he was starting to struggle as the ground grew ever more slippery. Raven heard a scream and a splash and suddenly the lad was in the water.

Raven made his way carefully down the slope to the flooded ditch and stretched out a hand. 'Come on. Don't be a fool. Take it.'

Denton thrashed around for a while longer in the green murk. But then the fight seemed to go out of him. He reached up and Raven seized hold of his arm, dragging him out. He pulled the lad safely onto the muddy bank and finally produced his warrant card. 'You could have made this a lot easier for both of us, son,' he said.

CHAPTER 11

'So,' said Dr Felicity Wainwright, snapping off her surgical gloves, rolling them into a tight ball, and depositing them into the clinical waste bin, 'I see there's a new DCI in town.'

The post-mortem had been routine and hadn't revealed any real surprises. Patrick Lofthouse had been dead before he entered the water, killed by a single gunshot which had punctured his heart. Felicity had retrieved the bullet and it would now be sent off to ballistics for analysis. They would also have to wait for the results of the toxicology tests to see if Patrick had imbibed any drugs or alcohol prior to being shot. Felicity had put the time of death, somewhat approximately given the circumstances, at anywhere between four o'clock and midnight on the Sunday, a window of eight hours.

Becca hadn't been best pleased when Raven asked her to attend the post-mortem on his behalf, apparently taking it for granted that she wouldn't mind. Why did people always assume that she was okay with hospitals? But she hadn't felt she could refuse, not while she and her new boss were still sizing each other up. She wouldn't have put him down as a squeamish type, but you could never tell.

'You've met Raven, then?' she said. Dr Wainwright didn't keep her opinions to herself and Becca was curious to hear her first impressions of her new boss.

'He popped in this morning on the pretext of saying hello,' said Felicity.

'You think he had an ulterior motive?'

'Macho posturing.'

'Do you think so?' said Becca.

'Of course. He wanted to make it clear who was in charge. I've seen that type before. They can be charming on the outside, but a tyrant underneath. Well, if he thought he could charm me, he went away disappointed.'

Felicity could be quite unforgiving, Becca had noticed before, when it came to members of the opposite sex.

'He couldn't hide his surprise though when he discovered I was a woman,' said Felicity.' Her tone was almost gleeful.

'At least he gets things done,' said Becca, wanting to stick up for her new boss. 'Unlike some people I could mention.'

'I assume you're referring to DI Derek Dinsdale?'

Bullseye! 'Dinsdale was originally in charge of the case,' said Becca, 'but Superintendent Ellis kicked him off as soon as DCI Raven rode into town.'

Felicity gave a tight-lipped smile. 'I bet that went down well.' The pathologist had never made any secret of her disdain for Derek Dinsdale. And to be fair, he had never shown much appreciation for the work done by pathologists and forensics experts. Dinsdale preferred to claim their glory for himself.

'He's prowling around the office like a bear with a sore head,' said Becca. 'I wish the Super would find something else for him to do. Or tell him to start drawing his pension.'

'Retirement's too good for him,' said Felicity darkly. 'I'd rather see him on my slab. Give him a good going over before putting him in the ground.'

Becca turned away. Sometimes Felicity's black sense of

humour went just a little too far for her liking.

'But speaking seriously,' said Felicity, 'this case has some similarities to one from a few years back. Wasn't Dinsdale in charge of that?'

'You've got a good memory,' said Becca.

'I never forget a corpse.' Felicity tapped the side of her head. 'Especially not one that's been shot and then dumped in the sea.'

'It is quite a coincidence, isn't it?' said Becca.

'Copycat killing?' suggested Felicity. 'Or did Dinsdale put the wrong man behind bars?'

'I don't know,' said Becca.

'But you think your new boss is the knight in shining armour who's going to find the truth?'

'We'll see,' said Becca. 'But if anyone can shake things up and get to the bottom of it, then it's DCI Tom Raven.'

*

The Shane Denton who sat across from Raven in the interview room at Scarborough police station was a considerably more subdued character than the one who had dared risk life and limb in the path of the 14:35 from Redcar Central to Middlesbrough. A cold dunking in a muddy ditch had left him forlorn and pitiful.

News of Patrick's death appeared to have come as a complete shock to him, but Raven wasn't convinced by his protestations of innocence. Why had he run if he had nothing to hide? Perhaps it was because of what they'd found in his mobile home. A cursory search of the property had unearthed a stash of cannabis and cocaine, poorly concealed amidst the detritus of a chaotic, aimless life. Raven would be charging him with possession, if nothing else. And with Shane's previous conviction for drug offences, it wasn't looking good for him.

He had already declined his right to legal representation. 'What's the point?' he'd asked mournfully. 'My gran says lawyers are all a bunch of crooks. Anyway, they did no good for me last time, did they?' Raven hadn't been able to disagree.

Now he sat hunched, ashen-faced and twitchy, a cup of hot tea nursed in his fingers, his eyes darting anxiously around the bare interior of the interview room.

Raven decided it was time to get stuck in. 'You worked for Patrick Lofthouse's father, Gordon Lofthouse' – Raven checked his notes – 'four years ago. Is that correct?'

'Yeah,' said Shane, 'I got a job at his car dealership. There's nowt in Redcar, not since the steelworks closed down.'

'What was your role at the dealership?' It was hard to picture Shane as a smooth-talking sales executive, especially with his marked use of Yorkshire dialect.

'I valeted the cars.'

Given the state of Shane's mobile home, that was perhaps even harder to imagine. 'How long did you work there?' asked Raven.

'About a year.'

'Why did you leave?'

'I were sacked.'

'After you abused the trust of your employer,' said Raven

Shane glared angrily at him. 'I never nicked owt. That were a lie.'

'You were convicted of drug offences.'

'Oh, that.' He shrugged. 'It weren't a lot. Just some weed.'

'Just some weed,' repeated Raven. Shane wasn't yet under arrest, although given what they'd found in his mobile home, he soon would be. And this time the charge would be more serious than just possession of cannabis. But it was Shane's relationship with Patrick that was Raven's most pressing concern. 'When did you and Patrick first become friends?' he asked.

'It were when I worked for his dad.'

'And you continued to see him after you finished working there?'

'That's right. We were mates.'

'When did you last see Patrick?'

Shane screwed up his face in concentration. 'Must have been at the end of August, start of September? Summat like that.'

'What about last Sunday?'

'What about it?'

'Did you see Patrick then?'

'No. Should I have done?'

'Patrick sent a message to his fiancée saying he was going to see you.'

Shane scowled. 'That stuck-up bitch. You can't believe owt she says. She never liked me.'

Becca hadn't yet returned from the post-mortem at the hospital, so Raven had asked DC Jess Barraclough to sit in on the interview. 'Why didn't Scarlett like you, Shane?' she asked.

'Said I were bad for Patrick's image. That's all she cares about, how things look.'

'Well,' said Raven, 'things don't look good for you right now. Scarlett wasn't lying about the message that Patrick sent her. So I'll ask you again. Did you see Patrick Lofthouse on Sunday?'

Shane threw up his hands in exasperation. 'I already said no, didn't I? Why don't you listen?'

Raven allowed the dust to settle a moment before asking his next question. 'When you and Patrick did get together, what did you do?'

Shane took a slurp of his tea. 'Just hung out. That's what mates do, isn't it?'

'So,' suggested Jess, 'you what, had a couple of drinks?'

'Yeah.'

'Smoked a bit of weed?'

'No. Well. Only in private, like…'

'Snorted cocaine?'

'You're trying to stitch me up now,' protested Shane. 'I never did owt.'

Raven glared at him. 'Don't be stupid, Shane. We

found the cocaine in your home and we'll be charging you with possession. You think that snorting coke is cool? That it's a victimless crime? Well, it's not. You're the victim.'

Shane flinched, averting his gaze, and Raven let it drop. He wasn't here to lecture Shane on his drug habit, and if they pushed him too hard he might clam up completely. For now he was talking, and Raven welcomed that. 'So, let's talk about what you did on Sunday. Where were you that day?'

'Where d'you think?' said Shane sullenly. 'In Redcar.'

'You'll have to be a bit more specific than that, Shane. What time did you get up?'

'I dunno. Ten? Eleven?'

'And then what?'

'I went to Tesco's for a few things. They've got CCTV in there, so you can check if you don't believe me. Then I went to see my gran. Did a couple of odd jobs for her, you know?'

'How good of you,' said Raven.

Shane shrugged. 'Afterwards, I went back to the caravan and had a couple of beers before going to bed.'

'Can anyone vouch for that?' asked Jess.

'I dunno.'

'But you're positive you never saw Patrick in all that time?'

'I already told you, no I didn't see him.'

'Could he have gone round to the caravan while you were with your gran?' asked Jess.

'He'd have called me if he were coming,' said Shane. A momentary doubt flickered across his face. 'He usually did.'

'But not always?'

Shane shrugged. 'He did turn up unexpectedly once or twice, I guess.'

'So it's possible that he came to the caravan when you were out?'

'No!' Shane shook his head in frustration. 'He would have phoned me, wouldn't he?'

'All right,' said Raven before Shane blew his top. 'Do you know who Tristan and Iseult are?'

Shane brightened immediately at the question. 'Of course. They're characters out of a medieval story. It were a tale of forbidden love. Chivalric romance and all that, with knights, princesses, heroic quests.'

Raven looked at him in surprise. It was as if a different person was suddenly speaking. Gone was the sullen, diffident youth to be replaced by a young man who spoke with confidence and assurance. 'You're interested in that kind of thing?' asked Raven.

'It were my gran who first got me into it,' said Shane. 'She used to tell me stories when I were little. Celtic and Norse mythology, King Arthur, the Vikings, all that stuff. She had a lot of books, still has, although they're getting a bit old now.' He looked across the table directly into Raven's eyes. 'Raven. That's a Viking name.'

'Yes,' said Raven gruffly. He had no desire to discuss his family history.

But Shane's enthusiasm showed no sign of dimming. 'In Norse mythology, ravens were an omen of death. The god Odin had two talking ravens. Every day, he sent them out to fly around the world and bring back news of what they saw and heard. Odin were the god of wisdom, but he were also the Viking war god, the god of death.'

Raven fixed him with a hard stare and Shane fell silent, aware that he had strayed into unwelcome territory. Raven's past was deep water, best left undisturbed.

'So can you tell us, Shane,' said Jess, 'why Patrick Lofthouse was wearing a ring engraved with the names Tristan and Iseult?'

'He were?' Shane looked surprised. 'I didn't know.'

'Where might he have got the idea?'

'Well, from me, I guess. We used to talk about all that stuff in our tea breaks at the car dealership. Patrick were bored stiff working there. He wanted to do summat more exciting with his life. Talking about myths and legends gave him summat to dream about.'

'Do you think that Patrick may have seen himself as Tristan?'

'Yeah.' Shane nodded vigorously. 'Yeah, that's exactly how he saw himself. A romantic hero. A forbidden lover.' A faraway look entered his eyes and he began to recite from memory. '"Fold your arms round me close and strain me so that our hearts may break and our souls go free at last. Take me to that happy place of which you told me long ago. The fields whence none return, but where great singers sing their songs forever." That's what Iseult says to Tristan just before they are parted forever.'

'Very romantic,' said Raven drily. 'So who was Patrick's forbidden love? Who was his Iseult?'

Shane shook his head. 'I've really no idea.'

*

'I'm off now,' said Jess, zipping up her parka and pulling the hood over her long blonde hair. 'Fancy going somewhere for a quick drink?'

'I'm good,' said Becca, holding up her mug of tea. 'Just want to tidy things up before I head for home.'

It had been late by the time she'd got back from the hospital and dropped the bullet off with ballistics, and most of the team had already gone home. She understood from Jess that Raven had charged Shane Denton with possession of cannabis and cocaine. They didn't have enough to pin Patrick's murder on him, although Shane's alibi was weak and still needed checking. Raven was currently in a meeting with Superintendent Ellis, updating her on the day's events. They had certainly achieved a lot more that day than when Dinsdale had been in charge.

'Don't stay too late,' called Jess, giving her a quick wave as she bounced out of the room.

Becca breathed a sigh and took a sip of her tea. At last she had the place to herself. Between visiting the Jubbs in the morning and attending the post-mortem in the afternoon, she'd hardly had a moment even to check her emails. And given the pace at which DCI Raven liked to work, who knew what tomorrow might bring?

It wasn't unusual for her to stay late at work, and she liked the peace that descended on the office after everyone else had left. The humming of the computers, the whispering of air through the heating vents, the background sounds of cars and people outside. Some evenings she went to see her boyfriend, Sam, some evenings she spent at home, but more often than not, this was where she would be found, catching up on the day's work and getting ahead for the day to come. She hated leaving admin to pile up and prevent her from focussing on her current duties.

Her brother often teased her, saying she ought to get out more and have some fun. Just last week he'd tried to persuade her to go out on the town with him and his mates. 'Come with us, Becs. We'll take you for a spin. There'll be drinking, there'll be dancing. It'll be a wild night, I promise.'

'I'm sure it would,' she had answered, laughing. 'That's why I'd rather stay at the office.'

She settled herself down in front of her computer with her mug of nice, strong tea – she'd tried other brands, but like her dad always said, you couldn't beat proper Yorkshire Tea – and got to work. She wrote up her notes from the post-mortem and then checked the time. Seven o'clock. She should probably call it a day. But there was no real hurry to get home. Her mum would keep something on a plate for her that she could re-heat in the microwave.

She shut down the police database and opened up her web browser. Ever since speaking to Scarlett Jubb that morning, she'd been itching to check out her online profile. It didn't take long to find it. Scarlett's YouTube channel had more than a million subscribers and consisted mainly of videos of her giving makeup tutorials while "applying" her face. Becca's own morning routine consisted of a quick wash with soap and a dab of moisturiser. If it was sunny – and it could be very bright in Scarborough during the summer months – she would use sunscreen if she was going to be out and about. Sometimes she forgot, or the sun would put in a surprise appearance, and her face would burst out in a rash of freckles. Her mum would smile and say, 'You've caught the sun.' But watching Scarlett's channel made Becca realise that moisturiser and sunscreen were only the very beginning of a girl's skincare regime. There were a hundred and one further steps to achieving the perfect face before you could consider stepping outside the front door. Despite herself, Becca found herself quite mesmerised as Scarlett leaned into the camera and explained how to apply foundation, concealer and do contouring. As for eyes, brows and lashes, they required whole videos of their own.

On Instagram, Scarlett had even more followers – a staggering ten million. There, she posed in skimpy swimsuits and designer dresses, worked out with weights and flexed herself into impossible yoga poses. Photos of her drinking green smoothies appeared with the hashtag *#cleanliving*. It was an image of perfection that few of her followers were likely to achieve themselves, but judging by the comments, they adored her. *OMG you look amazing! Wish I could have the perfect body like you! You rock girl!*

There were photos of Scarlett with Patrick too. In those pictures, the young man looked very different to the cold corpse that Becca had seen washed up on a cold Scarborough beach. In life, Patrick had been very handsome. Becca flicked through the pictures, seeing Becca and Patrick drinking cocktails in bars, splashing in the sea, and sunbathing on the deck of a yacht. They looked good together. A perfect couple. Now the glamorous lifestyle and promise of a happy future had capsized spectacularly. There had been no new photos or videos uploaded to Scarlett's accounts today. Becca clicked the "follow" button.

She checked the time again. It was gone eight o'clock. An hour had passed looking at someone else's life and she realised how the allure of social media could so easily capture and consume people's attention.

But Scarlett Jubb wasn't the only person Becca was curious about. On impulse she typed the words "DCI Tom Raven" into the search box and waited to see what she might find. It never hurt to have a bit of background on your colleagues, especially a new boss.

In contrast to Scarlett, Raven had no social media presence whatsoever. The fact didn't surprise her. After working with him for a day, Becca already had the sense that he wasn't the most sociable of people. But he wasn't completely invisible online. Scrolling down the page, she found his name coming up in relation to a couple of cases he'd worked on during his time at the Met. He'd been SIO during the high-profile murder investigation of a woman whose body had been found on Clapham Common. He'd also handled various rape cases, putting a number of perpetrators behind bars. A solid track record, then. An experienced detective. She wondered what had caused him to leave all that behind and return to Scarborough. His father's death had no doubt been the immediate catalyst, drawing him back to his home town for the funeral. But there must have been more to it than that. A push as well as a pull.

She almost missed it, then scrolled back up the screen to click on an old news article. Here was something interesting. In 1994, a Lance Corporal Thomas Raven had been deployed to Bosnia with the Duke of Wellington's Regiment. Their area of responsibility had covered the besieged enclave of Goražde. The regiment succeeded in pushing back the Bosnian-Serb Army in an engagement that saw one of their own killed compared with seven of the enemy soldiers. During a firefight between the opposing sides, Lance Corporal Raven had left his position and engaged the enemy in order to provide cover for two injured members of his patrol, enabling them to escape from danger. Raven was shot in the leg but received the Conspicuous Gallantry Cross in acknowledgement of his bravery.

'Still here?'

Becca jumped and shut down her browser before Raven could see what she was looking at.

'I was just wrapping up.'

'I think you've done enough for one day. Go home and get some rest. That's an order.'

Becca rose from her seat. 'Yes, sir.' She had to resist the urge to salute.

CHAPTER 12

The girl on the checkout is busy with a customer. There's no one standing nearby. It's now or never. He reaches out a hand for the CD and slips it inside his jacket before picking up another and pretending to study the list of songs on the back. He makes a show of putting the second CD back on the rack and walking away empty-handed, feigning an air of nonchalance that he doesn't feel. His heart is hammering in his chest and he fears that the square outline of the stolen item is burning a hole through the fabric of his bomber jacket. Now all he wants is to get outside where his girlfriend and Darren are waiting for him. The CD is for her. He can't afford to buy her one, but he needs a way to prove how much he loves her. And he doesn't trust Darren not to chat her up while he's in the shop. Woolworth's on Westborough, the Saturday hangout for Scarborough's teenagers, having graduated from the Pick'n'Mix to the record collection. He needs to get outside, quickly, but suddenly the aisle is blocked – a mother with a toddler throwing a tantrum, an old lady with a tartan shopping trolley on wheels, a group of younger kids from his school fooling about. And then the girl on the checkout – a young woman with bottle-blonde hair – points his way and screeches at the top of her voice, 'Stop, thief!' He tries to run but his legs are made of lead. He can see Darren standing in the doorway of the shop, watching and smirking. Laughing at him. The old woman with the tartan trolley suddenly produces an umbrella and beats him over the head with it. Someone blows a whistle…

Raven awoke with a start. The whistling sound was the alarm on his phone. He reached out a hand and turned it off. Six-thirty. Still dark outside, and would be for another hour at least. For a moment, he lay there, reliving the dream, the nightmare, bathed in sweat and waiting for his heart rate to return to normal.

The previous day's encounter with Darren Jubb had stirred memories that should have remained at the bottom of the deep ocean where Raven had dumped his past on leaving Scarborough all those years ago. It was true, he had once stolen a CD from Woolworth's – all in the name of love – although thankfully there hadn't been an umbrella-toting granny to administer justice. He hadn't been caught, but the euphoria of getting away with it had soon worn off, leaving in its wake a cold dread. He'd avoided Woolworth's for a long time after that.

He forced himself out of bed. He wasn't fifteen anymore and he had bigger matters to concern himself with, like a murder enquiry for one. He'd picked up the habit of rising early while in the army and it had served him well over the years. An early start helped him get ahead and stay in front, safe in the knowledge that most villains out there were still asleep. He washed and dressed quickly – it was too cold in the bathroom to hang around – then proceeded to the kitchen to rustle up breakfast.

He'd popped into Tesco Express the previous night to pick up the bare essentials – bread, milk, margarine, eggs, bacon, teabags, a frozen pizza for dinner. He'd realised it was time to stop living off takeaway food when he'd called in at the chip shop and the woman behind the counter had greeted him with the words, 'The usual?' It seemed that in the short time he'd been back in Scarborough he'd already become a recognisable face, his dietary preferences –

haddock and chips with curry sauce – duly noted.

As he rummaged in the kitchen cupboard for a frying pan, he thought of Darren Jubb in his big house up on the mount. He hadn't seen Darren's kitchen but judging from the rest of the house he imagined something shiny and spacious, all granite surfaces and chrome fittings. An American-style fridge-freezer. No expense spared.

His father's kitchen by contrast was small, dingy and hadn't been updated since Tom's childhood. He located a small frying pan at the back of the cupboard, its non-stick surface worn and blackened with age. The sight of it triggered another memory – his mum frying eggs every morning before his dad went out in the fishing boat. Joan, his mother, had done everything for her husband. Not that Alan had ever shown any gratitude. He took it for granted that his wife would run around after him, cook all his meals, do his laundry, clean the house. Alan Raven had exhibited the unenlightened attitude of a working-class man from another age. But his mother had never complained, immune to the feminist revolution that was underway all around her. When Joan had died, Alan hadn't been able to cope. Always a drinker, he'd found solace in the bottle. And he'd taken his anger out on his son.

The gas cooker hissed and Raven groped around for a box of matches. Striking one, he lit the flame, cracked a couple of eggs into a Queen's Silver Jubilee mug from 1977, and whisked them with a fork while he melted a knob of margarine on the hob. The markings on the cooker were so badly worn it was pot luck which ring you were turning on. He was pleased when he managed to produce an edible omelette without blowing himself up.

He scraped the omelette onto a plate with a faded flower design and sat at the kitchen table to eat it, powering up his iPad to check his personal emails. There was a message from Lisa, which he ignored, but nothing from Hannah, his daughter. He'd emailed her the previous night to let her know he would be staying in Scarborough for the foreseeable future and to ask her how she was getting on.

He was disappointed at the lack of response, but not surprised.

He wasn't having much luck with women at the moment. The pathologist, Dr Felicity Wainwright, had taken an immediate dislike to him, for no good reason he could discern. And Detective Superintendent Gillian Ellis had given him a hard time when he'd gone to her to report on his first day's progress. He'd expected her to be pleased that he'd already interviewed the prime suspect and had arrested and charged a second suspect in the case. Instead, she'd greeted him with the words, 'You didn't tell me you were an old friend of Darren Jubb's.'

'You didn't tell me that the MO was identical to a previous murder and that Jubb was the link between the two killings,' he'd responded.

'I told you what you needed to know, Tom. Make sure you tell me everything I need to know.'

'Such as?'

Her small eyes bored into him. 'You turn up out of the blue, just when Darren Jubb becomes number-one suspect in a murder enquiry. And now I discover that you and Jubb go way back. You were actually here in town before the victim's body was found.'

Raven raised his eyebrows. 'Are you suggesting I had something to do with the murder?'

'I'm saying I don't like unexplained coincidences.'

He shook his head, angry that his motives were being questioned. 'I came back for my father's funeral. Staying on in Scarborough was a snap decision. For personal reasons.'

'Perhaps you should have asked for compassionate leave instead of a transfer.'

'Are you going to send me back to London?' he demanded.

At that, she had relented a little. 'I'm not sending you anywhere, Tom. But I want you to get on top of this investigation quickly. Don't think you'll get an easy ride just because you've moved out of the big city.'

'Fine,' he said. 'I wasn't expecting one.'

She nodded. 'Good, then we understand each other. And by the way, don't you have another tie in your wardrobe?'

Raven looked down at the black tie he had been wearing ever since the day of the funeral. 'It's the only one I brought with me from London.'

'Buy yourself another, Tom. It makes you look like a funeral director. And a new suit wouldn't do any harm either, while you get that one dry-cleaned.'

She was right, of course. He'd brushed his trousers clean as best he could after his muddy encounter with Shane Denton, but the stain from the ditch water hadn't gone completely.

He'd retreated from her office feeling somewhat bruised, only to find Detective Sergeant Becca Shawcross googling him, although she'd tried to hide what she was doing. He wasn't sure how he felt about her delving into his past. Full marks for initiative, of course. It was precisely what he would have done himself if lumbered unexpectedly with a new boss. But at the same time, he wasn't sure how far she'd go, and he didn't want her raking over his life too closely. *'I could tell you a thing or two about your boss from back in the day,'* Darren Jubb had said to her, deliberately whetting her appetite for intrigue. '*Don't worry, Tom, your secrets are safe with me*,' he had promised. But nothing Darren said could ever be taken at face value.

Raven finished his omelette and cleared away the breakfast things before leaving the house. On his way out, he stole a quick glance at the photo of his mum, caught forever within her gilded frame in a moment of happiness. She would never know anything else now. She was dead. And Raven was to blame... Raven, and Darren Jubb.

CHAPTER 13

The corridor leading from reception to the foot of the stairwell smelled of coffee, stale tobacco and sweat, and it was there that Raven encountered the rotund form of DI Derek Dinsdale. The deposed SIO was leaning against the vending machine, feeding coins into the slot like a down-at-luck gambler hoping to finally win the jackpot. Raven nodded a tentative greeting, but the look that Dinsdale returned was filled with nothing but undisguised loathing.

Raven carried on past, saying nothing. He'd handled more difficult characters than Dinsdale during his time at the Met and had no time to waste on a disgruntled rival.

Detective Superintendent Gillian Ellis was a different matter however. His position in Scarborough was provisional and she had made it perfectly clear that if he didn't get results soon she wouldn't hesitate to send him back to London with a flea in his ear. She'd hired him at a moment's notice and she could fire him just as quickly. She was that sort of woman.

When he arrived in the incident room, he was glad to see that his team members were already in, nice and early.

'Team meeting in ten,' he announced to everyone on his way to his office.

'No croissants today?' muttered DC Dan Bennett.

'You should have had breakfast before you left home,' Becca told him.

Raven went into his office and threw his jacket over the back of the chair. He sat down and took a look around his new domain. It was even shabbier than he had appreciated on day one. Worn carpets, scuffed walls, mismatched furniture. The wear and tear of a well-used workplace. The room was small too, but he liked the fact that he was close to his team and that they could see him through the glass.

He scanned the surface of the desk. A keyboard, a screen, and a phone. Plus a whole heap of junk that Dinsdale had left lying around. Pens, pencils, Sellotape, crisp wrappers, jotting pads, car parking tickets. Raven scooped it all up and deposited it into the wastepaper bin. He liked his desk clean, just like his car.

He slid open the top drawer of the desk and peered inside. Lying at the bottom was an envelope with his name on it. He lifted it out, opened it and removed the scrawled, handwritten note it contained.

Watch your back.

He crumpled the paper into a ball and dropped it into the bin.

*

Ten minutes later his team was gathered around the whiteboard, Raven on his feet at the front of the room. Since the previous day he had added three names to the board. In addition to the victim's name – *Patrick Lofthouse* – were the names of the two suspects. *Darren Jubb* and *Shane Denton*. A photo printed from the website of *The Scarborough News* showed Darren beaming smugly at the camera during a publicity event at his nightclub, Vertigo. *Connections to two murders*, Raven had written next to the photo. Shane's photo, meanwhile, was less flattering, being a mugshot taken following his arrest. *Charged with possession of a controlled drug*. Cocaine – a class A drug. With a previous conviction for the same offence, Shane was facing the prospect of a custodial sentence. But the question that concerned Raven was whether Shane had seen Patrick on the day of the murder. If he had, then he was in the frame for a much more serious charge. He picked up the marker pen and scrawled *Alibis?* beneath each man's name.

'Right,' said Raven, 'I want a round-up of all the facts so far. Who wants to go first?'

He was unsurprised when Becca put aside her mug of tea and picked up her notes and printouts. He wondered if she'd done any more googling about him, and if so what she might have found. 'I've got a summary of the findings from the post-mortem yesterday,' she said. 'Dr Wainwright confirmed that the cause of death was the gunshot wound. A single bullet punctured the heart and Patrick was already dead when his body entered the water. Dr Wainwright estimated the time of death to be between four o'clock in the afternoon and midnight on the Sunday. It's difficult to be more accurate because of the body being in the sea.'

Raven wrote the times on the board. He knew from prior experience that when bodies were found in water, the job of the pathologist became harder and the estimate of the time of death more uncertain. They would need to rely on other evidence to narrow down the timeline. 'Anything on toxicology yet?'

'Not yet. We'll have to wait until we hear back from the lab.'

'Chase them,' said Raven. 'What about ballistics?'

'I took the bullet in for analysis myself,' said Becca. 'They said it might take a few days to produce a full report, but I can tell you that it's a 9mm round.'

'Most likely from an illegal handgun,' said Raven. 'That suggests the involvement of organised crime. We'll need to check Patrick's background thoroughly and see if he had any links to criminal organisations.'

Next he turned to DC Tony Bairstow who was clutching a large file of paper. The man certainly was thorough. 'What do you have for us, Tony?' he asked.

Tony cleared his throat. 'Although the body was discovered on the North Bay, it's possible that it was washed up there by the sea and that the murder took place elsewhere. I had a long conversation with the coastguard yesterday. It's a complicated business, calculating tide times and currents, and with the eight-hour window for the time of death, there's a lot of uncertainty–'

'Understood,' said Raven.

'–but if the body entered the water at the time of the murder or immediately afterwards, it might have drifted along the coast from as far as Whitby.'

Raven's mental map of the North Yorkshire coast positioned Whitby roughly halfway between Scarborough and Redcar, home of Patrick's myth-obsessed, drug-consuming friend, Shane Denton. 'What about Redcar?' he asked. 'Is that too far north?'

Tony looked doubtful. 'The coastguard said Whitby was the furthest point possible. It was more likely to be closer to Scarborough.'

'Then that appears to back up Shane's version of events,' said Raven. 'According to him, he didn't see Patrick on Sunday and wasn't expecting to. Patrick may never have gone to Redcar, after all.'

'Which suggests that Patrick sent that message to Scarlett so that he wouldn't have to tell her where he was actually going,' said Becca.

Raven acknowledged her quick thinking with a smile. 'Or who he was really planning to meet. Have we located Patrick's car yet? What did he drive?'

Again, it was Tony who had the information at his fingertips. 'An Audi A3, sir. Black.' He recited the numberplate. 'We've checked all the local car parks and it's not in any of them. The ANPR system didn't pick up the car leaving Scarborough on Sunday, but I've circulated details to other forces in the area, just in case.'

'Good work,' said Raven. He liked people who used their initiative and didn't have to be told what to do all the time. 'It must be out there somewhere. Where are we with Patrick's mobile phone records?'

Dan Bennett sat up in his chair, hastily swallowing the remains of a KitKat that he must have bought from the vending machine after discovering that Raven didn't plan to provide a free breakfast every morning. 'Sir, we've received a list of calls and text messages made and received from Patrick's phone. What we haven't got hold of yet is the tracking information from the masts which would tell us where the phone was at any given time.'

'Anything notable?' asked Raven.

'The number that Patrick called most often was Scarlett Jubb's, and there are other calls to and from family members in the days preceding his death. But the last contact with Shane Denton was a couple of weeks ago.'

'What calls did he make on the day of the murder?'

'None, sir. And no SMS messages either. But of course he may have sent messages that we can't track, like the one he sent to Scarlett. Unless we find Patrick's phone we have no way of knowing.'

'Did we find any messages from Patrick on Shane's phone?' asked Raven.

This time it was DC Jess Barraclough who responded. 'Nothing, sir. Shane was in the habit of deleting all the messages he sent and received.'

'Damn it!' Raven hated technology. For each new invention that made detective work easier, another one tipped the balance in favour of the criminal. The net result was to make the investigation process endlessly more complicated and bureaucratic.

'All right,' he said, 'here's what I want you all to do today. Jess, I'd like you to go to Redcar and speak to Shane's gran to verify his alibi. Speak to the other residents of the caravan park and see if anyone can vouch for his whereabouts.'

'Yes, boss,' said Jess, her ponytail bobbing enthusiastically. She looked pleased to be going out, even if it was Redcar he was sending her to.

'Dan, can you check Darren Jubb's alibis for Sunday? He claims to have had one engagement after the other all day long. Too convenient by half. There must be a gap or a discrepancy somewhere. And Tony, I'd like you to follow up with locating Patrick's car, and chase the phone company, toxicology and ballistics. Get hold of Patrick's bank records, too. We need information, and we need it quickly.'

Tony jotted down the instructions in his notebook.

'What would you like me to do?' asked Becca.

'You're coming with me,' said Raven. 'Let's go and sample the delights of Her Majesty's Prison Service.'

CHAPTER 14

This time, Becca didn't make the mistake of assuming she would be driving – although she had cleared the rubbish out of her car the previous evening, just in case. She wondered if Raven had learned his tidiness and discipline in the army. She had been intrigued to learn that he was ex-military and had seen action in Bosnia. A decorated hero, no less. Not that she had any intention of sharing her discovery with her colleagues. She enjoyed a good chinwag as much as anyone, but she wasn't a gossip. If Raven wanted the others to know his background, he could tell them himself. But as they walked towards his car, she couldn't help watching him for signs of the leg injury he was supposed to have sustained. She hadn't noticed it before, but he did appear to move his right leg more stiffly than the left one.

He stopped and leaned against the car. 'It's okay most of the time. Cold weather makes it ache. Hurts like hell if I try to run, especially over rough ground. I'm not cut out for chases anymore.'

She quickly averted her gaze. 'I'm sorry. I didn't mean to pry.'

'Don't worry about it.' He gave her a wink. 'It'll be our secret.'

As soon as they were on the road and heading out of Scarborough, Raven asked her to tell him everything she knew about the man they were going to see at HMP Full Sutton. This time around, she'd had time to read through her notes from the case.

'Lewis Briggs,' she said. 'A bouncer at Darren Jubb's nightclub. He pleaded guilty to shooting Max Hunt, a known drugs dealer. The evidence was conclusive. The gun was found at Lewis's home, with his fingerprints still on it. Gunshot residue was detected on the sleeve of his leather jacket. He had no alibi, and a witness placed him at the scene of the shooting.'

'Sounds almost too good to be true,' said Raven. 'Like he was framed.'

'But he made a full confession,' said Becca.

'Did he say why he killed Hunt?'

'He didn't give a reason. Said it was personal. Max Hunt was a regular at the nightclub where Lewis worked, so the two men knew each other from there.'

'How did the police know to search Lewis's home?' asked Raven.

'An anonymous tip-off.'

'The police must have had some idea where the tip-off came from.'

'It was from an untraceable mobile phone.'

'A man's voice? A woman's?'

'A man's,' said Becca.

Raven fell silent, mulling over the information she'd given him. They had left the hilly environs of Scarborough behind and were following the flat, straight road that led to York. The countryside here was low-lying and featureless and they drove past tiny hamlets and isolated farmsteads. In the distance, wind turbines turned briskly in the steady breeze.

'You told me that Lewis Briggs had a previous conviction for drug dealing?' said Raven.

'Yes,' said Becca. 'But he wasn't involved in the kind of large-scale operation that Max Hunt was running. Lewis was convicted of possession with intent to supply. Apparently he used to pass pills to some of his regulars at the door of the club.'

'So there was nothing to indicate that he was looking to muscle in on Hunt's turf?'

'No,' said Becca. 'That's probably why the investigation stopped once Lewis had confessed to the shooting. There was no reason to look for anyone else who might have been involved.'

Raven gave her a thin smile. 'But you no longer think that?'

'I think it's best to always keep an open mind. And to follow the evidence.'

'Two bodies washed up on a beach,' recounted Raven. 'In each case, a single gunshot wound to the chest. And Darren Jubb's name cropping up each time.'

Becca was pleased to hear that Raven's thoughts tallied with her own. 'Like I said, follow the evidence.'

'It might just be a coincidence,' said Raven.

'It might.'

Raven put his foot down and the pitch of the BMW's engine rose as they overtook a lumbering tractor. Becca couldn't vouch that Raven was sticking to the speed limit, but there was no doubt that they were making good time.

'Who was in charge of the investigation?' Raven asked.

Becca tried to keep her voice free of inflection. 'DI Derek Dinsdale.'

Raven raised one questioning eyebrow. 'Do you think Dinsdale followed the evidence? All of it?'

'Well,' said Becca, 'I suppose that since Lewis confessed and took full responsibility…'

'Where did Lewis get the gun?' said Raven. 'Why didn't he get rid of it after the murder? Who made the tip-off? Who benefited from Max Hunt's death? There are far too many loose ends in this case for my liking. They should have been followed up.'

He made it sound like an act of gross negligence, and Becca supposed it had been. When she didn't immediately respond, he continued, 'I'd understand if you felt a sense of loyalty to the Senior Investigating Officer at the time.'

'Dinsdale? God no!' said Becca before she could stop herself. She felt her cheeks colouring. She didn't want Raven to think that she wasn't a good team player. 'I mean, that is…'

He grinned broadly at her discomfort.

'What I meant to say,' she clarified, 'is that while I can be loyal to a fault if I'm working for someone I respect, DI Derek Dinsdale–'

'–lacks certain leadership qualities.' Raven finished her sentence for her. 'Don't worry. I'd already noticed that.'

This brought a smile to Becca's lips and she felt emboldened enough to express her true thoughts. 'So the question is, was Dinsdale simply incompetent, or did he deliberately fail to follow up the wider implications?'

Raven kept his eyes firmly on the road ahead. 'Who was Dinsdale reporting to at the time?'

Becca hesitated. She had few qualms when it came to Dinsdale, but she had no wish to cast aspersions on a woman she regarded as a role model. One of the few women in a senior position in the force.

'Well?' persisted Raven. 'Who was Dinsdale's boss?' She suspected he already knew the answer but just wanted her to say it.

'Detective Superintendent Gillian Ellis.'

Raven didn't ask her any more questions and Becca was content to sit and watch the fields flashing by. The BMW really did eat up the miles.

*

HM Prison Full Sutton was discreetly hidden from the main road behind a row of high trees. The sign for the turn-off was small and easy to miss if you were weren't looking out for it. Raven might easily have driven past and been none the wiser that he was yards from a high security prison holding some of the country's most dangerous criminals.

He pulled the car off the main road and approached the site. More densely-planted trees surrounded the high wall that enclosed the buildings. Built in the late eighties, the prison was a far cry from the Victorian hellholes of Wormwood Scrubs and Brixton that he had occasionally been required to visit in London. But it still had the same pervasive air of hopelessness and gloom, not helped by the fact that at this time of year the trees were bare. A biting wind swept across the flat, open landscape and Raven drew his black coat around him as he stepped out of the car.

'You've been here before?' he asked Becca.

'No.'

He flashed her a grin. 'Well, too bad. Your luck's just run out.'

Full Sutton was a maximum-security men's prison, holding category A and B prisoners. In recent years, at least two child sex offenders had been murdered here by other convicted prisoners, and a report had found that organised gangs were operating inside the jail, arranging "fight clubs" between prisoners. It was no surprise that the security checks to enter the prison were tight. After the hassle of signing in and handing over their phones, Raven and Becca were shown into a windowless interview room that smelled strongly of disinfectant. Raven had no wish to know what smell the disinfectant was trying to mask. They both declined the offer of a coffee.

A burly prison officer brought Lewis Briggs into the room and seated him at the table in the middle. The guard then positioned himself in front of the door, like the bouncer that Lewis himself had once been.

Raven took a seat opposite his adversary. Lewis was a big bloke and all muscle. Locked in a cell for most of the day, he no doubt spent his time doing push-ups, pull-ups, dips and squats. His hair was cropped close to his scalp, and his nose looked as if it had been rearranged for him on more than one occasion. He leaned back in his chair, his heavily tattooed arms folded across his chest, his body language screaming *uncooperative*.

Raven wasn't fazed. He knew how to handle men like Lewis Briggs. They pretended they didn't like you wasting their time, but in truth they had sod all else to do. There was no point trying to butter them up with small talk. It was best to cut to the chase.

'We're here,' said Raven, 'because a man's body washed up on the beach at Scarborough on Monday morning with a bullet in the chest. Sound familiar?'

'I didn't do it,' said Lewis, deadpan. 'It weren't my weekend off.' He jerked a thumb towards the guard at the door. 'Ask him, he'll vouch for me.'

Raven ignored Briggs's sarcasm. 'You see, what I think is that whoever paid you to kill Max Hunt also ordered this latest killing.'

'Then you're wrong. No one paid me to kill Hunt.'

'So why did you shoot him?'

Lewis shrugged.

'Did you know that Max Hunt was dealing in class A drugs?' asked Raven.

'Lots of people knew. Made no difference to me.'

'Because you were dealing in drugs yourself.'

'Might have been.'

'But it was just a side hustle for you, wasn't it, Lewis? You didn't have the ambition for anything bigger. You left all that to others.'

Lewis leaned forwards and his nostrils flared with anger. But he didn't rise to the bait. Instead, he turned his attention to Becca and smirked. 'She's a pretty one. Does she say anything, or is she just here for decoration?'

'I worked on the investigation that put you behind bars,' said Becca. 'So I know all about you. The thing is, Lewis, I don't think you have the brains to get hold of a gun.'

Lewis's smirk died on his face. 'Yeah?'

'So who gave you the gun?'

Lewis's eyes narrowed. 'I bought it from a bloke in a pub.'

'What bloke?' asked Becca.

'Can't remember. Can't remember which pub either.' Lewis's body language was back to his previous, closed position.

Raven glanced around the interview room, with its bare walls, linoleum floor and metal door. 'You want to spend the rest of your days in this place, Lewis? It doesn't have to be that way. You could help us out, tell us who ordered the killing. Just give us a name, that's all.'

Lewis said nothing.

'I'll tell you what,' said Raven. 'Let's play a game. I say a name, and you just nod your head if I guess the right one. How's that?'

'I don't like playing games.'

'Darren Jubb.' Raven let the name hang in the space between them. But Lewis gave no indication that he had even heard it.

Raven pressed on. 'You worked for Darren at Vertigo. What kind of work did you do for him?'

'I were a bouncer,' said Lewis. 'I bounced.'

'Anything else?'

'Nowt.'

Jesus, thought Raven, *he's a hard one to crack.* Usually you only had to offer guys like this a chance at freedom and they were singing like a canary. 'Come on, Lewis,' he coaxed. 'Cooperation could reduce your sentence. I could put in a good word for you, tell the parole board that you were coerced into pulling the trigger. Were you coerced?'

No response.

'So you're stuck here while Darren Jubb is living a life of luxury,' said Raven. 'That's not smart, and it's not fair. Is it?'

'Think about your wife and child,' urged Becca. 'Don't you want to be back with them?'

For a moment, a light flickered in Lewis's eyes, but then his face hardened again. 'Life's never fair to blokes like me,' he said, 'but this time I got what were coming to me.' He nodded to the prison officer. 'I'd like to go back to my cell now.'

Raven watched him go. However much guys like Lewis might protest and make a show of refusing to cooperate, a visit from a couple of detectives was the most stimulation they got in months, years even. They would often suddenly remember a whole slew of stuff they'd "forgotten" earlier just to prolong an interview. But not Lewis. He retained his obstinate silence as he allowed himself to be led away. He didn't even turn back to look.

'Do you think he was too scared to talk?' asked Becca as she and Raven left the prison and crossed the windswept tarmac back to the car.

Raven thought for a moment. 'Scared? No, I don't think so. He was far too relaxed for that. If anything, I'd say he was simply resigned to his fate.'

CHAPTER 15

It was a whole hour's drive back from Full Sutton, and by the time they reached Scarborough, Raven had grown thoroughly sick of the monotonous landscape and wind-blasted cottages that dotted the roadside. The morning's visit felt like a waste of time. So it was a relief when DC Tony Bairstow flagged him down on his arrival back in the incident room. He was clutching a sheaf of paper in his hands.

'What have you got for me, Tony?'

'Sir, I chased the lab about the toxicology report and they've just sent it across by email.'

'And?'

'It shows traces of cocaine in Patrick's bloodstream.'

Raven pictured the drug stash that had been recovered from Shane Denton's mobile home in Redcar. 'So both Patrick and Shane used coke.'

'That's right, sir.' Tony turned the pages of the report. 'The lab found unusually high concentrations of cocaine-derived metabolites in the blood, indicating that it had been taken shortly before his death.'

'So Patrick was high when he was killed. That's good

work, Tony.'

'Thank you, sir. There's one other finding in the report. As well as the blood, the pathologist sent a sample of Patrick's hair for testing, and the lab found significant amounts of cocaine metabolites in that too. The report says this indicates Patrick was a habitual user of the drug.'

Raven nodded. A new picture was beginning to emerge of Patrick Lofthouse. He wasn't quite the "good boy" his mother had described. He and his delinquent friend Shane had shared more than innocent tales of myths and legends. They had smoked weed and snorted coke together too.

'Is Jess back from Redcar yet?' Raven asked. The young detective's trip shouldn't have taken much longer than his visit to Full Sutton.

'Not yet, sir,' said Tony.

DC Dan Bennett approached, his shiny suit and highly-polished shoes failing to mask his nervousness in Raven's presence. Raven knew from long experience that he had a tendency to appear intimidating to junior members of his team. 'Yes, Dan?' he said encouragingly.

'You asked me to check out Darren Jubb's alibis for the day of the murder.'

'What have you found?'

'Everything he said checks out. His accountant confirmed that he met with Darren and Ethan on Sunday morning, and I checked with the restaurant where the Jubb family went to lunch. I phoned the North Cliff Golf Club and they confirmed that Darren Jubb played a round of golf there that afternoon. And finally I spoke to the organiser of the charity event at the Grand Hotel. She assured me that she had spoken with Mr Jubb herself and that he was there all evening.'

'Okay,' said Raven. 'But all that proves is that Darren went out of his way to make sure that his time was fully accounted for throughout the day. He might not have shot Patrick himself, but that doesn't mean he didn't order the killing.'

The door to the incident room opened and DC Jess

Barraclough entered, her parka zipped up to her chin. Raven turned to her expectantly.

'Sorry it took me so long,' she said. 'I couldn't get away from Shane's gran. She kept plying me with cups of tea and wanted to tell me everything about her grandson from when he was a bairn.' Jess undid her parka and shrugged it off her shoulders. 'If you can believe Mrs Denton's version of events, Shane was a little angel. At least, he was until he was about eight years old. Then his mother developed alcohol and mental health problems and got into an abusive relationship. Social workers applied for a court order to take Shane into care. He was already displaying some challenging behaviour. He spent the next few years in children's homes until his gran was granted custody of him. He lived with her until he was eighteen, then he went completely off the rails, getting into drugs and petty crime. But he still visits her every few days and helps with her shopping and other jobs.'

'So can she vouch for him on Sunday?'

'Yes. She was adamant that Shane was with her for some of the day at least. He came for lunch and stayed most of the afternoon. But I couldn't find anyone who saw him after that. From four o'clock onwards we have no proof of his whereabouts.'

'So he has no alibi for the time of the murder. We can't even be certain that he was in Redcar.'

'Should we bring him in for questioning again?' asked Becca.

'Not yet,' said Raven. 'We don't have enough to go on. Let's keep digging and see what else we can find.'

'What do you have in mind?'

'A visit to Patrick's parents. I'm not sure they've told us all they know about their son.'

*

Back in Raven's car, Becca felt her phone vibrate. On checking it she found a notification from one of Scarlett

Jubb's social media accounts. Tapping on the message brought up a video, and immediately Scarlett's tear-stained face appeared on the screen, her lower lip trembling with emotion. There were no designer dresses on display in this video, no heavy eye makeup, no pretence at glamour at all. Here, it seemed, was the real Scarlett, raw with grief, much like when Becca had sat next to her and held her hand

'So, today I have some awful news to share with you,' Scarlett told her followers. 'Patrick is dead. My darling Pat. He's gone, and my life will never be the same without him. Let me tell you how much he meant to me…'

Becca watched the video through to the end. Already the post had thousands of likes. The comments contained a huge outpouring of sympathy. The messages from Scarlett's army of followers appeared to be genuine and heartfelt, but Becca wondered how much comfort could truly be garnered from the words of strangers.

She showed the clip to Raven, who appeared unmoved. 'All right, change of plan. Let's swing by the Jubb house and talk to Scarlett again.'

'Do you think she's hiding something?' Becca asked.

Raven frowned, his dark brows knotting together. 'Of course she's hiding something. She kept quiet about Patrick's coke habit, didn't she? I wonder what else she didn't tell us.'

This time it wasn't Ethan Jubb who answered the door to the house on Oliver's Mount. Nor was it Darren. The face that stared back at Raven held hard eyes like polished orbs, thin lips, and a shock of hair that had once been chestnut and was now almost completely white.

Frank Jubb, the founder of the Jubb dynasty.

He wore beige trousers and a blue cardigan and walked with a stoop, but the outward appearance of a harmless old man was a paper-thin veneer. Raven knew that it concealed a bully who had lied, stolen and cheated his way through life – a man who cared nothing for others, apart from his own family, to whom he'd always been fiercely loyal and protective.

His lips twisted into a cruel sneer when he saw Raven. 'Darren said you'd returned. It took you long enough to crawl back here, didn't it? What were you afraid of, Raven?'

Raven had no intention of allowing the old man to needle him. That was how Frank had always got his kicks. He might lack the subtlety of his son, but he was equally adept at provocation. 'Nothing, Frank. Is Scarlett in?'

'You leave her alone. She's already suffered enough.' Frank gestured with his hands. 'Go on, clear off.'

He was about to shut the door when Ethan Jubb appeared behind him. 'What is it, Grandpa?'

'Bloody cops again,' said Frank. 'I just told them to clear off.'

Ethan came to the door, seeming embarrassed by the old man's rudeness. 'Detectives, can I help you?'

'We're here to speak to Scarlett,' said Raven.

Ethan looked doubtful. 'She's still very upset. She's been in her room all day. I don't think she wants to speak to anyone.'

'Why don't you ask her?' said Becca.

Ethan led the way upstairs and knocked at Scarlett's bedroom door. 'Sis, it's the cops again. Shall I tell them to go away?'

The door opened, and Scarlett appeared. She was wearing the same outfit that she'd worn for the video – a black cashmere sweater over black jeans. Black, the colour of mourning. Her gaze slid from her brother to Raven, before lingering on Becca.

'How are you, Scarlett?' said Becca. 'Can we come in? We only want a few words.'

'Okay,' said Scarlett. She went inside and sat down on her bed.

Scarlett's room was big and lavishly decorated, favouring shimmering satin curtains and art deco lighting. The walls were adorned with canvas-printed photos of Scarlett and Patrick, the images familiar from Scarlett's

Instagram. There was the swimsuit pose, the cocktails in the bar, the glamorous dresses and fancy backdrops. A large vanity table stood in one corner of the bedroom, packed with all kinds of makeup and hair products. This must be where Scarlett filmed her beauty tutorials.

'I know this must be upsetting for you,' began Raven, standing awkwardly in the doorway to this overtly feminine environment, 'but we have a few more questions to ask you about Patrick.'

'I understand,' said Scarlett. She appeared more composed today, and ready to face the world again. Perhaps the cathartic effect of making and releasing her video had helped her start to come to terms with the tragedy. Her phone was in her hand, and she clung to it like a comforter.

'Can you tell us about Patrick's drug use?' asked Raven.

Scarlett's face teetered once more on the brink of crumpling, but after a moment she regained her poise. When she spoke her voice was measured. 'Patrick snorted cocaine. For recreational purposes. Not every day, but generally at the weekends or when we went out together. He said it made him feel more alive.' Her face hardened. 'I hated it. I tried to get him to stop, but it was the one thing we couldn't agree on. When it came to drugs, I just couldn't reason with him.'

'He was an addict?' suggested Becca.

Scarlett nodded. 'Yes, I suppose he was. He always said he could handle it, but he couldn't really. That's what drugs are like, aren't they?'

'Yes,' said Becca.

'Do you know where he got his supply?' asked Raven.

'I think so. It was Shane who got him started, and I'm pretty sure it was Shane who kept him supplied. That's why he kept going back to Redcar.'

'Is that why you didn't like Shane?' asked Becca.

'Yes. It was all his fault. If Pat had never met that loser…' She looked up suddenly. 'Is this why Patrick was murdered? Was it the drugs that got him killed?'

'We don't know, Scarlett,' said Becca. 'It's one angle we're investigating.'

'Patrick went to see Shane the day he died,' said Scarlett. 'Did Shane–'

'–we're still trying to pin down Patrick's last movements.'

Raven had another question for her. 'Did your father know Shane Denton?'

'My father?' said Scarlett. 'Of course he didn't. What reason would Dad have for getting involved with that low-life? Why do you ask?'

'We're simply trying to establish the facts. Your father took you out for lunch on Sunday. Was that unusual?'

Scarlett hesitated, looking perplexed by Raven's twisting line of questioning. 'To go out for lunch? Not at all. We often did. My mum came too.'

'But not your brother. Any reason for that?'

'He was busy with work.'

'And was this lunch pre-arranged?' continued Raven. 'Or was it a spur of the moment thing?'

'I guess Dad mentioned it a few days before,' said Scarlett. 'Why does any of this matter? Why do you keep asking me about Dad?'

'Just establishing the facts,' said Raven. 'Thank you for your time.'

*

The Lofthouse family home was a substantial, detached house on Northstead Manor Drive, overlooking Peasholm Park. It didn't quite scream *money* in the way the Jubb house did, but the whitewashed exterior, paved driveway, and palm trees in big terracotta pots flanking the front porch all spoke of a comfortable, middle-class existence. It was the sort of house Raven's mother would have walked past and admired, secretly yearning for but knowing that she could never hope to live in such a place. *Respectable* was the word that sprung to Raven's mind as he and Becca waited for an answer at the door. The Lofthouses were respectable people who wouldn't want their son mixed up in the murky world of drugs. What parent would, come to that?

Gordon Lofthouse opened the door. He looked smaller and greyer than the last time Raven had seen him, as if he had shrunk into himself, grief hollowing him out from the inside. He didn't ask why the detectives were there, but seemed to accept their presence as an inevitable part of the way things were now. 'Come inside,' he said mechanically.

Raven was hoping that the efficient and friendly family liaison officer, PC Sharon Jarvis, would still be in the house, taking care of things – people who had received a devastating shock often didn't look after themselves properly, sometimes even forgetting to eat – but there was no sign of her.

'We sent her away,' said Gordon when Raven asked. 'We don't need someone to mollycoddle us. Come through to the lounge.' He led them into a large room with bay windows. It was furnished with a leather sofa and armchairs with a television in one corner. A glass coffee table displayed copies of the *Radio Times* and *The Daily Telegraph*.

The house was what Raven's mother would have called "spick and span" – nothing out of place and not a speck of dust to be seen. Everything in the room, from the beige carpet to the watercolour landscape above the mantelpiece to the glass vase on the windowsill, looked as if it had been chosen to blend in and not draw attention to itself. It was a comfortable home, certainly, but very bland and middle-aged. It was easy to see why Patrick Lofthouse might have been drawn to the more glamorous – and dangerous – world of the Jubbs.

Janet Lofthouse was sitting in the armchair closest to the bay window with a photograph album open on her lap. Raven caught a glimpse of pictures of a little boy playing on the beach with his bucket and spade before she put the album aside and rose to her feet. Her features were drawn, her hair limp, and there were dark smudges under her eyes, but Raven could see she was determined to be civil. 'Inspector, can I get you a cup of tea?'

Raven assured her there was no need. 'We don't want to put you to any trouble, Mrs Lofthouse. We just want to talk to you about Patrick, find out a bit more about what he was like. It would help us to understand him better.'

'You'd better sit down,' said Gordon.

Raven and Becca made themselves comfortable on the sofa. A framed school photograph of a fresh-faced Patrick aged about thirteen or fourteen stood on a side table close to Raven's elbow. The boy's blond hair was cut short – as an adult he'd worn it shoulder-length – and his tie was neatly knotted, the top button of his shirt done up. Raven recognised the striped tie and blue blazer of Scarborough College, the independent school near Oliver's Mount. That must have been where Patrick had first met Scarlett. Raven – and Darren Jubb for that matter – had gone to the local state school back in the day and wouldn't have been seen dead in the uniform that the "posh" kids wore. But the Lofthouses were clearly the sort of people who wanted the best for their only child. They must have thought they were doing the right thing, giving Patrick a good start in life, not exposing him to the rough and tumble of the playground. But sometimes you had to be careful what you wished for. If Patrick had gone to the state school, he would probably never have met the Jubbs and would still be alive today.

No doubt the same thought had struck the Lofthouses. Yet Raven knew all too well how toxic that way of thinking could be. If only I'd done this… if only I hadn't done that. Regrets about past decisions could swallow you up if you allowed them to.

Janet noticed Raven looking at the photograph. 'Patrick was a day pupil at the college,' she said with a sigh. 'He was fourteen when that photograph was taken.' She looked wistful, her hands clasped tightly in her lap. 'He showed so much promise at that age, didn't he Gordon?' She looked to her husband for confirmation as if she wanted – needed – him to tell her what a wonderful son they'd had. Once.

'Oh, yes,' said Gordon. 'We had high hopes for Patrick at that age. He played rugby and cricket for the school. He got good grades in most subjects. He was a good lad, back then.'

'But things changed?' asked Raven. He sensed the parents were mourning the fourteen-year-old boy as much as they were mourning the man Patrick had become. Maybe he had "died" to them a long time ago.

'When he was seventeen,' said Gordon, 'he started mixing with a new crowd. He gave up playing sport, said it wasn't cool, whatever that was supposed to mean. He dropped a lot of his old friends, boys he'd known since he was four or five. He started saying he didn't want to work in the family business.'

'Did this "new crowd" include Scarlett Jubb?' Raven asked.

A cloud passed over Gordon's face. 'We were dismayed when Patrick told us he was going out with Scarlett. She wasn't the kind of girlfriend we'd imagined for our son. The Jubbs might have money, but they're common as muck underneath. They're not our sort of people. They don't share our values, you see.'

'What values are those?' enquired Becca.

Gordon straightened his back. 'Hard work, decency, respect.'

'Did you express your views to Patrick?'

'Well, of course we did,' said Gordon. 'But it did no good.'

'We hoped it would fizzle out,' said Janet. 'Patrick and Scarlett, I mean. But the two stayed together.' There was a grudging respect in her voice.

'And then they became engaged,' said Becca.

'Yes,' said Gordon. 'We made it perfectly clear that we were against the engagement, but her parents insisted on throwing a party to celebrate.'

'We went along to be polite,' said Janet. 'But really, it

wasn't our kind of thing at all. All loud music and champagne.'

'Vulgar,' declared Gordon. 'Just an excuse for them to show off.'

'Did you see much of Scarlett's parents?' asked Raven, 'with Patrick and Scarlett being at the same school?'

'We ran into them a few times at school didn't we, Janet? But we weren't on speaking terms. That Darren Jubb is little more than a thug, what with his nightclub and his amusement arcades. There were always rumours circulating about him among the other parents. You'd hear things at the rugby matches on a Saturday morning.'

'What kinds of things?'

But it seemed that Gordon wasn't willing to make specific allegations. 'Look closely at his businesses, Inspector, and you'll find dirty money, I can assure you of that.'

His wife gave a tight-lipped nod. 'And Mrs Jubb isn't exactly what you'd call *respectable* either.'

'In what way?' asked Becca.

Janet pressed her lips together as if holding in her opinion. 'The word I'd use to describe her isn't a polite one, I'm afraid. But she always looks like she's dressed up for a night on the town. She doesn't dress her age. Frankly, she'd turn up to school events – parent assemblies, prize-giving days, that sort of thing – looking like a trollop. It wasn't a good example to set for her daughter, and look how Scarlett's turned out.'

'How has she turned out?' said Raven.

'Well,' said Janet, 'all she does is post videos and pictures of herself on the internet. I mean that's not a proper job, is it?'

'She seems to be good at it. And she earns good money.' Raven had taken a look at some of Scarlett's makeup tutorials before going to bed the previous night and thought they seemed like harmless fun.

'Money isn't everything, Inspector,' said Gordon, despite the fact that it had clearly paid for their comfortable lifestyle.

'I have some news that you might find upsetting,' said Raven, preparing the Lofthouses for what he was about to reveal. 'The post-mortem found traces of cocaine in Patrick's system.'

Gordon's face remained impassive but Janet dropped her gaze, not meeting Raven's eye. Her fingers twisted and coiled together like snakes in her lap.

'You don't seem surprised,' observed Raven.

'No,' said Gordon. 'I'm sorry to say that it doesn't surprise us at all.'

'How long had Patrick been using drugs?'

'A few years. It was that Shane Denton who got him started.'

'Is that the real reason you fired Shane?' asked Raven.

Gordon nodded. 'I had to get him away from Patrick. Patrick was too easily influenced, that was his problem.'

'Did you know that Scarlett tried to persuade Patrick to stop taking cocaine?' asked Becca.

Janet looked up, surprised, but her husband remained stony faced. 'Well, she didn't try very hard, did she?'

'On Sunday,' said Raven, 'Patrick told Scarlett he was going to visit Shane in Redcar. Scarlett thinks he intended to buy drugs. But we have no evidence that Patrick met Shane that day. We still haven't located Patrick's car. Do you have any information that might help us trace his movements?'

'I'm sorry, but we can't help you with that, Inspector,' said Gordon. 'Like we told you, the last time we saw Patrick was on the Saturday. We have no idea what he did on the day he died. Now will that be everything?'

'Just one more thing,' said Raven. 'Is it okay if we take a look at Patrick's room?'

*

Patrick's bedroom still bore signs of the teenager he had once been. The desk and chairs were functional and minimalist, unlike the fancy furniture in Scarlett's bedroom. Marks showed where posters had once been Blu-tacked to the wall. Raven remembered a phase of his own teenage years when he'd plastered his walls with images of bands torn from music magazines – the Cure, Joy Division, Bauhaus, the Sisters of Mercy. He'd bought CDs when he could afford them – he wasn't a habitual thief – and played the music turned up to full volume on his stereo until his dad hammered on the door telling him to, 'Turn that bloody racket off.'

There were no indications what Patrick's poster collection might have comprised, but well-thumbed fantasy novels were piled onto a bookshelf above the built-in desk – JRR Tolkien, George RR Martin, Ursula Le Guin. There was an anthology of Celtic mythology and even a copy of Thomas Malory's *Le Morte d'Arthur*. Raven picked up the anthology with his gloved hands and found the corners of various pages turned down, with scribbles in the margins and many passages underlined in ink.

'"In the midst of the lake Arthur was ware of an arm clothed in white samite, that held a fair sword in that hand",' Raven read aloud.

'What's that?' asked Becca.

'That,' said Raven, 'is the romantic longing of a young man who desperately wanted to do more with his life than take over his father's used car business.'

Becca sniffed. 'Hardly helps us find his killer though, does it?'

Raven smiled and returned the book to the shelf. The bedroom furniture was battered and marked, but a brand-new Apple MacBook occupied centre stage on the desk. Raven indicated the shiny laptop to Becca. 'You can take this to digital forensics.'

'Still no sign of his mobile phone,' said Becca, packing the laptop into an evidence bag. 'I expect it's somewhere at the bottom of the North Sea by now.'

While she rummaged through the other bits and pieces scattered across the desk, Raven inspected the bedside locker. Inside the top drawer were the usual random belongings of a young man – a pair of nail scissors, a pack of playing cards, a box of paracetamol tablets, a near-empty tube of spot cream and a pair of Ray-Ban sunglasses. There was also a half-full box of condoms, although it was hard to imagine Patrick bringing Scarlett back here for a night of passion under the roof of his disapproving parents.

'What do you make of this?' Becca showed him a sheet of writing paper that she had lifted from the desk. Good quality, thick and creamy, headed with a name and logo.

'Gisborough Hall. Isn't that a country house hotel?' Raven had heard of it, but had never been there. It wasn't the sort of place his family would ever have visited. In fact, as far as he knew, his parents had never been to any hotel, apart from the Grand Hotel where his mum had cleaned the rooms.

'Yes,' said Becca. 'My parents took me and my brother there for their silver wedding anniversary a few years ago.' She opened a map on her phone and did a quick search. 'It's about six miles south of Redcar.'

'Redcar, interesting. But is it the sort of place Patrick would be likely to meet Shane Denton?'

'Not unless they were both into fine dining.'

Scrawled across the paper was a handwritten date and time. *17 October, 7pm!* It was underlined twice for emphasis.

'Okay,' said Raven. 'Two questions. What was Patrick Lofthouse doing at Gisborough Hall, and what happened on the seventeenth of October, one week before he washed up on the beach?' He handed the sheet of paper back to Becca, who slipped it into another evidence bag.

Raven returned to the bedside locker and pulled open the next drawer. Socks. Underwear. He reached his hand inside and felt something hard beneath the socks. 'There's something in here.'

He slid the drawer out completely and placed it on the bed. Then he removed the randomly assorted socks and boxers until the hidden contents were revealed. No fewer than six mobile phones had been concealed beneath the clothes. A couple of Motorolas and some cheap-looking brands that Raven had never heard of. The Motorolas were unwrapped, but the others were still in their packaging.

'Burner phones,' said Becca, peering over his shoulder.

'Well, well,' said Raven. 'What were you up to, Patrick?' He exchanged glances with Becca and saw that she had reached the same conclusion as him – that Patrick Lofthouse hadn't been merely a user of drugs, he had been a dealer too.

CHAPTER 16

'You stay here to preserve the evidence,' said Raven. 'Call CSI and get them out here immediately. I want them to go over Patrick's room with a fine-toothed comb.'

'What, now?' asked Becca. She checked the time. 'It's the end of the working day. Can't it wait until tomorrow?'

'No, it damn well can't.' Since the discovery of the burner phones in Patrick's bedside locker, Raven seemed to have been gripped by a manic energy. His voice was louder, his movements quicker, as if someone had pressed the *fast forward* button on his remote. 'Get them to come here right away, and if they cause you any trouble, let me know. This could be the breakthrough we've been waiting for.' He turned and headed for the door.

'Raven?' said Becca. 'Where are you going?'

'I'm heading back to the station to get things moving at that end. I want Shane Denton brought in for questioning first thing in the morning. We got it all wrong. Shane wasn't supplying Patrick with cocaine – it was the other way around. We need to start throwing the net wider, find out who Patrick was dealing with, pin down his movements over the past few weeks. These phones could help us uncover his entire network. This is just the beginning of a wider investigation.'

Raven clicked his fingers and was gone like a departing whirlwind, leaving Becca feeling exhausted. She'd hoped to go and see her boyfriend, Sam, that evening, but that didn't look like it was going to happen. Resigned to the task he had set her, she dialled through to Holly Chang at CSI.

'Hi Becca, what have you got for me?' Holly's voice was upbeat as ever, but Becca wondered how she would react to the news of an unscheduled job just as she was probably preparing to head off for the day.

'I need you to go through a victim's home for me.'

'Victim? Is it that lad on the beach?'

'That's right,' said Becca. 'Patrick Lofthouse. We found some burner phones hidden in his bedroom.'

'Is that right?' said Holly. 'Patrick was a naughty boy, was he?'

'It looks that way. So Raven wants you to come out and do a thorough search in case there's anything else here.'

'Raven. That's your new boss, then? What's he like?'

Becca paused before answering. What exactly was Raven like? He could be a good boss at times. Calm, competent, courteous. But he was mercurial too. She had seen him punch the wall in frustration when things didn't go his way. He had very quickly got on the wrong side of Dr Felicity Wainwright. And he could spend long periods mired in silent introspection, like when he had driven back from Full Sutton that morning, his eyes on the road, his foot to the floor, the car filled with an ominous sense of foreboding. It didn't help that in his long black coat and tie he looked like an undertaker.

'He's, uh, very efficient,' she told Holly. 'He gets things done.'

Holly chuckled. 'Bit of a bastard is he?'

'Not at all. But he can be rather demanding at times.'

'Okay,' said Holly. 'Well, I'll schedule it for first thing

tomorrow.'

'Uh… actually, Raven wants you out here right away. He said it was urgent.'

A stony silence greeted her announcement. 'This evening?' said Holly after a beat. 'I had plans, actually. You know… family life?'

'Raven was very insistent.'

'Was he now?'

Becca waited, hoping she wouldn't have to call Raven and tell him that CSI couldn't make it.

'All right,' grumbled Holly at last. 'I'll round up some poor sod to help me, and we'll come straight over. And I hope that bugger Raven appreciates it.'

The line went dead and Becca prepared herself for another late night. At least she and Holly would be able to console each other by grumbling about Raven. You could say one thing for her new boss, he had a talent for making enemies.

*

The lights turned green and Raven nudged the BMW impatiently through the rush hour traffic. His instinct that Patrick was more than just an innocent victim had been proven right. Whatever was going on here, Patrick had been at the heart of it, and Raven was confident that by following this fresh lead they would make real progress.

He hoped he hadn't taken Becca for granted, asking her to stay on and supervise the CSI team. He hadn't even thought to ask her if she had any prior arrangements. A young woman no doubt had better ways to spend her evenings than doing overtime. But overtime was inevitable when you were a police officer and she would have to get used to it. He'd lost count of how many hundreds of hours he'd spent over the years poring over evidence, sitting in cars staking out suspects' homes, or simply filling in paperwork. An unavoidable hazard of the job. Yet look where that had got him. Absenteeism from family life had led to Lisa leaving him. Turning her back on a marriage of twenty-three years. Much as he had tried to shrug it off, the pain of her betrayal still pierced him like a knife. He didn't want the same thing to happen to Becca.

But the discovery of the burner phones was a real breakthrough, and it would be criminal to waste the opportunity.

On arrival at the police station, he was pleased to find all his team still there. He gathered them together around the whiteboard. 'All right, listen up. There's been a development. It now looks more than likely that Patrick was involved in some sort of criminal activity, quite possibly drug dealing.'

He watched their reactions as he explained about the discovery of the phones in Patrick's bedroom. There was initial surprise, but then quick acceptance. They had all felt that Patrick must have been involved in something.

'Specialists from digital forensics will examine the two Motorolas and Patrick's laptop,' he said. 'Meanwhile, I want to dig deeper into Patrick's activities. Where did he go during the days and weeks leading up to his murder? Who did he meet? Did he have enemies? Associates? He didn't keep that stockpile of burner phones to talk to himself. Tony, can you liaise with the forensics team and find out who Patrick called on those phones, and who called him?'

'I'm on it, sir,' said Tony, writing his instructions on his notepad.

'Excellent,' said Raven. DC Tony Bairstow was clearly someone who could be relied on to take on any task assigned to him and get it done. The sort who did what was required without looking for glory. He was the sort of hardworking copper that most SIOs would have cloned if they could.

'Dan,' said Raven, 'you have a list of all the numbers that Patrick called from his main phone. Can you speak to everyone on that list and see if you can piece together Patrick's movements for, say, the past two weeks?'

'Two weeks? All right, sir. No problem.'

Raven hadn't yet got the measure of DC Dan Bennett, but he sensed that the young man was ambitious. Which wasn't necessarily a bad thing. Raven had been ambitious himself during his time as a young detective clawing his way up the Met. But real ambition was backed up by hard work, a willingness to put in the grind. Raven sensed a shallowness to Dan's ambition born of impatience. Even now he was perched casually on the edge of his desk, jiggling his foot in a most distracting manner. Maybe Raven was being unfair, but there was something about the way Bennett dressed that irritated him. Dan clearly spent far too much time styling his hair, polishing his shoes and selecting his ties for Raven's liking. Which reminded him, he still needed to follow Gillian's instructions and remedy his own wardrobe malfunction. He would need to stop off in town on the way home for a quick round of shopping. It wasn't just a new tie he needed. He'd run out of shirts and underwear, and with no time to do any laundry, he would start to smell ripe if he didn't stock up soon.

He hadn't attempted to use the ancient washing machine in his dad's house for fear of flooding the kitchen. Would it even work after over thirty years of disuse? After his mum had died, his father had taken their dirty clothes to a launderette and stuffed everything into the same tub – delicates, colours and whites – so that all Raven's shirts had shrunk and ended up the same uniform grey. Nothing had ever been ironed again.

'What would you like me to do, sir?' The voice of DC Jess Barraclough's voice cut through Raven's thoughts. He still couldn't get over how young Jess looked. It was difficult to believe she was any older than his own daughter. Yet she seemed competent enough, and wasn't short of enthusiasm.

Raven held up the clear evidence bag containing the headed writing paper that Becca had found. 'This was discovered in Patrick's bedroom. It may not be significant, but we need to follow it up. The paper is from Gisborough

Hall, the country house hotel near Redcar.' Nods all round told Raven that the hotel, or at least its existence, was well known to the team.

He passed the note to Jess, showing her the handwritten message. *17 October, 7pm!* 'The seventeenth of October is precisely one week before Patrick's murder. What happened on that day that was so important to him? And how did he come to be in possession of this headed letter paper? Was he staying at the hotel on the seventeenth? Or was he there on some other date?'

'You want me to go to the hotel?' asked Jess, looking hopeful. Visiting a luxury hotel was obviously a more appealing prospect than another trip to Shane's muddy caravan park in Redcar.

'Yes, please,' Raven told her. 'That leaves one more job,' he said, as much to himself as the others. 'I'll arrange for a couple of uniformed officers to go and pick up Shane Denton first thing tomorrow morning and bring him in for questioning. But now, if you don't mind, I have some shopping to do.'

He glanced at his watch. If he was quick, he ought to have just enough time to pop into the menswear department of Marks and Spencer's before it closed.

*

Raven was on his way down the corridor when Derek Dinsdale appeared suddenly from a meeting room as if he'd been lying in wait for an ambush. The DI tried to make it look like a chance encounter, but Raven wasn't fooled. He tried to push past, but Dinsdale moved to block him.

Raven stopped to assess his antagonist and wasn't impressed by what he saw. A creased brown suit. A beer belly spilling over a straining waist band. Grey hair combed over in a futile attempt to conceal a growing bald patch.

'DCI Raven,' growled Dinsdale. 'I hear you paid a visit to HMP Full Sutton today.'

Raven didn't know where Dinsdale got his information, and couldn't be bothered to ask. He doubted he would get a straight answer. 'Then you'll know why.' He tried once again to continue on his way, but Dinsdale stood his ground.

'You're barking up the wrong tree, Raven. I ran the Max Hunt case. I put Lewis Briggs away. It was a cast iron conviction. You won't find any holes in that investigation, if that's your game.'

'I'm not here to play games,' said Raven. 'And if Lewis's conviction is as safe as you claim then you won't have a problem with me re-interviewing him.'

'Did he tell you anything?'

Dinsdale's gaze was challenging, provoking. Raven had a strong desire to punch that smug face.

'I thought not,' concluded Dinsdale in a self-satisfied tone.

Raven felt his anger growing, like a serpent uncoiling within his belly. 'What's your point, Dinsdale?'

The older man glared at him. 'My point is, leave it alone. You've already taken the Patrick Lofthouse investigation away from me. Don't think you can muscle in on the Max Hunt murder too. That conviction is sound, and the guilty man is in prison where he belongs. I had forensics, witness statements, a full confession too.'

'What about motive?' asked Raven.

A frown darkened Dinsdale's brow. 'Blockheads like Lewis Briggs don't need motive. They just have to get out of bed on the wrong side to want to kill someone.'

'Really?' said Raven. 'And yet Lewis went to the trouble of sourcing a firearm to carry out the killing. It was clearly premeditated murder. Do you have any idea how a "blockhead" like him managed to get his hands on a gun?'

Dinsdale sneered. 'Just because we're not in London, it doesn't mean that illegal firearms aren't in circulation. You probably think this is just some sleepy seaside town, but it's only a two-hour train ride to a city like Leeds, and not much longer to Manchester. Call in at the right kind of pub at the wrong end of town and you can buy anything you want. Pistols, shotguns, even automatic rifles. And the ammo to go with them.'

'Was there any evidence that Lewis Briggs travelled to Leeds or Manchester in the days before he carried out the shooting?' demanded Raven. Dinsdale's silence told him all he needed to know. 'I thought not. You may have extracted an admission of guilt from Lewis, but his confession was remarkably short on detail. He was unable to give a reason why he wanted Max Hunt dead. He refused to say where he obtained the weapon. Did you even consider the possibility that a third party had ordered the shooting and supplied the gun?'

Dinsdale bared his teeth in frustration. 'Listen, Raven. I'm telling you that the conviction was watertight. There was no third party, no complicated motive, no mystery about how that scumbag got his hands on a gun. He's behind bars, and no good will come from asking questions. So stay away from Lewis Briggs. And stay away from Darren Jubb too, if you know what's good for you.'

Now Raven really felt his fury growing. He took a step forward, pushing his face closer to Dinsdale's sweating features, conscious that he was half a head taller than his adversary. 'Why?'

The older man cowered back. 'Because Jubb's not a killer. He's no angel, but he's not into anything like that. You're wasting your time if you think he's involved in this.'

'Is that right?' said Raven. 'You seem to have already decided the outcome. Is that how you solve all your cases?'

'Of course not.'

'Then let me give you some advice of my own.' Raven shoved Dinsdale's chest, forcing him back against the wall of the corridor. 'I'm in charge of this investigation, and I'll run it however I see fit. If I want to interview Lewis Briggs, I'll do that. If I want to re-open any of the loose ends that you failed to follow up, I'll do that too. And if I want to question Darren Jubb or anyone else for that matter, I won't be asking for your permission. Is that clear?'

Sweat prickled on Dinsdale's forehead and he struggled to pull away, but Raven grabbed a fistful of his shirt, twisting it tight.

'I said, is that clear?'

'Are you threatening me?' asked Dinsdale.

There was naked fear in the other man's eyes now, and Raven realised that he'd gone too far. He released the DI, who scuttled back to a safe distance.

'It was you who threatened me,' said Raven. 'I know you left that note in my desk. "Watch your back". Well, I don't like threats.'

'It wasn't a threat,' protested Dinsdale. 'It was a warning.'

'Meaning?'

'What it said – watch your back.' Dinsdale straightened his shirt, struggling to reclaim some dignity. 'You know nothing about the way this place works. You're just a pawn.'

Raven scoffed. 'What does that make you, Dinsdale? The king?'

The detective shook his head. 'I'm just another lowly pawn. All I'm saying is, watch out for the queen.'

So that's what this encounter was really about. Dinsdale's resentment after being side-lined by Gillian. His existential angst about being a washed-up has-been. His fear of becoming a nobody.

'I don't have time for this nonsense.' Raven side-stepped Dinsdale and headed for the exit. He needed to get outside before he did the man an injury.

Dinsdale had deliberately provoked him, but Raven knew that he'd crossed a line. He should never have pushed the other man, should never have grabbed hold of him. His rage had got the better of him, and now he felt a wave of fresh anger, directed at himself. And disgust too. Disgust at what he'd done, and what more he might have done if the fear in Dinsdale's eyes hadn't checked him.

He pushed through the building's exit and stepped out into the cold. He could use a cigarette to calm him down.

And yet he hadn't smoked in over twenty years. Funny how the old habit could suddenly rear up out of nowhere and clamour for his attention.

But Raven wouldn't succumb to the temptation. He knew where that path led. His father's anger and violence had been fuelled by a similar addiction – alcohol – and Raven had done everything in his power to avoid becoming his father's son. He hadn't touched a drink since that terrible night, when he was just sixteen, that had pushed him out of Scarborough and defined the rest of his life. He had worked his damnedest to suppress any trace of his father's anger. But here he was, a grown man of forty-seven, being rattled by a bloody idiot like Derek Dinsdale.

'Shit!' He caught a glance of his watch and realised that he was about to miss his chance to go shopping. Steeling himself against the inevitable leg pain that he knew would result from a run, he began to hurry along the street, heading into town.

CHAPTER 17

His mum is coming down the creaking staircase, her dressing gown wrapped close around her. He remembers the green quilting, the high neck, the floral design at the front. He waits for her at the bottom of the stairs among the shadows, like a ghost. She stops when she sees him. 'What is it, Tom? Can't you sleep?' She's been crying. He can see that. Even though he's only – what? – seven years old? He's been crying too. He goes to her, feels her arms curl snugly around him, and feels safe. He wants to stay there forever. 'I heard a noise,' he tells her. 'It woke me up.' She doesn't ask what kind of noise, just takes his hand. 'Come back to bed, Tom. It's late.' He lets her lead him back upstairs to his room, lets her tuck him in. He can see the bruising on her face, the eye that's already blackening. He knows that in the morning it will look even worse. 'Did you fall over again?' he asks her. She says nothing, just kisses his forehead and turns out the light. 'Sleep well, Tom. Sleep well…'

The next day began, like so many others in Scarborough, with the screeching of the gulls. The noisy buggers were swooping and diving outside Raven's bedroom window. Perhaps they had found a rubbish bag that had spilled its contents into the street. Or perhaps they were doing it just to torment him. He wouldn't put it past them.

He clambered out of bed, wincing as his leg took his weight. He had run as quickly as he could the previous evening, but the shop had been closed when he reached it. So now he had no options. It would be the black tie again, and a used shirt and underwear to go with it. He really would have to make time to stock up on some fresh clothing today.

He hurried through his bathroom routine giving his armpits an extra blast of deodorant for good measure, then engaged in his daily battle with the gas cooker in the cramped kitchen. He'd been so exhausted the previous evening, he hadn't bothered to cook. Instead he'd called in again at the chippie for more haddock and chips with curry sauce. And why not? With a side order of mushy peas it was almost a balanced meal.

After munching through his breakfast of bacon and eggs and leaving the all-too-sticky non-stick frying pan to soak in the bowl in the sink, he made his way outside. Cold wind blasted his face, channelling its way through Quay Street off the sea. It always amazed him that the house could stand just yards from the harbourfront yet still not have a sea view. Quay Street occupied a prime location in the old town, but the road itself was more wind tunnel than street, scarcely wide enough for a single car to squeeze between the tall brick houses. They crowded so snugly together in places that if you leaned out of an upstairs window you could almost shake hands with your neighbour opposite. In the summer it could be charming, garnished with hanging baskets brimming with flowers. In October, its appeal lessened, and in the bleak midwinter, he knew the old house would become an ice box, its windows rattling as easterly gales blasted the glass, sending chilly fingers into the corners of every room.

He made his way along the road to the car park at the end. It was a pokey area with space for no more than a couple of dozen cars, and he wondered what he would do if he ever found it full. He would have to drive up East Sandgate, he supposed, and take his chances in the maze of tiny streets between Castlegate and Longwestgate on the steep hill that led up to the castle. So far he had been lucky, and he was grateful that it was off-season.

The M6 was where he had left it, glowing pewter grey beneath the leaden morning sky. He unlocked it and was about to open the driver's door when he noticed a mark on the paintwork. He stooped to get a closer look and realised that it wasn't just a mark, but a scrape. Some bastard had gouged a line a foot long in the bodywork.

His finger ran along the scratch, testing its depth. This was no accidental bump from another car. It was a deliberate act of vandalism. A key or some other tool had been used to score the metalwork.

'Fuck.'

Was this the work of kids? Or had he been deliberately targeted? Dinsdale's words came back to him. *Stay away from Darren Jubb, if you know what's good for you.*

If this was a clumsy attempt at intimidation, then Dinsdale – or whoever was responsible – had seriously underestimated him. He climbed into the driver's seat and drove away, the engine revving hard, the rear wheels spinning as he accelerated out of the car park and down the cobbled road that led to Sandside.

*

Raven was in a foul mood this morning and was making no secret of it. *Fine*, thought Becca, but it wasn't Raven who'd had to stay late the previous night at the Lofthouse's home, supervising an uncharacteristically grumpy Holly as the CSI team leader and her assistant scoured Patrick's bedroom for further evidence. In the end they'd found nothing of significance, and Holly had finally left around nine o'clock, cursing Raven once more for his unreasonable demands.

When Becca had got home, she'd found that her mum had kept a steak and kidney pie warm in the oven for her, and was quickly able to rustle up some peas and potatoes to accompany it. Not to mention some apple crumble and custard to finish.

'You're a star, Mum,' Becca had told her, making her beam in delight.

Raven, by contrast had no smiles for anyone today, barely acknowledging the fact that she and Holly had worked several hours of unscheduled overtime to satisfy his demands.

'And there was nothing else in Patrick's room?' he asked her. 'Nothing at all?'

'What were you expecting?' she asked, but he had no answer to give her. Instead, he wanted to know where he could get the paintwork on his car repaired.

'It got scratched last night,' he explained. 'Kids mucking about, I expect.'

'You could always ask Gordon Lofthouse,' she suggested. 'Lofthouse Cars does servicing and repairs as well as sales.'

Raven's face remained stern. 'I don't mix business with pleasure.'

'Leave it with me then,' said Becca. 'I'll ask my brother. He always knows who to recommend.'

As long as you don't mind cash-in-hand, no questions asked, and no money-back guarantee. But she kept that thought to herself. Her brother meant well, and Raven was in no position to quibble. If he couldn't be bothered to find a repairer himself, he would have to make do with whoever Liam suggested.

He clapped his hands to gather everyone's attention. 'All right. Tell me what you're all up to today.' He pointed to Dan. 'You first, Dan.'

Dan swallowed nervously and adjusted his already-straight tie. He was obviously desperate to impress his new boss and terrified of making a mistake. Becca felt some sympathy for him. Raven could be intimidating when he was in one of his dark moods. 'Sir, you asked me to piece together Patrick's movements for the past two weeks.'

'Good. Any problems with that?'

'No, sir. I'll get onto it straightaway.'

Raven's eyes shifted to his next team member. 'What about you, Tony?'

'Liaising with forensics about the burner phones, sir, and also continuing the search for Patrick's car.'

'Excellent.' Raven peered around the incident room. 'Where is Jess this morning?'

'She drove straight to Gisborough Hall to check on the headed letter paper,' said Becca. 'She'll probably be back by lunchtime.'

Raven nodded with satisfaction. 'And what about you, Becca?'

'You haven't assigned any tasks to me yet,' said Becca, 'but Shane Denton's been brought in for questioning. I wondered if you'd like me to sit in with you for that?'

Finally, a faint look of satisfaction lit up Raven's Stygian features. 'I'd like that very much. Let's go and see what he has to say.'

*

'So,' said Raven, with a thin smile, 'here we are again. We seem to be making a habit of this, Shane.'

Shane Denton's eyes darted nervously between Raven and Becca as he took in his surroundings. He had been roused from sleep at some unearthly hour by a couple of uniformed coppers and brought to the interview room at Scarborough, where he had waited at Raven's convenience to be interviewed. His hair was unwashed, his chin unshaven, and he looked to be wearing the same change of clothing that he'd worn last time Raven had interviewed him.

That makes two of us, thought Raven glumly.

'You can't drag me back here,' protested Shane. 'It's not right. You already nicked me once for possession. You can't arrest me again.'

'You aren't under arrest, Shane,' explained Becca. 'You're here to be interviewed under caution.'

'Is that what you call it?' said Shane. 'Your bully boys came for me in the middle of the bloody night. They kicked my door in and dragged me out of bed.'

'I'm sure they didn't,' said Raven, 'but if you'd like to make a formal complaint, I'll give you the relevant paperwork to fill out later. For now, I'd like to talk to you about where you acquired your supplies of cannabis and cocaine.'

Shane immediately fell silent, his desire to complain about police harassment apparently forgotten.

Raven placed a photograph on the table, showing a bag containing white powder. 'This cocaine, to be precise.' He placed a second photo next to it. 'And this cannabis.'

Still Shane said nothing.

'We have witness statements,' said Raven,' stating that it was you who first introduced Patrick to drugs. It would be logical to assume that you supplied them to him, wouldn't it?'

Shane opened his mouth as if to speak, then thought better of it. He seemed unable to lift his gaze from the photographs on the table.

'A sample of Patrick's blood taken during the post-mortem was found to contain traces of cocaine,' continued Raven. 'Tests showed that he was a habitual user. We know that he made regular visits to you at Redcar. Any reasonable person would conclude that he came to you to buy his cocaine. Do you know the maximum penalty for supplying drugs, Shane?'

Shane looked up, but still no words came.

'The maximum sentence for supplying class A drugs is life imprisonment.' Raven let the implications of that sink in. 'That's a lot more serious than the offence that you're currently charged with.'

'I didn't do it,' said Shane.

'What didn't you do, Shane?' asked Becca.

'I didn't supply owt. I just bought the drugs for my own use.'

'So where did you get them? Who sold you the cocaine?'

Shane looked as if he wished the floor would open up and swallow him, but he muttered, 'It were Patrick. Pat sold me the drugs.'

Raven nodded in satisfaction. It was exactly as he'd thought. 'Where did Patrick get the cocaine?'

Shane shook his head. 'I dunno. He told me he could get it whenever I wanted. I admit it were me what got him started using weed and coke, but soon he were the one buying it and passing it on to me. I dunno where he got it though. I never asked.'

'You never asked,' repeated Raven. 'Look, Shane, here's my problem with all this. You've admitted buying coke from Patrick, and we know from Scarlett that Patrick was on his way to see you when he was murdered. You've been unable to provide an alibi for your whereabouts at the time of his death' – Shane opened his mouth to protest, but Raven waved him to silence – 'the testimony of your gran notwithstanding. And Patrick's body was put into the sea somewhere between Scarborough and Redcar. So that leaves you in a very tricky position. You see, you're now the number-one suspect in our murder enquiry.'

Shane's mouth dropped open in horror at Raven's announcement.

'You had an obvious motive,' continued Raven. 'The theft of drugs that Patrick was bringing to you. You had opportunity. All we have to do is prove that you had access to a firearm, and you'll be facing not only a drugs charge, but also a charge of murder.'

'No,' blurted Shane. 'I never. I didn't. It weren't me.'

Raven leaned forward across the table, bringing his face up close to Shane's. 'Then tell us what you know, Shane. Tell us everything you know about Patrick.'

CHAPTER 18

DC Jess Barraclough was very happy to be out of the police station, driving across the North York Moors in the ancient Land Rover her dad had taught her to drive in. The car was a bit of a wreck, and had over a hundred and fifty thousand miles on the clock, but her dad didn't believe in throwing anything away. 'Look after it well and it'll last you a lifetime, Jess, love,' he'd told her on handing her the keys. Anyway, she couldn't afford anything better for the moment and had developed a fondness for the old workhorse with its crashing gearbox and spluttering exhaust.

She'd joined the police force so she wouldn't have to be stuck behind a desk all day, and she'd been delighted when DCI Raven had asked her to visit Gisborough Hall to enquire about Patrick Lofthouse's visits there. The drive would take about an hour in total, during which time she was quite content to sit back and enjoy the scenery.

Even on a wild and windy day like today, she found the moors breath-taking. Where some people saw a bleak, almost treeless landscape, to her the expansiveness of the heather-clad moors always made her heart sing. This was her native land, having grown up in Rosedale Abbey, a tiny village in the middle of the moors. By comparison, she found Scarborough big and noisy, the amusement arcades along the sea front brash and tacky. She tolerated the bustle of the seaside resort because she enjoyed her job, but she was always glad of an opportunity to leave the town behind. At the weekends, if she wasn't visiting her family back in Rosedale Abbey, she was usually to be found hiking along the Cleveland Way or cycling the cinder track along the coast to Ravenscar or up to Highwood Brow. In the summer she'd spent a fabulous two weeks tackling the whole of the Pennine Way, from Edale in Derbyshire to Kirk Yetholm in the Scottish borders. Yes, the moors were definitely the place to be. Not that you wanted to be caught out there in a snowstorm. That had happened to her on one occasion and she'd had to take shelter in the nearest pub until the snowplough could get through. But today, all she had to contend with was the car being buffeted by the wind and the threat of a downpour from the lowering clouds. She put her foot down and pressed on towards Whitby.

It was a relief too, to be away from DC Dan Bennett. Dan was an attractive guy, but Jess wasn't interested in dating a fellow police officer. The last thing she wanted when she finished a long day at work was to talk to someone who did the same kind of job as her. And if she was honest, Dan could be a bit of an idiot and was always just a little too eager to hit on her. It was almost embarrassing to watch.

Besides, Jess had more on her mind than love. At twenty-one, she was the youngest member of the team, having only got out of uniform back in the summer. She hadn't been to university like Becca and Dan, and didn't have Tony's years of experience on the job. She was aware of being the most junior detective at Scarborough. But that made her all the more determined to prove herself and show what she could do.

She welcomed the arrival of the new boss, DCI Raven.

Although he could be a little terrifying with his stern expression – not to mention his coal-black hair, black coat and black tie – he was shaking the place up after Dinsdale's plodding lead. And he had placed his trust in her, already giving her two assignments to complete on her own. First Redcar. Now Gisborough Hall.

The entrance to the hotel was only a short distance off the main road. Following the sign to reception, she drove slowly along a short tree-lined avenue, the skeletal branches of the leafless trees arching overhead. The path curved to the right and she passed a long topiary hedge before pulling up in front of the hotel. Built in the nineteenth century in the Jacobean style, the former country house was all mullioned windows, steep gables and tall chimneys. At this time of the year, the dark stone walls were cloaked in a deep, red Virginia Creeper.

Jess pushed open the large wooden door and presented her warrant card to the young, black-waistcoated woman on the reception desk.

'DC Jess Barraclough from Scarborough CID. I'm investigating the murder of Patrick Lofthouse whose body was found on the beach at Scarborough three days ago.'

If the receptionist, whose name badge read *Kirsty*, was disconcerted at the arrival of a police detective or the mention of a murder enquiry, she was too professional to let it show. This was an upmarket hotel, and they clearly invested in their staff. 'I heard about that on the local news,' said Kirsty. 'How can I help?' Her accent was pure Middlesbrough.

'We believe that Mr Lofthouse may have stayed at this hotel before he died. We found this among his personal possessions.' Jess produced the headed notepaper from a black folder. 'Can you confirm that this writing paper is from Gisborough Hall?'

'Yes, that's our logo,' said Kirsty. 'All our rooms have writing paper. It doesn't get used much these days, but it's a nice touch.'

'Thank you,' said Jess, returning the sheet of paper to

the folder. 'Now what I'd really like to know is, when did Patrick Lofthouse stay at the hotel? And did he come here on multiple occasions? Is that something you could find out for me?'

Kirsty hesitated. 'I'm not sure. That sort of information is confidential.'

Jess flashed the receptionist a short smile. 'Then perhaps I need to speak to your manager. Could you call them for me, please?'

She hoped that the prospect of requiring Kirsty to summon her manager for help would encourage the receptionist's cooperation. She could get a warrant for the information if she needed to, but it would be so much quicker and simpler if Kirsty would just agree to check the hotel's database here and now.

Kirsty was thinking it over. 'I suppose it can't do any harm if I just look through the bookings for you. You are the police after all…'

'Exactly,' said Jess. 'No need to bother your boss.'

She could see that Kirsty was actually quite enjoying this. No doubt it would give her something to tell her mates, the next time they met for a drink. 'What dates would you like me to check?'

'Let's start with the seventeenth of October,' said Jess. That was the date written on the headed notepaper.

Kirsty tapped at the computer keyboard, her eyes scanning up and down the screen. 'No one called Patrick Lofthouse stayed here on the seventeenth.' She sounded disappointed. But Jess knew you had to be more patient when carrying out investigations.

'What about anyone with the name of Tristan?' she asked.

Kirsty scrolled up and down the list of bookings. 'No, sorry.'

'Okay, not to worry, let's just go back before the seventeenth.'

She waited patiently while Kirsty worked through the list of bookings. The walls of the reception area were hung with landscapes and line drawings. A middle-aged couple dressed for walking in waxed coats and thick boots came down the stairs and headed outside. Although the grounds of the hotel were stunning and the location was ideal for walking, this wasn't the sort of hotel that Jess stayed in on her hiking trips. Her limited budget only stretched to family-run B&Bs and youth hostels. A favourite was the hostel just up the road in Whitby, on the top of the cliff next to the ruined abbey.

'I think I've found him!' Kirsty sounded gleeful.

'Excellent,' said Jess. 'When was he here?'

'He booked a double room for one night on the tenth of October. In the name of Tristan Lofthouse.'

'A double room,' said Jess, noting down the date. 'So was he with someone?'

'Well, when I say a double room,' said Kirsty, 'that's really just a standard room. They're all either double or twin. We don't have single rooms here.'

'Understood. But was he on his own?'

'The booking is just in his name,' said Kirsty. 'There's no one else mentioned.'

'This is a long shot,' said Jess, 'but I don't suppose you were working that day? Do you remember him checking in?'

'I'm sorry,' said Kirsty.

'Well, then, did he stay on any other date?'

'Just let me check. Would you like a coffee while you're waiting?'

Jess declined the offer but asked if she could see the room Patrick had stayed in.

'Let me see if it's occupied,' said Kirsty. 'No, you're in luck, it's empty at the moment.' She programmed a passkey and gave Jess directions to the room.

The room, on the first floor, was just as grand as Jess had expected. The mahogany four-poster bed was made up with crisp, white linen, the walls were decorated in floral wallpaper, and the view from the leaded windows looked out over a croquet lawn and the surrounding countryside. The room boasted an original fireplace, a crystal chandelier, and a marble ensuite bathroom. Very nice indeed. But what was Patrick Lofthouse doing here? And what was so important about the date and time he'd written on the headed notepaper?

When she returned to reception, Kirsty greeted her with the news that she'd found four other occasions when a Tristan Lofthouse had stayed at the hotel. She gave Jess a printed sheet, showing that he'd stayed here twice during August and twice during September, always in the same room.

Jess thanked Kirsty for her help.

'My pleasure,' said Kirsty, beaming. 'If you need anything else, just give me a call.'

Jess headed back outside to her car, wondering whether Kirsty was already messaging her friends with the news that she'd helped the police with their investigation into a murder.

CHAPTER 19

'So he knows nothing,' concluded Raven. 'Except that Patrick was a dealer.'

He and Becca were making their way back to the incident room after concluding the interview with Shane Denton. Raven had already released Shane, sending him back to Redcar in the company of the two coppers who had brought him in earlier that morning. They had sounded amused when told of Shane's accusations of police brutality. 'Middle of the night?' said the first. 'It was seven o'clock at the earliest. He should have gone to bed at a decent time, then he wouldn't have minded so much.'

'And we didn't kick his door down,' said the second indignantly. 'Just banged on it until he opened up to find out what all the noise was about.'

'Well, don't worry,' Raven reassured them. 'He's not filing a complaint. He's just glad to get out of here without being arrested a second time.'

'And you believed his story?' Becca asked Raven as they reached the door to the incident room.

Raven considered the question. 'He was scared when I told him he was a suspect in a murder enquiry. Terrified.

So he was either telling us everything he knew – which was nothing we hadn't already worked out for ourselves – or else he really did shoot Patrick, and was lying desperately to save his skin. But for now we have nothing to charge him with.' Raven pushed open the door and waited for Becca to walk through.

'Do you still think there's a link between this case and the Max Hunt murder?' she asked.

'There's a strong parallel, at least,' said Raven. 'Max Hunt was a dealer, and so was Patrick. The question we have to ask ourselves in both cases is, who benefits from their death?'

Tony was waiting for them, and came over as Raven entered. 'Sir, there's been a development on Patrick's car. It's been found on Salt Pans Road. A walker reported it after noticing that it had been parked on the grass verge for several days.'

'Salt Pans Road,' said Raven, dredging up long forgotten geographical memories. 'That's north of here, isn't it?'

'Yes, about two miles up the road,' said Tony. 'Just past the village of Cloughton. Salt Pans Road is a single-track road that leads right down to the coast. The car was abandoned at the end of the road.'

'Is it possible that's where he was killed and thrown into the sea?'

'It's consistent with what the coastguard said, sir.'

'Excellent,' said Raven. 'This could be a very important development. We need to get CSI on the scene right away.'

'I've already organised a team to go and collect the car,' said Tony. 'They're bringing it back now so that forensics can check for prints. And CSI have gone out to search the area.'

Raven smiled. This was just the kind of news he needed. 'Good work, Tony,' he said, giving the DC a friendly pat on the back.

Tony received the compliment with a short nod.

*

Raven looked out across the bleak stretch of coastline. Salt Pans Road was nothing more than a single-lane track crossing empty farmland to the sea. Driving to its end was like travelling to the edge of the world. A nowhere place where land, water and sky collided. The wind made waves in the long grass and the surf crashed gently against the narrow strip of beach below. The CSI team was out, combing the ground. If this was the place where Patrick had been executed, then there was a chance that some item might be found. His missing phone. A trace of blood. But it was a large area to search and so far they'd found nothing.

'The walker says that the car had been here since Monday morning,' said Becca. 'It may have been left on the Sunday evening, but we can't be certain.'

The most obvious scenario was that Patrick had driven here to meet someone, and that person had shot him dead and dumped his body in the sea. This was a desolate spot, the kind of place you might come for a bracing walk. Or if you wanted to meet someone and not be seen. But if Patrick had been shot in his car, or in the killer's car, and dragged down to the beach, there would be signs. Blood. Crushed vegetation. And there were no such indications. So had he gone for a walk along the beach with his unknown assailant and been killed there? If so, the sea may well have swept away any evidence.

Raven watched the CSI crew go about their work. The team leader, a woman, was directing them. She had spoken briefly to Becca on their arrival but had pointedly ignored Raven and had her back to him now. Yorkshire folk could be gruff at times.

'We'll need to carry out door-to-door to find out if anyone saw anything,' said Raven. He turned around, sweeping his gaze in a full circle. Not a single building was visible. And no sign of human presence, apart from the road that led here and a single bench that looked out across the rocky bay. But the place wasn't entirely the back of beyond. The person who'd reported the abandoned car wouldn't be the only one who came here to walk. And there were houses further back up on the main road.

He cast his eye one last time over the clumps of trees and tufts of grass that clung stubbornly to the ground, then returned to the shelter of his car.

'That's a nasty scratch,' said Becca, eyeing the bodywork of the M6.

'Yes,' agreed Raven. 'Very nasty.'

*

On arriving back at the police station, Raven was startled to come face to face with Detective Superintendent Gillian Ellis. The Super's features were set like stone and she regarded him through cold, hard eyes. Raven didn't need his years of experience as a detective to divine that she was raging mad.

'I'll see you later, DS Shawcross,' he said, and watched as Becca scurried away gratefully down the corridor.

'My office,' said Gillian. 'Now.'

He followed her into the office and stood before her desk, waiting for her to take a seat. None was offered to him in return.

'DCI Raven,' she began without preamble, 'it has been brought to my attention that you and DI Dinsdale had a bit of a "set to" yesterday.'

'That's true,' said Raven. There was no point denying what she already knew. 'But with respect, ma'am, the man deliberately provoked me.'

Gillian raised a hand to stop him. 'Provoked or not, I expect my officers to maintain the highest professional standards. An altercation between two grown men in a corridor is unacceptable. Do you hear me? Unacceptable!'

'Has DI Dinsdale lodged a complaint against me, ma'am?'

'No,' conceded Gillian. 'He has not. But that is not the

point. The point is that your behaviour fell far short of the standards expected of a senior detective. Of any police officer, in fact. I've already had cause to give you one verbal warning. Give me a good reason why I shouldn't just send you back to London, or have you dismissed on the grounds of gross misconduct.'

Raven kept his mouth shut. He knew that nothing he might say would influence Gillian's opinion of him. She would make up her own mind about what to do.

She rubbed her fingertip against her nose, watching him. 'I understand that you made a visit to HMP Full Sutton yesterday. Why?'

'Ma'am, it was to conduct an interview with a prisoner. Lewis Briggs. He's serving a life sentence for the murder of–'

'I know who Lewis Briggs is,' she snapped. She fixed him with her small eyes, her mind engaged in some intricate calculation that only she was privy to. 'Do you have any evidence suggesting a miscarriage of justice?'

'No, ma'am.'

'Then do you think that Lewis Briggs may have some involvement in the current investigation?'

'No, ma'am.'

She narrowed her eyes further until they were little more than slits. 'Well, then…?'

'There are parallels, ma'am, between the Max Hunt killing and the murder of Patrick Lofthouse. I wanted to explore those parallels.'

'And did you gain any insight from your prison visit, DCI Raven?'

'No, ma'am.'

He could tell that she appreciated his straight answers. She nodded infinitesimally, before framing her next question. 'What exactly did DI Dinsdale do to provoke you, DCI Raven?'

Raven sensed a trap. Was this a test of his loyalty? If he answered her question honestly, would she regard him as a snitch? If he failed to disclose what Dinsdale had said, would she consider herself betrayed? He wanted to tell her how Dinsdale had failed to follow up obvious leads during the Max Hunt case. He wanted to tell her that Dinsdale had warned him off investigating Darren Jubb. He wanted to tell her that he had accused Gillian of being the queen in some sinister plot.

'Nothing, ma'am. The incident was entirely my fault.'

Her nodding head told him he'd given her the answer she was hoping for. 'Then we'll speak no more about this, DCI Raven. Unless I have cause to summon you here again. You've had two warnings now. Don't fool yourself into thinking there'll be a third chance.'

'No, ma'am. Thank you, ma'am.'

'You still haven't bought a new tie.' She sighed in exasperation and dismissed him with a curt wave. 'Now get out of my sight, Tom. And make sure you find yourself some clean shirts too. You stink.'

*

Mindful of his urgent need for new clothes, and aware that he'd only narrowly escaped being dismissed from his job, Raven made sure that he left the office on time and went into town for a much-overdue shopping trip.

The town centre had changed a little over the years – the branch of Woolworth's where he'd nicked his first CD had closed down and been taken over by Poundland – but the overall layout and feel was exactly as it had been during his teenage years. Marks and Spencer occupied the same spot as it always had, on the adjacent road of Newborough. He entered the store and went straight to the menswear department. He'd always bought his shirts, socks and underwear at M&S despite Lisa's attempts to get him to broaden his horizons. His unadventurous approach to clothing had driven his wife to distraction, but secretly Raven was in no doubt why he so obstinately clung to his old habits. His mum had always bought his clothes for him at M&S, and continuing to shop there was one of the few ways he could keep her memory alive. It was tragic, really.

He scoured the racks of clothing, searching for the same shirts that he always bought. The shop had changed its range many times over the years, but Raven still sought out the same style every time. Slim fitting, hundred percent cotton, pure white. He scooped half a dozen off the shelf, added a generous helping of plain grey socks and piled some of his regular boxer shorts on top. His arms filled with his bounty, he went to the checkout desk and paid.

He was just about to leave the shop when he remembered. Returning to menswear, he selected a plain navy tie and checked out a second time. 'You're a big spender,' quipped the woman on the till.

'Don't you believe it.' Raven winked at her. 'You won't see me again for another twelve months.'

After dropping the BMW off in its usual place, he carried his purchases along the dark, narrow corridor of Quay Street, fumbling with his keys. He could have killed another fish supper but was determined not to show his face at the chippie again until at least the weekend. Friday night at the earliest. It would have to be frozen pizza instead.

Ahead of him, a car door slammed shut. He was surprised to see a red Porsche parked outside his house, blocking the street. A woman was standing in the light cast by a streetlamp, her strawberry blonde hair tumbling over her shoulders, her slim form silhouetted by the lamp.

A shiver went through him. It couldn't be. It wasn't possible.

'Donna,' he gasped. 'Donna Craven.' But it was his teenage voice that spoke out of his man's body.

She stepped towards him and her features came fully into view, her hair backlit like a halo. 'Hello, Tom. I heard you were back in town.'

CHAPTER 20

Old oak beams, exposed stonework, and a glowing log burner in the corner. The warm lighting of the hotel bar played well against her smooth skin and brought a sparkle to her eyes.

'You don't look your age, Donna,' said Raven. 'No one would ever guess that you were–'

She pressed a manicured finger to his lips. 'No need to say it out loud, Tom. Let people make their own guesses. And you look good too. You always did.'

'You're just flattering me now, Donna.' He grinned. 'But don't stop.'

Raven had driven her to this place once he'd recovered from the shock of meeting his old girlfriend. A hotel a few miles outside Scarborough. A cosy, informal atmosphere in which to catch up. 'A discreet little venue where no one will bother us,' Donna had explained, 'and the food is fabulous.'

'I'll drive,' Raven had told her. 'You can leave your car in the car park.'

On arrival they'd ordered food, Raven a steak and chips, Donna a salad with pan-fried scallops, prawns and langoustines. He had declined to share a bottle of wine, saying that he was driving. 'I'm happy with mineral water and a twist of lime,' he'd told her. Donna had ordered a large glass of Chenin Blanc for herself.

'So, how long has it been?' she asked. 'Thirty years?'

'Thirty-one.'

'Sounds like you've been counting.' She peered at him playfully over the rim of her raised glass and took a sip of the wine. 'So what have you been doing with yourself all this time?'

'It's complicated.'

'Good. You know I hate listening to boring stories.'

'Well…'

How could you sum up thirty-one years in a few short sentences? The five years he'd spent in the army had felt like a lifetime. He'd joined up as a raw sixteen-year-old, anything to get away from his life in Scarborough. His mother's death, his father's drinking and increasing violence. His anger at Darren, and shame at his own behaviour. The army had offered a solution to all his problems. The discipline, the camaraderie, the sense of shared purpose. It had given him the safe environment he yearned for. A chance to recreate himself anew, and put his past behind him. Then, at the age of nineteen, he'd been sent to Bosnia. It was the first time he'd been abroad, and he was dropped straight into the middle of a war zone. No amount of training could prepare you for that.

The complex situation in the Balkans had been a mystery to him, but he understood that soldiers were only deployed when all attempts at political solutions had failed. They were there to keep the peace, but that didn't mean they weren't expected to fight if the situation called for combat. The engagement in Goražde had lasted a mere fifteen minutes, but at the end of it one of his friends was dead and he was injured and had to be stretchered off the battlefield. He hadn't intended to risk his life that day. It had been an instinctive reaction to help his fellow soldiers in need of assistance. He wasn't even aware that he'd made a decision until it was all over.

They'd operated on his leg, patched him up as best they could, and given him a medal. But he would never be the same again. Would he still be in the army now if he hadn't been shot? It was an unanswerable question, just one of many.

After Goražde, the army had lost its appeal. It had served him well enough, enabling him to get away from Scarborough and grow up, but the heat of battle had forged yet another version of Tom Raven and it was time to move on. And so he'd gone south to London, joined the police force, worked his way up the Met to the rank of Detective Chief Inspector. In the meantime there had been marriage, a daughter, and then a separation. So far, so predictable. He gave Donna a potted summary, leaving out the bits that bored him or that he preferred to avoid.

The food arrived and he cut into his steak. It was cooked just the way he liked it – well done on the outside, almost raw underneath. Blood oozed out over his plate as he divided the meat into sections.

Donna sipped her wine, cupping the glass with her slim fingers, her long nails painted a vibrant shade of red. Almost the same colour as her car.

'Detective Chief Inspector,' she said. 'Who would have thought it? Caught any shoplifters recently, Tom?' She smiled at him, her crimson lips curving into a half moon, letting him know that she meant no mischief, that this was just a shared joke between them.

Donna Craven. He could hardly believe he was sitting here with the woman – she'd still been a girl when he'd last seen her – who had stolen his heart all those years ago. The sexiest girl in the school, that had been Donna. With her long hair and amazing figure, she had walked the school corridors with the confidence of a supermodel. All the boys fancied her like crazy. The girls hated her, although they pretended to be her friend. She'd been out of his league, or so he'd thought. He couldn't believe the way fortune had smiled at him when she'd suggested they go to a nightclub together. They were underage of course, but they got away with it. Donna could always pull off a stunt like that. With her makeup and her stilettos, she could easily pass for eighteen or more. The toughest nightclub bouncers were putty in her hands. He still remembered their first kiss, sheltering from the November cold around the side of the Futurist Cinema. Tentative to begin with then suddenly fierce and passionate. She had ignited something inside him that he hadn't known existed. They had shared a cigarette afterwards, and he had thought himself so grown-up. He thought he had found the love of his life. And perhaps he had.

He tried to turn the conversation away from himself. 'I can't believe you look so amazing, Donna.' It was true. At sixteen she'd been naturally slim. Now, at forty-seven, she had the body of a woman who clearly worked hard to keep herself in shape. Her sleeveless dress revealed toned upper arms, she had retained her flat stomach and narrow waist, and her face was suspiciously light on wrinkles. Her perfume wafted across the table, musky with a hint of vanilla.

'I like to keep myself trim,' she said with a shrug and a smile.

'You're doing all right then?'

'I can't complain.'

'And the Porsche?' Like him, Donna hadn't come from a wealthy family. Quite the opposite. Her father had done odd jobs. Her mother had worked as a district nurse.

'I married a wealthy husband. You know that was always my masterplan.'

'Well, congratulations on achieving it. Are you happy?'

'Happy enough. I have a husband to adore me, and two gorgeous children. What more could a woman want?'

'You tell me, Donna.' He'd noticed she'd said "adore", not "love". And that she hadn't said anything about loving her husband back.

She set aside her knife and fork, picked up her wine glass, and fixed him with a look. 'I made my choice, Tom.

Just like you made yours.'

He felt his mood slip in the face of her accusation. 'I'm sorry I went away.'

A single tear slid from the corner of her eye, glinting in the soft light. 'You broke my heart, Tom. You didn't even tell me you were leaving.' Her voice was fragile, trembling, as if it might shatter at any moment. 'I thought you'd be back in a few days. Then the days turned to weeks, and the weeks into months. I kept hoping, for the longest time.'

He swallowed. 'You know why I had to leave, Donna.'

'No. I know why you thought you had to go. But you had a choice. You could have stayed.'

What if I had?

But he had made his choice. He had made it on a cold winter's night, almost a lifetime ago. Choices couldn't be made a second time. You only got one shot at life.

Donna blinked away the tear. When she spoke again, she had recovered her poise. 'I see that you walk without any trouble. I would never have known you'd been shot. Does it hurt?'

'Only in cold weather. So you've been stalking me online, have you?'

She smiled. 'Don't flatter yourself. I read about it in *The Scarborough News* years ago.'

'*The Scarborough News*, eh? So I reached the dizzy heights of fame.'

'Briefly.'

A waiter cleared away their plates and brought Donna a second glass of wine. 'Cheers,' she said, raising it to her lips.

'Cheers.' He drank his mineral water and lime.

A silence fell between them, an echo of the deep quiet that had endured for thirty-one years. A space filled with memories, desires, regrets. They had been a boy and a girl back then. A simple story, destined for a happy ending. But then the darkness had come.

'Tell me about the others,' said Raven.

Donna raised her thin brows in surprise. 'You mean

Darren? Do you really want to know? He's doing very well for himself actually. He took over from Frank and moved into the entertainment business.'

'His nightclub, you mean?'

She tapped his arm. 'You already knew!'

'I'm a policeman. It's my job to know everything. What about Harry?

Harry Hood. The fourth and final member of their little gang. Another reprobate – slimier than Darren, more avaricious than Donna, less principled than Raven. He was the worst of the bunch. Raven pictured him languishing in some jail somewhere. It was hard to imagine that he had made anything of his shabby existence.

'You don't know?' said Donna. 'Really?'

'No.'

'He's become a criminal lawyer.'

'I don't believe it.' Raven was aware that his mouth had dropped open.

'I don't know why not. He's a poacher turned gamekeeper, Tom. Just like you.'

'It's not the same!' Raven had joined the police because it had seemed like an obvious career move after leaving the army. But deep down he knew that it was a kind of atonement, a desire to make amends for his many youthful transgressions. He could hardly believe the same to be true of Harry Hood. Repentance had never been on Harry's agenda, only a desire to line his own pockets. 'Lawyers earn good money,' he said uncharitably. 'Unlike policemen.'

Donna scowled. 'Don't start feeling sorry for yourself, Tom. You know I hate that.'

Now Raven regretted asking about the others. Asking questions was a professional habit, but sometimes it was better not to know the answers. He wished he'd kept the conversation firmly in sunny waters, steering away from murky depths and hidden reefs. He feared that he'd allowed his unexpected reunion with Donna to run aground.

He began to wonder if returning to Scarborough after spending so much of his life avoiding it had been a huge mistake. The town was full of ghosts, and not just those of the dead. The ghost of his own past dwelt here, and also the ghost of his lost hopes and dreams. All of his wrong choices and missed opportunities were gathered together, dragging him down like weights around the neck of a drowning man. He suddenly needed air.

'Let's get the bill,' he said.

'I'll pay,' said Donna. 'It's my treat.'

'No, really,' he said, reaching for his wallet, but her hand closed around his.

Her fingers pressed down, warm and soft, yet firm. 'I insist,' she said. 'It's my husband's money. He likes it when I spend it.'

The slim gold band around her ring finger told its own story, yet Donna's touch wasn't the innocent brush of an old friend's. It was a lover's caress. He knew he should pull his hand away, but he didn't. He let her stroke his skin, sending waves up and down his spine.

'It's getting late,' she said softly. 'We could see if they've got a room.'

He was tempted. God, he was tempted. But something held him back. Donna was a married woman, and he a married man. Maybe he was being old-fashioned, but that was how he was.

'I should get back,' he said, withdrawing his hand. 'I've got an early start in the morning.'

'Of course.' She smiled sweetly. 'But I have enjoyed this evening. We should do it again.'

'Maybe.'

She opened her wallet and slid out some crisp notes. She left them on the table, tipping generously. 'Come on, then, Tom. Let's go.'

He rose to his feet, and she joined him, looping her arm through his. Together they made their way towards the exit.

Donna smiled at the barman as they passed.

'Goodnight, Paul.'

He returned her farewell with a brisk nod. 'Goodnight, Mrs Jubb.'

Raven froze. 'Jubb?' It seemed to take a huge effort to get the word out. 'You're married to Darren Jubb?'

Donna smiled once more, her red lips parting to reveal a neat row of pearly teeth. 'Didn't I mention it, Tom? Well, I suppose you never really asked. But then again, I thought you knew everything.'

CHAPTER 21

Becca woke to the smell of frying bacon. If it had been left to her, she'd have made do with a slice of wholemeal toast and marmite and a mug of tea before going into work, but she knew her mum wouldn't let her out of the door without "a proper English breakfast" inside her. 'It'll set you up for the day,' her mum always said. She was probably right.

At the age of twenty-seven, Becca hadn't expected to be still living at home in her parents' Bed & Breakfast, sleeping in her childhood room on the top floor. She'd come very close to moving into a place of her own with her long-term boyfriend. But that had fallen through at the last minute. Now she was resigned to living at home for a while longer. The family home was a place of refuge and comfort, and she was grateful for her parents' support, yet she feared that if she didn't move on soon, she would be stuck here forever, her waistline gaining inches year on year.

Her parents, Sue and David Shawcross, ran a guest house in a four-storey Edwardian house on North Marine Road close to the old town and with views over the North

Bay. An "award-winning" guest house, as Sue would remind anyone who cared to listen. And it was true that the wise owl logo of the *TripAdvisor Travellers' Choice Awards* was proudly displayed in the front downstairs window. In the summer months they were always fully booked, often with regulars who came back year after year, appreciative of the warm welcome, comfortable rooms and good food. But in the winter months, most of the rooms were empty, save for the occasional business traveller. This week the schools were on their half-term break and an extended family from Leeds – parents, three children and two sets of grandparents – were booked in for a few days, braving the wind and rain in their brightly coloured waterproof coats and Wellington boots.

On her way to the kitchen, Becca encountered her dad carrying platefuls of food to the dining room, all freshly cooked to order by her mum.

'Need a hand, Dad?' Becca offered.

'All under control, love,' said David. He was a pro when it came to carrying three plates at once, a skill that Becca had never entirely mastered. 'There's plenty more in the kitchen if you want a bite before you leave.' Sue always insisted that if she was cooking for a dozen guests then it was no more trouble to rustle up a plateful for her own family.

'Here you go, love, get that inside you before you head out.' Sue started piling scrambled eggs, grilled tomatoes, rashers of bacon and thick juicy mushrooms – not to mention a slice of traditional Yorkshire black pudding made from dried pigs' blood, suet and oats – onto a plate as soon as Becca appeared in the kitchen. 'It's blowing a gale out there.'

Becca sat to eat at the kitchen table. As soon as she tucked into the food, she realised just how hungry she was.

'You've been putting in long hours,' said her mum. She placed a mug of strong tea in front of Becca and took the chair opposite, cradling her own mug in two hands.

'It's this new case,' said Becca between mouthfuls of

food. 'A murder investigation always takes top priority.'

David returned to the kitchen and started feeding slices of bread into the industrial-sized toasting machine.

'I've been following it in *The Scarborough News*,' said Sue. A copy of the newspaper was lying on the table. 'A local lad, and engaged to be married too. Shocking business. I know you can't go into details, but do you have any idea what happened?' Her mum had learned over the years that Becca couldn't divulge details about ongoing investigations, but she still liked to fish for snippets of information that she could share with her army of friends and acquaintances.

'We're working on some theories,' said Becca, noncommittally. Although, she reflected, talking of *theories* made it sound as if they had multiple leads when in actual fact, they had little to go on. 'DCI Raven thinks there might be a connection to a similar case from a few years ago.'

'I remember it,' said Sue. 'But the man who was killed then was a horrible drugs dealer, wasn't he? This latest victim sounds like a nicely brought-up lad. His parents run a local business.'

'That's right,' said Becca. 'But like I said, we're following up a number of theories.'

'So, how are you getting on with this new boss of yours?' asked Sue. She was always more interested in the people Becca worked with than the actual crimes they were solving. 'He works you hard. I've hardly seen you this past week.'

Becca took a sip of her tea. 'We get on all right, actually. He's certainly a lot more dynamic than Dinsdale. But he doesn't like to talk much about himself. He's more the strong, silent type.' She wondered about mentioning Raven's army background, but thought better of it. If she told her mum that Raven had been awarded a medal for bravery, it would be all over Scarborough before nightfall.

'There used to be a Raven family living down by the harbour,' said Sue. 'The boy went to the same school as me. His father was a fisherman, his mother worked at the Grand Hotel.'

'Really?' said Becca. 'Do you remember much about them?'

'Not really. The mother died, the boy moved away. I haven't seen the father in years.'

'Raven's father died recently. That's why he returned to Scarborough.'

'Well, that sounds like the same family,' said Sue brightly. 'Now, how did the mother die? I really can't remember.'

The kitchen door swung open and Becca's brother, Liam, sauntered in. He gave his mum a kiss on the cheek. 'That smells good. Got any spare?' He sat down at the table, turning down the collar of his leather jacket. 'I could do with something hot. It's ball-freezing weather out there this morning.'

'Then you should wear a scarf,' said Sue. 'And a proper winter coat, too.'

'Nah, I'm good.' Liam stretched out his feet under the table and waited with his hands in his pockets while Sue bustled around, fetching food for him and boiling the kettle for more tea.

'And a good morning to you too,' said Becca. 'I'm very well, thanks for asking.'

Despite being three years older than her and owning a very nice second-floor apartment right on the Esplanade overlooking the South Cliff Gardens, Liam treated his parents' B&B like a second home, always expecting to be fed on demand whenever he turned up. Sue, much to Becca's irritation, pandered to his every request, indulging him shamelessly.

'So, what's new in the detective business, sis? Caught any villains lately?' Liam smirked at her. He'd never taken her job seriously. Becca suspected his attitude might have a lot to do with the fact that he sailed very close to the wind himself where the law was concerned. His job – if you could call it that – involved wheeling and dealing in the property market. He was always buying up properties at knock-down prices, doing them up and selling them on for a profit or renting them out as holiday homes. His extensive network of builders, plumbers and decorators were all cut-price cowboys as far as Becca could make out. Whenever she saw him, he spent half his time jumping up to take calls on his mobile and darting out of the room to hold hushed conversations with his dodgy associates. She hoped that the tax authorities never decided to take a close look at his activities.

Not waiting for her answer – he clearly hadn't expected one – he pulled the copy of *The Scarborough News* across the table and started reading the article on the front page. *Body on Beach Investigation Continues* ran the headline. Becca had glanced at it earlier. The paper was clearly trying to make the most out of the few facts that had been released by the police. The article was a mix of speculation and rehashed material that had already been reported. A photo of Patrick appeared, quite possibly one downloaded from Scarlett's social media accounts, with the footer, *Patrick Lofthouse: son of local car dealer, Gordon Lofthouse.*

'I bought my car from Lofthouse Cars,' said Liam. Her brother owned a petrol-guzzling sports car that Becca disapproved of. 'Patrick sold it to me. I got him to knock a couple of grand off the asking price.'

Liam liked to haggle over everything he bought and then boast about how much he'd saved. Becca didn't know how much of his bragging she could really believe. But despite herself, she was interested to hear that Liam had come across Patrick.

'Here you go, love,' said Sue, planting a huge plate of bacon, eggs, sausages and baked beans in front of him.

'Thanks, Mum,' said Liam, grabbing his knife and fork and tucking in as if he hadn't eaten in days.

'So, what was he like?' asked Becca.

'Who?' Liam had already lost interest in the story and turned to the sports pages at the back of the paper.

'Patrick Lofthouse. I'm on the team investigating his

murder.'

'Don't think he was really into selling cars,' said Liam with his mouth full. 'That's why it was so easy to knock the price down.' He laughed. 'Poor bugger. Getting shot like that. And just when he was going to become a member of the Jubb family. He could have given up selling cars for good then. Have you any idea how much money Scarlett Jubb makes as an online influencer? I tell you, Becs, you're in the wrong job. All you need these days is an iPhone and a willingness to bare your soul to the world, no holds barred.' He took a quick slurp of his tea, spilling some over the table. Sue produced a cloth and quickly wiped it away.

'Wait a minute,' said Becca. 'You know the Jubbs?'

'Yeah, sure,' said Liam, seeing off a pork sausage in three bites. 'Ethan Jubb's in the same business as me, isn't he? Buying and selling properties.'

'So, do you know him well?'

'Well, I bump into him at his dad's nightclub now and again.'

'What about professionally?' Becca didn't like the idea that Liam might actually be connected to the Jubb family's business dealings.

'Oh, we're just acquaintances,' said Liam, shrugging it off. 'Rivals, I suppose you could say. He's often bidding for the same properties I'm interested in.' He wiped his plate with a slice of toast and finished off the dregs of his tea in one swift movement. 'Well, I must be off. I've got a meeting with some builders down in Cayton Bay.'

'Wait,' said Becca. 'Before you go, can you recommend a good bodywork repairer? My boss's car got scratched and he's new to the area.'

'No problem,' said Liam. 'I'll shoot you over a name and number later.' He leaned over to peck Sue's cheek once more. 'Sorry, Mum, got to dash. Thanks for the grub.' He was out of the door faster than Becca had ever seen him move.

'Well,' said Sue. 'He was in a hurry.' She picked up the empty plates and loaded them into the dishwasher.

Yes, thought Becca, *he certainly was. And just as soon as I started probing him about his relationship with Ethan Jubb.*

*

They're seated together in the corner of the bar. Him, Donna, Darren and Harry. The Albion on Castle Road isn't their usual haunt, but Darren's somehow managed to sweet-talk the barmaid into serving them, so here they are. Sixteen years old and drinking pints. All apart from Donna, who's trying a Bacardi and Coke for the first time. 'What do you think?' he asks her. 'Not sure.' She pulls a face. 'Would you prefer your usual? Vodka and orange?' She nods, and he makes his way over to the bar, trying to attract the attention of the barmaid without drawing the gaze of the old men who are ranged around the bar on stools. When he returns to the table, Donna's giggling and Darren has that look on his face, like the cat that got the cream. 'What?' demands Raven. 'Nothing,' says Darren, but his eyes catch Donna's and she can't stop herself laughing again. 'Are you laughing at me?' asks Raven. 'Course not,' says Darren. 'Don't be a twat.' Harry pushes his chair towards him with one lazy foot. 'Come on, Tom. Stop making a fuss. Sit down.' But Raven knows when he's being made a fool of. He dumps the glass on the table and storms out of the pub. Outside, the air is wet. That damp persistence that's not quite rain but seeps through to your bones and leaves you frozen. The droplets get into his eyes and sparkle like diamonds. Or are they the bitter sting of tears? He brushes them away, then pushes his hands into his pockets and heads for home.

The ironing board was tucked away at the back of the understairs cupboard. Raven shifted aside some old boxes and hauled it out, setting it up in the middle of the front room. He unwrapped one of his new Marks and Spencer's shirts, which had been sealed in plastic and folded like a complex work of origami, and stretched it out across the board. He was proud of his ironing abilities. Taking care of his own clothes was a skill the army had taught him well. Even when he'd lived with Lisa he'd insisted on washing and ironing his work shirts, and when Hannah had started at secondary school he'd ironed her shirts too, finding the activity strangely soothing. There were few things in life more satisfying than crisp, white cotton shirts.

His mum's old Morphy Richards was covered in dust and cobwebs – his dad had obviously never used it – but once he'd brushed the dirt away, he was pleased to find that the iron still worked. The lead was attached to the plug with insulating tape, and would never pass an electrical inspection, but the house lights stayed on, and apart from an initial smell of burning, everything seemed to be okay.

The sight of the old ironing board brought an image of his mum to mind, standing right where he was now, a basket at her feet, full of his school shirts, jeans and T-shirts. She'd had a quiet passion for laundry and had even ironed his socks and underpants. He smiled at the recollection.

Memories were flooding back now, thick and fast. Take cooking. Every Sunday she had worked a small miracle, roasting a rump cut of beef in the tiny gas oven, with roast potatoes, veg and a giant Yorkshire pudding oozing dark brown gravy. On Mondays she made a stew from the leftovers. Tuesdays were pork sausages, fried in the pan and served with mashed potato. On Wednesdays she would do a Shepherd's Pie, on Thursdays, fresh fish from the day's catch, and on Fridays she took him with her to buy fish and chips from the chip shop on the seafront. Every Saturday they had sandwiches made from white, sliced bread and filled with corned beef or slices of ham. It might not have been the healthiest of diets, but it was wholesome and cooked with love. He'd missed it when he'd left. Army food had been very much like school dinners. He'd never eaten an aubergine or an asparagus until he went to London.

He tested the iron by licking his finger and tapping the metal plate, the way he'd seen his mum do. The spit hissed and he began carefully working the iron around the shirt, starting with the sides and back before moving on to the arms, cuffs and collar. Pleased with the result, he left the iron on the kitchen counter to cool off and went back upstairs to finish getting dressed.

He glanced out of the window, half-expecting to see the Porsche parked cheekily on the double yellow lines, daring a traffic warden to slap a parking ticket on its windscreen. But of course it was gone. The street was empty and Donna was nowhere in sight.

He had driven her back in silence the previous night, his mind combing furiously through the evening's conversation. It had been a set-up, obviously. And he had fallen for it, hook, line and sinker. What possible motive could she have had other than to ensure that he had been spotted taking her out for a drink? She had clearly known the barman. The joint might even have been one of Darren's. Raven could have kicked himself for his carelessness. This could easily compromise the investigation, should the spotlight turn on Darren as a suspect. Donna had staged the whole show in order to protect her husband.

And yet, she had invited him to go to bed with her. If he had accepted, would she have followed through? He was pretty sure that she would.

At least I would have got something for my trouble, he thought sulkily. Instead, he was the biggest fool in Yorkshire.

Now he didn't know what to do. Go to Gillian and tell her what had happened? Which was what, precisely? A cosy chat between old friends. Or a blatant attempt to subvert his independence. He would be out on his ear before you could say the words *professional standards*. Tender his resignation, then? Or just carry on, hoping that his indiscretion might not come back to haunt him.

Before getting out of his car, she'd leaned over and kissed him tenderly on the cheek. 'Thanks for a lovely evening, Tom,' she'd said in a low, sultry voice. 'I've enjoyed it. We should do it again sometime.'

And then she'd vanished into the night with a flash of

red paint and a screech of tyres.

What galled him most was that she hadn't lied to him once the entire evening. *Two gorgeous children. A wealthy husband to adore me.* The clues had all been there, if he'd had the wit to follow them.

He buttoned up his new shirt, tied the blue tie around his neck and checked his appearance in the mirror.

You're a fool, Tom, his reflection told him. *A stupid bloody idiot.*

CHAPTER 22

'Nice tie, sir,' said Dan as Raven entered the incident room.

'Thank you, Dan.'

DC Dan Bennett seemed to have overcome his previous nervousness around Raven. This morning he was like a schoolboy sucking up to his teacher. Spouting compliments. Presenting a gift of an apple. Hoping for preferential treatment.

But at least he had spotted the new tie. Perhaps he would make a decent detective after all.

Now that he had Raven's attention, he followed him over to his office. 'So, what was it like being a DCI in the Met, sir?' Dan waited at the doorway, obviously hoping for tales of excitement and thrills.

Raven had none to give him. 'It was tough, Dan. In my time in London, I investigated armed robbery, murder and rape. Plus a lot of more mundane crimes. If something's against the law, I probably know someone who's done it. But don't make the mistake of thinking it's a glamorous job. It's not. It's the exact opposite.'

Dan didn't seem convinced. 'I wouldn't mind having a

go though, sir. In a big city, I mean. Leeds, maybe. Or Bradford. That's where I'm from originally. I'm a city boy at heart.'

Raven thought he'd detected a trace of West Yorkshire in Dan's accent. He wasn't surprised to learn that he hadn't come from Scarborough originally. 'So what brought you to the seaside, then?'

Dan shrugged. 'Just chance, really. Life's like that, isn't it? Sometimes it's simply the luck of the draw.'

Raven supposed that it was. Bad luck, in his case, or so it often seemed. A vision of strawberry blonde hair and a dress that revealed as much skin as it covered flashed though his mind. 'Life's not about luck, Dan,' he told the young man. 'It's what we make of it that counts.'

Wise words, from the mouth of a fool.

Raven waited for the rest of the team to fetch their morning teas and coffees before gathering them around the whiteboard.

There were still only two suspects pinned to the board, and precious few facts to incriminate either of them. *Darren Jubb. Shane Denton.* Having interviewed both suspects and got precious little information, Raven's guess was that the most promising source of new leads would be the dead man himself. What had Patrick Lofthouse been involved in that had got himself gunned to death? Already a picture was beginning to emerge, but Raven needed specifics.

'All right,' he said. 'Let's run through what you've got. Becca?'

'The CSI team didn't find anything over at Salt Pans Road. There was no indication that Patrick had been dragged from the car. If he was killed there, then it must have been down on the beach itself, and there's nothing left after the sea washed it clean. I ran the door-to-door enquiry like you asked. The nearest settlement is the village of Cloughton. It's a small place – two pubs and a church. Nobody remembers seeing Patrick or his car.'

'It was worth a try,' said Raven. 'Jess?'

Jess nodded eagerly. 'So it seems that Patrick did stay at Gisborough Hall, on several occasions in fact. But not on the seventeenth. So I'm not sure that moves us any further forward.'

'Okay,' said Raven. 'What about you, Dan? Can you tell us where Patrick was on that date?'

Dan's face fell. 'Not on the seventeenth, sir. I've been working through all Patrick's phone contacts, calling people and asking them when they saw him recently. But I haven't got anything for that particular date.'

'It must mean something,' said Raven. 'Keep working through the list.' Finally he turned to Tony. 'Any news from forensics about the car yet?'

'Nothing of any great interest was found in the car, sir. No blood. And the only fingerprints were Patrick's himself, and close family members.'

Raven grimaced at the lack of headway. Four days into the investigation – five since the murder took place – and they had little to show for it. Nothing more than hints and hunches. It was hardly the fast progress that Gillian was demanding.

'But we do have something from Patrick's mobile phone company, sir,' said Tony. 'They've now supplied the tracking data from Patrick's main phone.'

'About time,' said Raven. 'What does it show?'

'Well,' said Tony, 'it's a bit surprising, really. Although when you think about it, it does make sense.'

'Spit it out, Tony,' said Raven.

'Well, the thing is, the data from the phone masts indicates that Patrick's phone was last used out at sea.'

Raven shook his head, not sure that he'd heard correctly. 'At sea?'

'Yes.' Tony produced a map and began to unfold it. 'I've plotted the coordinates here for you.' He pointed to some pencil marks on the plan. 'There's a fair amount of uncertainty, as you'd expect, but from what I can gather, the final location of the phone was here at 17:01 on the Sunday. After that, there's nothing. So either the phone was switched off, or else–'

'It's lying at the bottom of the sea,' concluded Raven. He leaned over the desk to study the plan more closely.

The map showed the area of the North Sea coast from Bridlington Bay south of Scarborough to Harwood Dale, halfway to Whitby in the north. Tony's pencil marks sketched out a cross-hatched area of roughly one square kilometre. The village of Cloughton appeared on the map, but that wasn't where Patrick's phone had last been used. Instead the marks were out to sea, some five kilometres offshore.

The conclusion was inescapable. 'His body was dumped from a boat,' said Raven. 'That's why there was no blood in the car or near the beach. He was shot onboard and pushed over the side. What the hell was he doing on a boat? And more to the point, whose boat was it?'

'Darren Jubb owns a yacht,' said Becca. 'It's called *Sea Dreams*. He keeps it in the harbour.'

Of course. Darren Jubb. Every clue was pointing in the same direction. 'Okay, then,' said Raven. 'Let's bring him in.'

*

The red Porsche was parked on the driveway and it was Donna who opened the door when Raven rang the bell at Jubb Towers. She was wearing a fur-trimmed camel coat, belted at the waist, with black high-heeled boots.

'Tom!' She tilted her head to one side when she saw Becca standing beside him, and gave him a smile that was half triumph, half seduction. She leaned towards him and placed a hand on his arm. 'You should have called. I'm just on my way out. I'm taking my daughter for some much-needed retail therapy.'

Scarlett. The family resemblance was obvious now that Raven knew. Scarlett had the same high cheekbones as her mother. Her hair was darker, favouring her father, but the slender curves and seductive eyes were exactly the same.

Raven was aware that Becca was studying him and Donna with heightened interest.

'I haven't come to see you, Donna,' he said. 'I'd like to ask Darren to come to the station with me.'

'What for?' Donna's tone was at once hurt and accusing, as if she expected better from a man she'd taken out to dinner and had offered to sleep with. 'Darren hasn't done anything wrong.'

'I'm not arresting him,' said Raven. *Yet.* 'But I do need to speak to him. Is he in?'

'He's in a meeting with Ethan,' she said, grudgingly moving aside to let Raven enter. 'Darling,' she called out, 'the police are here to see you. It's Tom.'

Raven steadfastly refused to meet Becca's questioning look.

At that moment, Scarlett appeared, coming down the stairs, all dressed up for the promised mother-and-daughter bonding experience. Raven supposed the trip would involve lots of shopping, lunch at an expensive restaurant, and perhaps some kind of beauty treatment. He was no expert on retail therapy, but he guessed it would take more than a day out with Donna for the young woman to get over her fiancé's murder. They said that time healed everything, but Raven wasn't so sure.

'Hello, Scarlett,' said Becca. 'How are you?'

'Good.' Scarlett acknowledged the police presence with a tight smile. She was calmer than the last time Raven had seen her, but he couldn't say she looked any happier.

Donna steered her daughter towards the door. 'Come on, sweetheart, let's leave the police to do their work.' The front door closed behind them.

A door opened and Darren Jubb emerged from his office. 'Tom, how can I help?' He was all smiles and affability today. *A good actor*, Raven reminded himself. Ethan stood in the doorway behind, shoulders hunched, hands in pockets, shooting suspicious looks in Raven's direction.

'I'd like you to come to the station with us to answer a

few questions,' said Raven.

Darren pasted a pained look on his face. 'Right now? It's just that Ethan and I are in the middle of some important business and–'

'Yes, right now,' said Raven. 'There's a car waiting outside.'

Darren's smile disappeared completely. 'Am I at liberty to decline this invitation?'

'The interview is voluntary at this stage. But it would be in your best interest to cooperate.'

'That sounds ominous. All right then, I'll come with you, but I'm going to call my lawyer first.'

'That might be advisable,' said Raven.

CHAPTER 23

'Get up to anything last night?' enquired Becca casually.

Raven glanced across the table of the interview room at her, trying to read the meaning of her question. He'd seen the way she'd looked at him and Donna and wondered how much she had guessed.

'I did some shopping. How about you?'

'I spent the evening with my boyfriend.'

He waited, but she didn't seem eager to share more details.

Fine. That makes two of us.

They were waiting for Darren Jubb to finish his briefing with his solicitor before the interview got under way. Unlike Shane Denton, whose faith in the legal system had been eroded to nothing, Darren clearly wanted to be fully lawyered-up before he said a word under caution.

He always did like to cover his back.

'Raven,' said Becca, 'about Darren Jubb…'

'Don't believe a word he says,' Raven cautioned her. 'He's a polished liar, always has been.'

'You two go way back.'

'A very long way.'

She hesitated. 'Would it be better if someone else did this interview? Someone less... involved. I could handle it, with Dan or Jess.'

'No,' said Raven. 'Darren Jubb is mine.'

The door opened and Darren entered, his legal representative following close behind. A tall, thin man, with a slight hunch to his shoulders. Raven met the man's face and a shock of recognition hit him like a thunderbolt.

Harry Hood. Of course.

After the conversation with Donna it should have come as no surprise at all.

The man was thirty years older than the schoolboy Raven had last seen, but his weasel features were just the same. Beady eyes, aquiline nose, that mouth that could so easily twist into a mocking sneer but never seemed to smile.

Harry Hood and Darren Jubb – two bad apples at the bottom of the barrel.

'Tom Raven! Well, it's been a long time. Darren told me you were back in town, but I had to see it for myself.' Harry offered his palm, and Raven accepted it reluctantly. Harry's eyes twinkled with glee, as if he'd just won some major triumph. He kept hold of Raven's hand. 'Darren and I had a wager on how long it would take you to return to Scarborough. I never imagined it would be thirty years.'

'Thirty-one,' said Raven.

'My money was on three months tops.'

'So you lost your bet.'

'No,' said Harry, 'I won. My guess was closer. Darren said you would never return.' He released Raven's hand and motioned for Darren to take a seat.

Becca switched on the recording machine and introduced everyone for the tape.

'So my client is being interviewed under caution,' said Harry, once the formalities were completed. 'But this interview is entirely voluntary. Mr Jubb wishes it to be known that he is here to help the police with their enquiries, being an upstanding citizen of impeccable reputation, and that he is free to leave at any time.'

'He's free to leave,' confirmed Raven. The part about Darren being an upstanding citizen was harder to swallow.

And yet it was my fingers on that stolen CD in Woolworth's.

Darren had simply instigated the theft, egging Raven on, then stepping back and directing the operation from outside the shop. No doubt his skills at manipulation had only increased over the years.

'Then let's get started,' said Darren. 'I'm sure we'd all like to be out of here before lunchtime.'

Raven knew that the case against Darren was full of holes. But he was hoping there would be fewer holes by the end of the interview. 'Mr Jubb, I'd like to begin with your relationship with Lewis Briggs. Can you tell us how you came to know Lewis, and exactly what the nature of your dealings with him were?'

'Lewis Briggs?' said Darren, his eyebrows raised. 'I haven't heard that name for a while. Lewis worked as a bouncer at my nightclub. I employed him to work the door, keep the riff-raff away, deal with any troublemakers inside the club. My "dealings" with him were entirely of a professional nature.'

'Did he work for you in any way other than at the nightclub?'

'No.'

'Did you know Max Hunt?'

'I knew him,' said Darren. 'He was a regular. But he wasn't a friend. And before you ask, I had no "dealings" with him at all.'

'And can you think of any reason why Lewis Briggs would have wanted to kill Max Hunt?'

Harry interjected before Darren could respond. 'I'm going to have to stop you there, DCI Raven. It really isn't appropriate for you to expect my client to speculate about the motives of a third party.'

'Then were you aware that Max Hunt supplied illegal drugs?' asked Raven.

'No,' said Darren. 'If I had, I would have instructed Lewis not to let him inside my club. I can do without that kind of hassle.'

'Did you know that Lewis Briggs also sometimes sold or distributed illegal drugs to your clientele?'

'No. Again, if I had known I would have dismissed him immediately.'

'Okay,' said Raven. 'Now let's talk about Patrick Lofthouse. What was your relationship with Patrick?'

'He was engaged to be married to my daughter.'

'And were you aware that Patrick was dealing in illegal drugs?' Raven had stepped away from known facts now into the realm of conjecture, but he didn't think he was far wrong.

Darren gave him a sceptical look. 'Patrick a drug dealer? Do you have any proof of that?'

'Just answer the question, please.'

'No,' said Darren. 'I didn't know.'

'Were you aware that Patrick used cocaine?'

'Certainly not.'

Raven indicated that Becca should ask the next question.

'Mr Jubb,' she began, 'can you confirm that you are the owner of a boat called *Sea Dreams*?'

A big smile spread across Darren's face. 'Certainly. She's a real beauty, a Beneteau Monte Carlo 5. Fifty feet long, seating for eight, integrated TV with Bose speakers, sun lounger, all the latest electronics. I paid half a million for her. Tax deductible, according to my accountant.' He winked at Raven. 'I must take you out for a spin one day, Tom.'

'And can you confirm that you keep the boat moored at Scarborough harbour?' asked Becca.

'That's right.'

'When did you last use the boat, Mr Jubb?'

Darren wrinkled his forehead. 'It was probably a few weeks ago. She doesn't get used so much at this time of year. I doubt I'll take her out much now that winter's almost here, unless we have a spell of bright weather.'

Raven was growing tired of Darren's manufactured affability. 'Can you provide us with a specific date for when you last used the boat?'

'I'd have to check. But I would say not in the past three weeks.'

'What about the twenty-fourth of October? The day of Patrick's death.'

'Definitely not,' said Darren. 'I've already given you a detailed breakdown of my activities that day, Tom. A meeting with Ethan, lunch with Donna and Scarlett–'

'The golf club, the charity dinner,' concluded Raven. 'Yes, you certainly were very busy that day.'

'I like to make the most of my leisure time.'

Harry leaned forward. 'DCI Raven, if you don't mind me saying, this interview doesn't appear to have much focus. Was it really necessary to waste my client's time by bringing him here to the police station?'

Raven ignored the rhetorical question. 'I wonder if your client would have any objections to us conducting a search of his boat?' he asked.

'And what exactly are you expecting to find onboard?'

Raven put his question directly to Darren. 'Will you give us permission for a search?'

'No,' said Darren. 'I don't want your people crawling all over her, thank you very much.'

'Despite being an upstanding citizen keen to help us with our enquiries?'

'Your "enquiries" seem to amount to little more than harassment, Chief Inspector,' said Harry. 'Mr Jubb has declined your request. Do you have any further questions?'

Raven glanced sideways at Becca. 'Just one more,' she said. 'Mr Jubb, where were you on the seventeenth of October, at seven pm?'

Darren seemed blindsided by the question. 'The seventeenth? That's ages ago. I don't even know what day of the week it was.'

'It was a Sunday,' said Becca. 'The Sunday before

Patrick Lofthouse was murdered.'

'I don't remember,' said Darren. 'I'd need to check my diary...'

'There's no need for that,' said Harry. 'I can tell you exactly where you were, Darren. You were at my house, remember? You and Donna came over for dinner.'

'Barbeque ribs,' said Darren. 'How could I have forgotten?' He stood up, his chair scraping on the floor. 'And now I really do think it's time for lunch.'

Raven watched him leave, Becca escorting him out.

Harry lingered, waiting until he and Raven were alone. 'Don't be a sore loser, Tom. No hard feelings, eh? There's no need to take this personally.'

'I'm not. And I haven't lost.'

Harry sighed. 'I think you have, Tom. I don't think you were even in with a chance of winning this game.'

'It's not a game, Harry.'

Harry chuckled. 'Oh, but it is. Haven't you realised that yet? Police, criminals, lawyers... we're all playing the same game. Just for different teams.'

'Keep telling yourself that if it helps you sleep at night.'

Harry smiled a lizard grin. 'Oh, I have no trouble sleeping, Tom. None at all. A bottle of Rioja over dinner sees to that.' He tapped his forehead. 'See you around.'

CHAPTER 24

Raven emerged from the interview with Darren Jubb feeling somewhat bruised and battered. He'd known that he was on weak ground, but Darren and Harry had swatted away every question without even breaking a sweat. What had Raven learned? Next to nothing.

'I want a warrant to search that boat,' he said once he was back in the incident room. 'Tony, can you arrange it?'

'I'll get onto it right away, sir.'

'Anything else happened while I was entertaining Mr Jubb and his lawyer?'

'As a matter of fact, yes,' said Tony. 'A couple of things. We've had a tip-off from a member of the public. They reported seeing Patrick Lofthouse having an argument with someone on the day he was murdered.'

'Where was this?'

'Outside the Jubb house, sir. The witness is one of Darren Jubb's neighbours, a Mrs Overfield. Jess's gone to see her now to take a statement.'

'Okay. And what was the other thing?'

'We've received a list of calls made from Patrick's

burner phones. Only one of them has ever been used, but on the seventeenth of October, five calls were made between the Motorola and a number registered to a network in the Netherlands. I've contacted the Dutch authorities to see if they can identify the number, but the chances are it's another untraceable burner phone.'

'And where was the Motorola when these calls were made?' asked Raven. 'The UK or the Netherlands?'

'The Netherlands.'

Raven quickly processed the new information. 'So this suggests that Patrick was in the Netherlands on the seventeenth of October. That must be what the date and time on the notepaper referred to. He had a meeting arranged with someone in Holland.'

'It looks like it, sir.'

'A drugs deal?' suggested Dan.

'Could be, Dan. Get onto the airports and check the passenger lists to the Netherlands in the days before the seventeenth. See if Patrick took a flight.'

'I'm on it,' said Dan.

*

Oliver's Mount wasn't exactly open countryside and it certainly couldn't compare with the high moorland of Jess's family home of Rosedale Abbey. But it was one of her favourite parts of Scarborough, and commanded a spectacular view over town and sea, all the way to the castle on the headland. The hill had once been known as Weaponness but had changed at some point to its present name. The town of Scarborough had seen heavy fighting during the English Civil War and the castle had come under sustained bombardment from the Parliamentarian forces. But as far as Jess could make out, Oliver Cromwell had never himself visited either the town nor the hill that now took his name.

Be that as it may, she was glad of the opportunity to exercise her own initiative, driving out to the Mount to visit the witness who had phoned in that morning. She parked her Land Rover outside the house on Weaponness Park, and took in the view from the driveway. The house was directly opposite the entrance to the Jubb's, and she could clearly see the house and garage, in front of which a black Range Rover was parked.

She rang the doorbell and waited. After a minute she heard movement from within and the door opened a few inches on a brass chain.

'DC Jess Barraclough, Scarborough CID.' Jess held up her warrant card so that it could be seen through the crack.

The door closed again and reopened to reveal an elderly woman.

'Mrs Overfield?'

'Yes. Come in, come in.' The old woman beckoned Jess inside. She led her through an elegant hallway into a lounge decorated in pastel wallpaper. 'Have a seat. I'll fetch us a nice cup of tea.'

'There's really no need, Mrs Overfield.'

'Oh, I insist. I don't get many visitors, so when I do I like to look after them properly. Now you wait there, dear. I won't be long.'

Jess took a seat on a wide sofa opposite a fireplace. It was clear that the old lady was determined to make the most of her visit. Jess had noticed this with witnesses before. Some of them lived lonely lives and seemed to find a visit from the police the highlight of their week. It would be quicker to accept the tea than to protest.

The woman returned after a few minutes bearing a tray with a teapot, two china cups and saucers and a plate heaped with biscuits. 'Help yourself,' she said as she poured the tea. 'I do love the pink wafers, don't you?'

Jess took the tea and a biscuit and waited politely.

'Now, I don't want you to think that I'm a nosey parker, spying on my neighbours,' said Mrs Overfield.

'Of course not,' said Jess. 'We always welcome information from members of the public. They're our eyes and ears.'

The old lady nodded appreciatively. 'Well, my eyes and ears aren't what they used to be, but when someone makes a scene like the one I witnessed, I could hardly not notice, could I?'

'Perhaps you could tell me exactly what happened? From the beginning?'

'Of course. Well, it was last Sunday morning. I know it was, because I was getting myself ready for church.'

'So what time would that be?' asked Jess.

'About a quarter to ten. Now, as I was going downstairs, I heard a commotion outside. It's not the first time I've heard noises from the Jubb house. And it's not the first time I've had cause to complain. Parties going on late into the night, car doors slamming at all hours… they really are the neighbours from hell.'

'I can imagine,' said Jess. 'Now when you say a commotion–'

'It was a man shouting. An older man, middle-aged at least. And a younger man replying. But it was the older one who was really angry.'

'Did you catch any of what he was saying?'

'I wouldn't have done,' said Mrs Overfield, 'except that as I say, I was on my way to church. So I went outside and listened.'

'From your front garden?' Jess pictured the garden with its tall hedge and large conifers. The house was set well back from the road and she wondered just how good the old woman's hearing was.

'I know what you're thinking,' said Mrs Overfield. 'But my hearing's perfectly good when I'm wearing my hearing aid, and besides, I crept right up to the hedge so I could get a better view. I wanted to see who was causing such a dreadful disturbance. I could already tell from the voices that it wasn't Darren Jubb, or his son, Ethan.'

'So who was it?'

'Not someone I'd seen before. But I recognised the younger man. It was Scarlett Jubb's fiancé, Patrick.'

'That would be Patrick Lofthouse?'

'Yes. I've seen him around. And of course he's all over the news now. Shocking.'

Jess had been following the newspaper coverage herself. Inevitably, the murder had been the front-page story every day. 'But you don't know who the older man was?'

'I didn't at first, but from what he was saying, I deduced that he was Patrick's father. I knew I was right when I saw his photograph in *The Scarborough News*. It was Gordon Lofthouse. I'm positive.'

'And he was shouting at Patrick?'

'A dreadful racket,' said Mrs Overfield. 'And the language, too. Awful. Anyway, the row was all about money. Stolen money, if I'm not mistaken.'

'What stolen money would that be?' asked Jess.

'Well, I don't know, dear. But the father was accusing his son of taking it. And not a small amount, from what I could gather. He went on and on about it. "A disgraceful breach of trust… what would your mother say… shameful act…" He really did pile it on thick. Anyway, at the end of it all he seemed to deliver a kind of ultimatum. A car drove past just then, so I didn't catch every word, but the gist of it was that something would happen if Patrick didn't return the money that day. "It's your final chance to do the right thing", he bellowed. "And if you don't…" well, that's the bit I missed.'

'And what was Patrick's response to his father?'

'Well,' said Mrs Overfield, 'that's really what surprised me most. He didn't try to deny what he'd done, and he didn't apologise. He didn't even seem to be sorry. All he said was, "You haven't got the guts to do a thing!"'

*

Becca descended the stairs to the locked basement beneath the police station where old case files were kept. It wasn't a room she had cause to visit very often, and the place was dark, deserted and rather creepy. She unlocked the door, waited for the overhead fluorescent lights to flicker on, then began to search for the section she was interested in.

The records were stored on floor-to-ceiling metal racks arranged in date order. Moving along the rows was like stepping back in time. 2022, 2021, 2020… The advent of the digital age didn't mean that each case didn't accumulate a huge mound of paperwork, photographs, physical evidence and other random miscellaneous items. You never knew what you might find down here amid the shadows, cobwebs and the smell of dust and ageing paper. She fancied herself as a bit of an archaeologist, hunting among forgotten artifacts of the past for clues. Or as a librarian, perhaps, scouring the archives for some hidden letter or manuscript. She carried on along the gloomy ranks of files until she located the year she was looking for. 2019.

Becca was convinced that the solution to the current case lay in the previous investigation into the murder of Max Hunt. The investigation that DI Dinsdale had led, when she had been a detective constable, carrying out many of the dogsbody jobs that Jess and Dan were doing now. At that time she had been just a cog in the machine, not privy to the big picture. She had no knowledge of what information Dinsdale had seen or what had led him to make the decisions he had. Why had he not interviewed Darren Jubb? Why had he not followed up the possibility of a drugs connection? How had Lewis Briggs obtained an illegal firearm, and who had made the anonymous tip-off? There were so many unanswered questions. Becca had read through the summary reports in the database, but the original notes and evidence were all down here. Trawling through the entire case notes would be a monstrous task, but it wouldn't hurt to take a quick look round and see if there was anything obvious.

She worked her way carefully along the shelves, referring to the contents catalogue. Here it was. 19-496A. She stopped. And stared.

The files were missing.

Where they ought to have been, there were only empty

shelves. She checked to either side, but there could be no mistake. The Max Hunt case files had been taken. And no one had signed them out.

CHAPTER 25

'Let's go into the garden,' said Gordon Lofthouse. 'Janet's upstairs having a rest. I don't want to disturb her.'

Raven followed him around the side of the house and into the rear garden. The square lawn was neatly trimmed, the shrubbery around the deep borders cut back for autumn, all the dead leaves and twigs piled into a compost heap at the back. In the greenhouse, tomato plants were still growing, fruits dangling from the stems in cascades of red and green.

Gordon sighed, looking around as if he were a stranger to his own home. 'She hasn't been able to sleep at all. Not since we heard the news. The doctor's prescribed sedatives, and she's finally managed to nod off.'

'It must have been a terrible shock for you both.'

Gordon nodded absently. 'Do you have any children, Chief Inspector?'

'A daughter.'

'Children can be such a burden. Do you find that?'

Raven left the question unanswered. 'I'd like to talk to you about Shane Denton. When I first spoke to you, you accused him of stealing.'

'That scoundrel!' Gordon's nostrils flared. 'Yes. It was one of the reasons I sacked him. And he was taking drugs too, of course.'

'Shane denies stealing any money from you.'

'Well, he would, wouldn't he?'

'The thing is,' said Raven, 'I believe him.'

Gordon fell into silent introspection. He reached out to touch a rose bush, pruned back to a bare framework of branches in readiness for winter. His thumb rubbed along a stem, studded with thorns. 'You do, do you?' he said at last. 'Well, maybe you're right. The truth is that money kept disappearing even after Shane was sacked.'

'You suspected that Patrick was taking it?'

'I didn't suspect. I had proof.'

'And did you confront him about it?'

Gordon closed his thick fingers around the stem of the rose. 'We talked,' he admitted. 'But Patrick denied everything. He said I was mistaken. But I wasn't.'

'Did you speak to your wife about this?'

'No. It would have broken Janet's heart. Patrick had disappointed her enough already. This would have been the final straw.'

'So what did you do?' asked Raven.

'Nothing, at first. I hoped that warning him I was onto him would make him stop. But it didn't.' Gordon looked at Raven as if beseeching him to understand. 'I couldn't just go on pretending it wasn't happening. In the end I had to act.'

'You set him an ultimatum,' said Raven. 'When you confronted him outside Darren Jubb's house.'

Gordon looked surprised. 'You already knew that?' His eyes narrowed. 'I told him he had to pay back the money that day.'

'Was that a realistic prospect?'

'I don't know. Maybe not. But I lost my temper. He was stealing from his own flesh and blood!' Gordon's voice grew louder and the tendons in his neck stood out. 'What kind of a son does that?' he bellowed.

'So what did you tell Patrick you would do if he didn't pay it back?'

'Cut him out of the business,' said Gordon. 'Disinherit him. I told him that a son who steals is no son of mine.'

'And what was his reaction?'

'He just laughed at me. Imagine that! He laughed at his own father!' Gordon's face had turned the colour of a beetroot. He squeezed the stem of the rose bush and snapped it between finger and thumb. A drop of blood welled up where a thorn pierced his skin.

'You lied to me,' said Raven. 'When I asked you when you'd last seen Patrick you said it was the Saturday, the day before his death.'

'I couldn't tell you that I'd been to see him on the Sunday. Not in front of Janet. She'd only just learned of his death. This news would have killed her!'

Raven stared at him, saying nothing.

A trickle of blood was running down Gordon's finger, but he seemed unaware of it. 'Oh come on, Inspector,' he said breathlessly. 'You can't think I had anything to do with Patrick's death! You're mad. He was my own son! I gave him everything. All I wanted was for him to show some gratitude!'

'And he stubbornly refused,' said Raven. 'Instead, he humiliated you.'

Gordon jabbed a finger at Raven's chest, leaving a spot of blood on his new white shirt. 'You think I killed him? Do you? Is that what you think?'

Raven met the accusation placidly. 'What I think, Mr Lofthouse, is that you'd better calm down.'

*

'There's nothing left?' said Raven. 'Are you sure?'

'All of the paperwork has been removed,' said Becca. 'Everything.'

She'd spent the whole of the past hour running over the

possibilities in her mind, but it was impossible to come up with any legitimate reason why the Max Hunt files might have gone missing. No police officer would remove case files from the station unless they were up to no good. The only innocent explanation she could think of was that Raven himself had taken them, but a cursory inspection of his office had ruled that out.

So she was faced with a hard truth – the files had been stolen. But by whom?

It must have been someone involved with the current investigation. She couldn't believe that Tony would have done such a thing. He was far too straight and above-board. Dan wasn't averse to bending the rules, but he was too new to have been involved in the Max Hunt case, and lacked the wit to pull off a stunt like this. Jess certainly had the necessary resourcefulness, but again, she had only been a detective for a few months, so what possible interest could she have had in the previous case? In any case, Becca trusted her. There was only one person she couldn't rule out.

Derek Dinsdale.

The more she thought about it, the more sense it made. Dinsdale had led the Max Hunt investigation and, as Raven had pointed out, he had missed a number of important leads. Now that a second murder had taken place, maybe Dinsdale was trying to cover his tracks and make sure that nothing could be done to undermine the conviction of Lewis Briggs. Maybe he was trying to protect his own reputation and scupper any possible enquiry into his conduct. Was he, in fact, in the process of destroying evidence?

Becca waited for Raven to return from his interview with Gordon Lofthouse before following him into his cramped office. Then, after a brief hesitation, she pulled the door closed behind her. He had made it clear from the start that his was an open-door policy – he wanted them to come to him at any time with their ideas or concerns. But this was different. The matter was confidential.

Raven looked tired and dishevelled, as well he might after the bruising interview with Darren Jubb and that smart-arse solicitor of his. There was even a spot of blood on what looked like a new shirt. He was absent-mindedly flicking through an old copy of *The Scarborough News*. Becca hated to bring this latest bad news to him, but it was better that he knew, and best that he knew soon.

'What do you think happened to them?' asked Raven.

Becca paused, reluctant to put her thoughts into words. No one liked a tell-tale, and she had absolutely no proof of who had stolen the files. She hated the idea of accusing a fellow officer of tampering with evidence, even if that officer was DI Dinsdale. Why couldn't the man just retire and leave them all in peace? Why was he still here, prowling the corridors like a bad smell? Besides, Becca still didn't know Raven well enough to gauge how he might react to an accusation. He hadn't asked her to go looking for the files in the first place. Maybe he would think she'd gone beyond her remit, that she didn't trust him to lead the case.

'I don't know,' she said.

Raven nodded. 'No. Well, thanks for letting me know, Becca. You did the right thing coming to me.'

She felt a sense of relief at his words. 'So, what are you going to do about it, then?' she asked.

'You leave it with me,' said Raven. 'Let's keep it to ourselves for now.'

*

Raven sat alone in his office, contemplating the news that Becca had just brought him. While she had been too diplomatic to point the finger at a possible culprit, it hadn't been hard for him to guess what she thought. It didn't take a genius to pinpoint Derek Dinsdale as the most likely suspect. Dinsdale was the detective most closely associated with the Max Hunt case. He had the most to lose if the case were to be reopened and the decision process that had led to the conviction of Lewis Briggs re-examined. Raven wondered what Dinsdale had thought, the day that a second body had washed up on the beach, a gunshot wound to the chest. The parallels with the previous case must have been obvious, even to a halfwit like him.

And if, as Raven firmly believed, the two cases were linked, then it was possible that Dinsdale had removed the files in order to deliberately sabotage Raven's investigation. It would be very much in Dinsdale's interests if the new SIO from London were to fall flat on his face. Raven pictured Dinsdale crowing to Gillian, telling her that she should never have brought Raven in as his replacement. The man was a creep and would enjoy every moment of it.

But could there be an even more sinister aspect to Dinsdale's motives? Was he, in fact, in the pocket of Darren Jubb? Had Dinsdale removed some vital clue that linked Darren to the murder of Patrick Lofthouse?

Raven closed his eyes and rubbed the bridge of his nose with his thumb and forefinger. The interview with Darren had left him feeling tired and out of sorts. Maybe he was getting too old for this game. Darren had always been top dog in their relationship. As a teenager, Darren had been the one to call the shots, bending those around him to his will, charming them with his charisma. And he'd won Donna in the end, hadn't he? What more proof was there that Darren always got his way? He'd bided his time, played the long game, and scored a win. Scarborough was Darren's playground, and he did what he liked here. He wasn't so much a big fish in a small pond, but a shark in a fish tank. And he would continue to do exactly as he pleased unless Raven could prove his involvement in the killing of Patrick Lofthouse.

Raven's gaze returned to the open copy of *The Scarborough News* he'd been studying when Becca had come to him. The edition was from the start of the week, dated Monday, the day of his father's funeral, the day that the sea had given up the body of Patrick Lofthouse. The headline on the front page was all about the possible redevelopment of the site of the old Futurist Cinema, where Raven had stolen his first kiss so many years ago. But it was an article on the inside pages that had caught his eye.

Charity Dinner Raises Thousands for Good Causes

This, then, was the event that Darren Jubb had attended, now that he was one of the great and the good of Scarborough. The event that provided him with a perfect alibi for the time Patrick Lofthouse was most likely murdered. Raven began to read the article.

Council officials, business leaders, and notable public figures gathered in the ballroom of the Grand Hotel on Sunday evening for a charity event hosted by BBC Look North presenter Raymond Agnew.

The article went on to explain how more than a hundred guests had attended the dinner, donating a combined sum totalling tens of thousands of pounds. The money raised would go to a range of good causes, from extra funding for a mobile library to a grant for a new community vegetable allotment.

But it was the accompanying photograph that interested Raven. Smiling for the camera, a glass of wine in her hand, and flanked by an assortment of Scarborough's brightest and best, was none other than Detective Superintendent Gillian Ellis.

Raven could easily believe that someone in Gillian's position would be invited to an event like this. A senior police officer was undoubtedly a "notable public figure" and must be well known to council and business leaders. He applauded her charitable sentiment.

But did that mean that she knew Darren Jubb personally?

Darren wasn't pictured in the paper, but there had been more than a hundred people at the event, and only a few had been singled out for photographs. There was no reason to think that Gillian was particularly close to Darren. But if they moved in the same circles, they must have encountered each other on occasions.

Raven wondered what they might have talked about.

CHAPTER 26

Becca returned to her desk pleased that Raven had taken her concerns about the missing files seriously. He had assured her that he would treat the discovery in the strictest confidence. And she hadn't been obliged to name Dinsdale, so she had nothing to worry about on that score.

Raven was certainly the best boss she had worked for, despite his occasional dark moods, but he still remained something of a mystery. What exactly was the nature of his relationship with Darren Jubb and his wife? Why had he stayed away from Scarborough for so long? And why had he returned now? She knew, of course, that his father had just died and that he'd come back to bury him. But had the two of them really not spoken in thirty-one years? Becca couldn't imagine such a thing. She spoke to her own parents every day. True, she still lived at home, but if she ever moved out, she'd be sure to speak to her mum on the phone every few days and pop in whenever she could for a cuppa and a chat. Wasn't that what normal people did?

Raven was a mystery to be solved. And Becca was a detective. Now that she had scented the trail, she knew she wouldn't be able to rest until she'd followed it. She made herself a strong mug of Yorkshire tea, settled down at her computer, and began to type.

If Raven had left Scarborough thirty-one years ago, then that would have been 1991. Four years before she was born. What had been going on in Scarborough at that time? She logged on to the online edition of *The Scarborough News* and clicked on the archive link, but it only went back as far as the year 2000. She could always call in at the local library and see if they kept old copies of the paper, but in any case it was likely that whatever had driven Raven from Scarborough was a personal matter and not reported in the local rag.

Where else might she look? She didn't expect the police database to yield any useful information, but once she'd had the idea of checking it, she couldn't resist. It would only take a matter of seconds to run a search, and if she didn't find anything she would let the matter drop.

She entered "1991" and "Raven" as keywords and waited while the computer consulted its extensive database. She was so convinced there would be nothing to find, that when it returned a result she stared at the screen in astonishment.

A hit and run driving accident on 3rd June 1991. The victim was a Mrs Jean Raven, aged 45, of Quay Street, Scarborough. Occupation: chambermaid at the Grand Hotel. Mrs Raven had been walking along the Foreshore Road at approximately 11pm when a car had mounted the pavement at speed, killing her outright. Despite appeals to the public for information, the driver of the car had never been identified. The case had been left unresolved. Next of kin was named as Alan Raven. In a statement to the police, Alan Raven reported that his wife had gone out to look for their sixteen-year-old son, Thomas, because she thought he should be at home studying for his GCSE exams.

Becca sipped her tea and thought about what she'd just read. It would appear that Raven had gone out, presumably with friends – quite possibly Darren Jubb – when he should have been at home with his head in a textbook. People didn't have mobile phones in those days. His mum, who must have been worried about her son's prospects if he didn't pass his exams, had gone out to look for him. And by a random quirk of fate she had been killed by a drunk driver. What must that have been like for a sixteen-year-old boy? To lose a parent in those circumstances was horrendous enough, but to think that you had unwittingly been the cause of your mother going out in the first place didn't bear thinking about. And what about Raven's relationship with his father? Had Alan Raven blamed his son, unfairly, for his wife's death? Was this why Raven had left Scarborough at such a young age and not returned until it was time to bury his old man?

*

Raven stood at the end of the pier – it was more of a breakwater really – looking back at the old town. The South Bay traced out an almost perfect semicircle, from the harbour nestling beneath the headland to the tip of White Nab jutting out beyond Oliver's Mount. Halfway along the curve of the bay was the spa, the place where modern Scarborough had been born. A spring had been discovered there in the seventeenth century by the wife of a prominent citizen. The acidic water was said to cure all kinds of ailments, and thousands of visitors had flocked to the town in search of a miracle. Whether or not they found it, word of the spa spread, and by the middle of the eighteenth century, Scarborough had established itself as Britain's first seaside resort. A plethora of hotels and other hostelries sprang up to cater for the needs of the incoming tourists who came to sample the delights of its famous bathing machines. At the peak of the town's fame, the Grand Hotel was the largest hotel in Europe. These days, the spa no longer sold bottled water but had become a venue for concerts and theatre. Its elegant façade stood bathed in golden light.

Along the rest of the beachfront the gaudy illuminations of the amusement arcades, fish and chip shops, pubs and cafés glittered enticingly, their reflections shimmering off the shifting mirror of the sea. Further back from the shore, the dimmer lights from houses and hotels twinkled softly. And above them all rose the dark mass of the castle mound, looming over the town as a reminder of distant and more dangerous times.

A light breeze twitched Raven's coat, bringing with it a snatch of music from one of the various entertainments on offer along the Foreshore Road. Behind him, the boats moored in the Old Harbour bobbed gently in the water. There was Darren's luxurious yacht, *Sea Dreams*. And there too was the more modest cabin cruiser, *Kittiwake*, that Tony had informed him belonged to Gordon Lofthouse.

The pier itself was all dark, apart from the lighthouse that stood at the entrance to the Outer Harbour, directing its narrow beam out across the black water into nothingness.

Raven reached into the bag he was carrying and pulled out the object it contained.

The urn was a simple one, the most basic that the crematorium had to offer. No point spending money on something elaborate when it was only going to be used once. His dad had never spent a penny more on anything than was necessary, so Raven thought he might appreciate it. *Eyt all, sup all, pay nowt.* That was the traditional Yorkshire refrain, and it could almost have been Alan Raven's personal motto.

He unscrewed the lid of the urn and upended it, spilling ash out over the edge of the pier, watching it flutter down into darkness. No ceremony. No words. No tears.

The sea was calm, but the surf high, waves beating steadily against the solid wall of the breakwater. Soon the tide would turn, taking the ashes out to sea, where his father had spent much of his working life, going out on fishing boats day after day, year after year. It was an appropriate final resting place.

Who knew – if things had worked out differently, if the fishing industry hadn't gone into such savage decline, if the money had been better, if there hadn't been long bouts of unemployment and insecurity – perhaps Alan Raven would have turned out differently. He must once have been a good man or else Jean wouldn't have married him. But the tides and furies of life had battered against him, breaking down his strength, sapping his energies, stealing light and ushering in the dark. By the time Raven left Scarborough, his father was a ruin of the man he'd once been. A wreck on the sea floor, stirring only when the storms came, rising up in anger. His hands were no longer fisherman's hands. They held no rod, only a pint of beer or a glass of spirit. They hauled no nets, but curled into granite fists, ready to dish out a nightly beating to his wife or son. To share the misery and pain among those he ought to have loved.

He had been a bastard, and Raven had hated him. But he was gone now, floating away on the waves that rose and fell and cared for no man.

Raven turned around. Two young men were approaching him from around the side of the lighthouse. Jeans. Hoodies. Trainers. The universal uniform of male youth. But this pair wore black balaclavas drawn tightly over their faces, only their eyes visible through narrow slits.

'Evening, lads,' said Raven. He tossed the empty urn over the side of the pier and clenched his fists in readiness for what was coming.

The men held wooden batons. They raised them as they drew nearer, separating out in order to cut off his escape.

Raven moved away from the edge of the pier, not relishing the prospect of being pushed twenty feet into cold, black water.

The strangers said nothing. Instead, at a nod from one of them – a taller, leaner, older individual – they advanced, limbs fluid, batons in fists, shadowed eyes fixed firmly on his.

Raven assessed his adversaries. The tall one was clearly in charge. The other, while shorter, was built like the proverbial brick shithouse, his neck as thick as a bull's, his shoulders broad and muscular. Raven didn't fancy his chances with that one. He waited until the two of them were within striking distance, then made his move, diving to his left, throwing all of his weight against the slim leader.

The man drew back, trying to get out of harm's way, but Raven wrapped his arms around his waist in an attempt to tackle him to the ground. The lad struggled in his grip, hampered by the wooden baton in one hand, and Raven brought him crashing down, landing hard on the stone paving of the pier.

But his victory was short-lived. The second man came to his mate's assistance and delivered a cracking blow across Raven's back.

Raven roared with pain, but had the sense to get out of the way in case a second blow was coming. He rolled sideways across the paving slabs, away from the pier's edge, and tried to struggle to his feet. But the big lad bore down on him and lashed out again. The wooden stick caught his shoulder this time, sending shock waves racing along his arm. Raven raised his hands to protect his face as the thug came in to deliver another blow.

This time it came in the form of a kick to his belly. Raven writhed on the ground, clutching his stomach where the bulk of the force had landed. He opened his eyes to see the gorilla lifting the rod for a third time. He tried to slither away, but his injured shoulder buckled under his weight and his guts screamed in agony. He curled into a ball, shielding his face with his hands to protect himself from the next crack of the baton. But the dreaded strike never came.

'Enough!' cried the leader.

The voice sounded vaguely familiar, but there was no time to think about that now.

The gorilla kicked him one more time for luck, and then the two of them were off, racing away along the pier back towards town.

Raven rolled over and lay flat on his back, panting and looking up at the stars. Once he had his breath back, he ran his palms over his injuries, checking for bleeding, but they came away clean. Tentatively he sat up. His bodied ached in a dozen different places, but after a minute he was pretty sure that there were no broken bones, just a few ripe bruises.

If they'd intended to do him a really serious injury, they could have. Easily.

So this was a warning. *Stay away, if you know what's good for you.*

Raven rose slowly to his feet and found to his relief that he could walk unaided. He began to hobble along the pier, heading for home.

It had been an unexpected and brutal end to the evening. An unwelcome echo of his father's unrestrained violence.

But at least the beating had confirmed one thing. He was getting closer to his quarry.

CHAPTER 27

He's in the Lord Nelson this time, drinking shots with Donna and Darren on a warm night in early summer. His relationship with Donna has moved on, well beyond just kissing and fumbling around at the back of the cinema, and he's hopelessly in love. Harry's not with them tonight. He's at home revising for tomorrow's exam, and Tom knows that he ought to be doing the same. How many lines of Romeo and Juliet can he quote by heart? Not half as many as he needs to if he hopes to scrape a pass. But Donna insisted on going out, and if Darren's with her, then Tom needs to be too. Darren may not have the advantage of Tom's looks, but he has the knack of charming the pants off any girl, and his sights are firmly set on Donna. Donna doesn't care about exams. She says her looks will get her through life, and she may well be right. Darren doesn't care either. Once he leaves school he'll be joining his dad at the amusement arcade. Who needs English Lit when you've got slot machines to empty by the bucketload? Donna laughs at some clever remark Darren's just made. 'What do you think, Tom?' she asks. But Tom's distracted. There's some commotion outside. Police sirens. An ambulance, maybe. Normally they would keep well clear of the cops. It's not smart to be seen coming out of a pub when you're sixteen going on seventeen. But Tom's curiosity is aroused and it's very nearly chucking out time anyway. He downs his shot and gets to his feet. 'Come on,' he says, taking Donna by the hand. 'Let's see what's going on.' Outside, the night is broken by flashing blue lights. Police cars have closed the seafront and there's a single ambulance standing in the middle of the road. 'Let's get out of here,' says Darren, but Tom drags Donna with him towards the action. They don't get far before a policeman stops them. 'What's happening?' Tom asks him. 'Hit and run. Did you see anything?' Tom shakes his head. The cop's turning away, when Tom calls out, 'Was someone killed?' The policeman glances idly back. 'A woman. Mrs Jean Raven. Did you know her?' The words hit Tom like a body blow and he buckles over, bending down, retching in the gutter. The next thing he knows, he's flat on the ground. The hard pavement presses against his back, and all he can see is the stars wheeling far above.

Raven's side hurt too much for him to roll over. He manoeuvred himself gingerly out of bed, sliding sideways across the sheets and lowering his feet carefully onto the thin carpet. He raised himself cautiously into a sitting position, wincing as the bruising in his side reminded him that it wasn't going away anytime soon. The beating had aggravated the old wound in his thigh, and his leg was aching like a bastard. At times like this he wished he was a drinker. A bottle of wine to push himself to oblivion and take away the pain. But teetotallers had to face the world without the crutch of alcohol. Instead, Nurofen Plus and Panadol Ultra were his only friends. He pushed two tablets out of the pack by his bedside and swallowed them down.

It could have been worse. The thugs that beat him up were only wearing trainers. Steel-capped boots would have done far more damage.

He rose to his feet and made his way to the bathroom to conduct a quick inspection of his injuries in the mirror. Purple bruising on one shoulder. A red stripe across his back. More bruising around his middle and side. Not pretty, but he would live. He eased himself into the tub and made do with a quick wash of the parts of his body he was still able to reach. There didn't seem much point in shaving, so he let the stubble grow.

It was the weekend, but that meant little to Raven. When he was working on a murder enquiry, the investigation took precedence over everything else. Besides, what else might he have done on a Saturday morning? Join Darren for a round of golf? Drop in on Donna for a nice cup of tea and a cosy chat about the old days? Or hang around the house, wallowing in misfortune and allowing the gloomy memories that lurked around every corner to drag him down.

What did normal people do with their weekends? Raven had little idea. Lisa had always assigned tasks for him to do on his days off. Shopping trips, jobs around the house, mowing the lawn. Another reason for him to stay at work. Another reason she had left him.

He checked his email briefly to see if Hannah had got round to replying to him yet, but there was still nothing. He put on his suit, leaving his tie off and his collar open, and drove to the station.

*

On arrival in the incident room, Raven was surprised to find Becca already working at her desk. 'It's Saturday,' he said. 'Aren't you taking the day off?'

'Aren't you?'

Perhaps he wasn't the only one with workaholic tendencies. She ought to be spending time with her boyfriend on a weekend, or else she would also find herself nursing a broken relationship.

He tried to hide his limp but Becca's eyes were too sharp. 'Is something wrong?' she asked.

'Just a bit stiff this morning. Old age.'

She wasn't convinced. 'You've hurt yourself. Did you have an accident?'

'Not exactly.' He wondered how much to tell her.

Becca was smart and not much got past her. Perhaps she would be able to provide some useful insight. 'I'd like to bounce an idea off you. In the strictest confidence.'

She sat up, intrigued. 'Of course.'

Raven leaned against her desk, silently cursing the bruising on his side.

'You really are hurt, aren't you?' she said. 'What happened?'

'A couple of guys beat me up.'

Her eyes widened. 'What? When?'

'Last night. Down by the harbourside. They must have followed me there.'

'What were they after? Your wallet? Did they take anything?'

'No, it was nothing like that. They wanted to send me a message.' He studied her face as she absorbed the information. 'They were warning me off the case.'

She shook her head. 'But that's ridiculous. You must be imagining things.'

'A couple of good hard kicks in the ribs proves I'm not.'

She reached out a hand to touch him, then drew it back. 'Have you been to the hospital? You need to get yourself checked out. I can drive you over there now, if you like.'

'No. I'm fine. There's nothing broken. The thing is, this isn't the first warning I've been sent.'

'What do you mean?'

'That scratch on my car. That wasn't kids messing about. That was deliberate. Someone was telling me to back off.'

'Back off from what?'

He didn't answer her question directly. 'Someone's trying to block the investigation. The scratch on the car was a subtle warning–'

'Which had no effect,' said Becca.

Raven smiled. 'So they took more direct action.'

'Removing the old case files?'

'Precisely. And then, just to make sure there could be

no misunderstanding, they arranged for me to be given a more persuasive deterrent.'

Becca stared at him. 'You think that whoever removed the files also sent a couple of guys to beat you up?' She shook her head. 'That's absurd.'

'Is it? To me, it seems like the only logical explanation. There's a saboteur at work – someone who doesn't want us to get to the bottom of the Patrick Lofthouse murder. That person has access to the records archive here, which means they're a serving police officer.'

'Dinsdale?' Becca whispered the name.

'It's one possibility.' He considered telling her about the scrawled message Dinsdale had left in his desk drawer. *Watch your back.* With hindsight, the words seemed less like a threat, more like a warning. 'What I'm wondering,' he continued, 'is whether the rot goes higher.'

'What do you mean?' A frightened look had crept into Becca's eyes. She knew exactly what he meant.

'The supervising officer in the Max Hunt murder investigation was Detective Superintendent Gillian Ellis. And we both know the shortcomings in that investigation.'

'But it was Gillian who appointed you as SIO on the Patrick Lofthouse investigation,' said Becca. 'Why would she do that? If she didn't want the case solved, surely it would have been better to leave Dinsdale in charge?'

He chuckled. 'Quite possibly. But then again, just as the investigation begins, I turn up on her doorstep looking for a job. An outsider. Easy to manipulate. Knowing nothing of the Max Hunt case. Perhaps she thought I was bound to fail.'

He remembered how angry Gillian had been when she discovered he knew Darren Jubb. And then there were Dinsdale's clumsy attempts to warn him about the "queen". *Watch your back. You know nothing. You're just a pawn.*

Becca's eyes took on a hard edge. 'With all due respect, sir,' – she stressed the last word, deliberately not using his name – 'you can't possibly think that Detective

Superintendent Ellis has anything to do with the missing case files.'

'How can you be so sure?'

'I've worked at this station for five years,' said Becca, the obvious implication being that Raven was just a newcomer, 'and during that time I've developed the highest respect for Detective Superintendent Ellis. I can't believe that she would be involved in anything improper.'

'No? Wait here.' Raven hobbled over to his office and retrieved the copy of *The Scarborough News*. He opened it and showed Becca the photograph of Gillian at the charity dinner. 'Have you seen this?'

Becca scanned the article briefly. 'So? What does this prove?'

'It proves that Gillian and Darren attended the same event. The event that provides Darren with an alibi for Patrick's murder. Don't you find that odd?'

'Not really. Detective Superintendent Ellis attends a lot of public events. She has a high standing in the town.'

'I'm sure she does,' said Raven. 'A woman like that and a man like Darren Jubb could be useful to each other.'

Becca gave her head a sharp shake. 'You're accusing her of corruption now?' Her voice was rising, almost angry.

'I checked up on where she lives,' said Raven. 'It's a big five-bedroom detached house in Scalby. Must be worth a million or more. How does a police officer – even a superintendent – afford somewhere like that?'

'You've been spying on her?' said Becca indignantly. Apparently she had forgotten that Raven had found her googling him the other day. 'Well, perhaps you ought to get your facts straight. Superintendent Ellis's husband is a businessman. So there's no mystery about where she gets her money, and there's no reason to suspect her of doing anything wrong.'

'Okay.'

Becca had stood her ground, and Raven had to give her credit for that. But she hadn't given him the support he'd hoped for, and for that he felt disappointed. He lifted the newspaper from her desk and went back into his office.

Before long Becca packed her bags and left.

Raven sighed. *Great.* He'd managed to alienate one of his few allies just when he needed her most. Whatever he did next, he would have to do it alone. But he was used to that. He switched off the lights in his office and went out.

CHAPTER 28

The warrant had come through the previous evening, but it had been too late to carry out the search of Darren Jubb's yacht then. Instead, Jess had arranged for it to take place on the Saturday morning. Now she was standing on the pier, watching as Holly and the rest of the CSI team disembarked from their van to begin their examination of *Sea Dreams*.

'Thanks for agreeing to do this on a Saturday,' said Jess.

'No problem,' said Holly. 'I don't mind working at the weekend if I have advance notice. My husband is usually around to look after the kids. It's late shifts that I can't handle, and sudden changes of plan. Like when your new boss called me out the other night. I didn't even have a chance to arrange childcare.'

Holly's normally cheerful face had turned thunderous and Jess made a mental note never to call her out without giving her plenty of time to make all the necessary arrangements first.

Jess herself hadn't got anything particular planned for this weekend. If the search warrant hadn't come through, she would probably have gone walking or cycling. It was certainly a beautiful day for being outdoors and she was glad to be away from the office. Dan Bennett had been hanging around her again, even though she'd done her best to discourage him. The guy just didn't seem to take a hint. His behaviour was becoming borderline harassment.

'She's a beauty, isn't she?' said Holly, turning to admire the boat. 'I wouldn't mind one of these myself.'

'Are you a sailor, then?' asked Jess. She didn't know the head of CSI very well, but had taken a quick liking to the older woman on the few occasions they'd worked together.

'Don't know my midships from my mizzen,' said Holly. 'But I fancy the idea of sunbathing on deck while some gorgeous young man brings me cocktails.' She shrugged. 'Knowing my luck, I'm more likely to find myself stuck in a rowing boat with my husband paddling us around in circles.' She turned and set off down the floating wooden ramp that led out to where the yacht was moored.

It was a glorious late autumn day, with blue skies and sea to match. Sunlight glinted off the gently lapping water of the Old Harbour. The white and blue motor cruiser berthed in the marina could almost have been on the French Riviera. Jess adjusted her sunglasses and followed the CSI team leader down to the boat.

Sea Dreams certainly added a big splash of glamour to Scarborough. It was one of the largest boats in the harbour, and probably the nicest looking. Jess was no expert, but she'd once spent a week sailing around the Greek islands on a thirty-foot schooner with five other girls. It had been hard work but great fun. Darren's boat was nothing like that however. It was powered for a start, with two engines, and was much larger than the yacht Jess had sailed on. It was luxuriously specified, with an open plan saloon and three cabins below deck, two of them with en-suite shower rooms. A pair of sun loungers were positioned on the front deck, and a hydraulic platform at the stern gave easy swimming access to the sea. A flybridge offered commanding views of the sea for the pilot, and provided an outdoor galley with seating and a table for dining.

'I am definitely in the wrong job,' said Holly, unloading her gear inside the main galley.

'Me too,' agreed Jess, surveying the white leather décor of the interior. The yacht was more sumptuously furnished than her own studio apartment.

'Well, we're not going to find anything just by standing here gawping,' said Holly. 'Let's get on with it. Are we looking for anything in particular?'

'Blood, DNA, anything that can prove Patrick Lofthouse was on the boat last Sunday.' Jess grinned hopefully. 'And if you can locate the murder weapon or the victim's mobile phone, that would be awesome.'

'You want me to see if the Easter Bunny's stowed away on board too?' quipped Holly. 'Don't expect miracles, especially at weekends. Anything else?'

'We'd like to try and find out if the boat was used last weekend, and if so where it went. Does the navigation computer keep records?' The boat was certainly equipped with an impressive array of electronics, including a large flat screen next to the steering controls.

'Scott's my resident nerd,' said Holly. 'He understands GPS and all the gizmos.' She waved her hand in the direction of a young man who had just come on board carrying a metal box. He was about Jess's age, slim, and good-looking. Jess noted his bronzed face and light sandy beard. He scurried past, looking up briefly and giving her a shy smile as he went.

'Keep your eyes on the road, Scott,' said Holly, an amused smile playing on her face.

Scott ducked his head again, and carried on over to the instrument panel, Holly close on his tail, giving him orders.

Jess went back out on deck, smiling to herself and enjoying the feel of warm sunshine on her skin.

*

Becca was furious with Raven. Who did he think he was?

Just because he'd come to a small town from the bright lights of London, didn't mean he could start throwing around outrageous accusations. Especially when he'd been here for less than a week and hardly knew anyone. And especially when all he had to back up his claim was a photograph in the local paper. Becca had the highest regard for Detective Superintendent Ellis. She was a strong woman doing a difficult job, and the idea that she was complicit with Darren Jubb undermined everything that Becca believed. She refused to accept it.

And why had Raven been so keen to dismiss her suggestion that Dinsdale had stolen the case files? Instead he'd fabricated an elaborate theory that the scratch on his car and the assault at the harbour were all part of some grand conspiracy. Perhaps he was just paranoid. The kind of person who thought the world revolved around him.

Fortunately, she had a job to do that would take her mind off Raven. She went outside to her car, fished her phone out of her bag and dialled. After a few rings, her brother picked up. He sounded surprisingly bright and breezy for this time on a Saturday morning.

'Hey, Becs, how's it going? I've got that name you asked for – a guy who can fix your boss's car.'

'Oh that,' said Becca. She noted down the name and number Liam gave her. 'Thanks, but that wasn't why I was calling.'

'It wasn't?'

'No. I wanted to ask you about Patrick Lofthouse.'

Liam's response told her immediately this wasn't a subject he was keen to talk about. 'Yeah, I'm busy right now. Can it wait until another time?'

'No it can't. Have you heard any rumours about him?' Liam was always picking up info from the dubious people he hung out with. Sometimes it turned out to be completely wrong. Once or twice, it had proved useful to her.

'What kind of rumours?' he asked guardedly.

How many kinds have you heard? wondered Becca. 'I

want to know if Patrick was involved in any kind of criminal activity.'

'Hey, aren't you the one who's supposed to know about that?'

Liam's response told her that he knew something. Why couldn't he have told her the other morning over breakfast? Sometimes her brother could be infuriating.

'Come on,' she said. 'I just need you to tell me if you've heard of him being linked to anything dodgy.'

'How dodgy are we talking about?'

'I'm not interested in parking offences.'

'Well, you can't believe everything you hear on the grapevine, sis. But as it happens, I have heard that he was into drugs.'

This time, it seemed that Liam's source – whoever that might be – was reliable, at least in part. 'Using or selling?' she asked.

'Bit of both.'

'What kinds of drugs?'

'Some serious shit, from what I heard. Coke. Crack. Heroin. But that's just what a guy in a pub told me.'

'A guy in a pub?'

'I forget his name.'

'Sure you do.' This didn't sound like the kind of lead that could ever be used in a court of law. Liam's tips never were. And so far he'd told her nothing she didn't already know. Perhaps that wasn't surprising. Smart criminals didn't blab to their mates about what they were up to. And whatever Patrick had been, Becca was pretty sure he wasn't stupid. Far from it. 'Listen, we think that Patrick may have made a visit to Holland recently. Do you know anything about that?'

'So you already knew about the drugs,' said Liam petulantly. 'Well, maybe you know this too, but I did hear that he and his business partner took delivery of a fresh supply of cocaine recently.'

Becca blinked in surprise. 'Wait, his business partner? Who's that?'

'I couldn't say. Will that be all? Only I really do have a load of stuff to get done this morning.'

Becca sighed. She knew she wouldn't get any more out of Liam over the phone. Perhaps if she worked on him in person later, she might be able to prise more out of him. Then again, this talk of a mysterious business partner might just turn out to be useless gossip. 'That'll do for now, bro. Talk to you later.'

*

The house at Weaponness Park was becoming very familiar to Raven. He pulled the BMW into the driveway, parking it behind Donna's Porsche. The two cars made a nice pair, one silver, one red. Only the scratch along the side of the M6 marred the picture. That, and the fact that the Porsche had almost certainly been paid for with Darren's ill-gotten gains.

Darren Jubb had been a thorn in Raven's side for as long as he could remember. Right from the start, Darren had been trouble, encouraging Raven to skip school and steal sweets from the corner shop. Raven knew it was wrong. But he'd been flattered by the other boy's attention, aware that Darren had street cred among the other kids, and knowing that some of that respect rubbed off on him whenever he was at Darren's side. Later, the two of them had graduated to drinking cans of beer in Peasholm Park and smoking cigarettes behind the bicycle sheds at school. And then Darren had brought Harry into their circle, no doubt recognising a fellow mischief-maker when he saw one. The addition of Harry to the group had made Raven try even harder to please Darren. Under Darren's guidance, he had started stealing CDs and other low value items from the shops in town. Stupid, mindless actions. If Raven had stayed in Scarborough, who knew how he might have ended up? Darren exploited everyone around him, finding their weak point and using it to make them do whatever he wanted.

Donna Craven had been Raven's biggest weak point. And she had been his downfall.

He had gone over the events that led up to his mother's death countless times. If only he'd done what she asked and stayed home to revise, she would never have gone out that night to look for him. She might still be alive today. But Raven knew that he'd never even had a choice. Like a line of collapsing dominos, the chain reaction had been set in motion well before that fateful night. As soon as Donna had appeared on the scene and chosen Raven instead of Darren, a bitter rivalry had been set up – one that could only ever have ended badly.

Raven knocked on the door and stood back, breathing hard. It was time to have this out with Darren once and for all. He'd gone too far this time, and if he thought he could bribe police officers, arrange for evidence to be destroyed and pay thugs to give Raven a beating, then he needed to be brought up sharp. Raven wasn't sure exactly what he was going to say, but he knew he ought to have said it years ago. He'd been too weak and timid to oppose Darren as a teenager, but he wasn't weak now.

The door opened, but it wasn't Darren who stood there. It was Darren's old man.

'You again,' said Frank Jubb, blocking the entrance. 'What do you want this time?'

'I want to speak to Darren.'

Frank sneered. 'Well, you're out of luck. He's gone down to the harbour to find out what you lot are doing with his boat.'

'His boat?'

'You didn't know? Apparently one of your juniors has got a warrant to search it.' A sly smirk spread across Frank's ugly face. 'Don't you even know what your own people are doing, Raven? You'd better smarten up or you'll be heading back to London with a kick up the backside. And if you think you can pin that murder on Darren, you're a half-arsed clown, just like your dad.'

Raven glared at the old man. 'You always were a nasty

piece of work, Frank.'

'Nasty? Tough, you mean. Willing to make hard choices to find success.'

Raven had heard similar self-justification from low-life crooks like Frank Jubb countless times. Small-timers who attributed their modest success to shrewd business acumen. 'Face it, Frank. You just happened to get into amusement arcades just as they were taking off in a big way. You got lucky.'

Frank bared his teeth, his pride affronted. 'Luck, you call it? There's no such thing. Luck is for the little people. Luck is for the punters who come to my arcade and lose their wages for a chance to win. Luck's a story they tell themselves when they feed their coins into the slots of my fruit machines. Do you know where those slots lead? Straight into my bank account.

'I'll tell you something else that doesn't exist, Raven. A rich fisherman. That's why your old man died a pauper. Anyone could see the way the fishing industry was going around here. By the time your dad left school it was already down the toilet. He should have done what I did – invest in a growing business. But he was a stubborn fool. He followed his own father into the family trade. No wonder he ended up the way he did. An embittered drunk, blaming anyone but himself for his bad luck, and using his fists against anyone who said otherwise.'

Raven felt his anger rise and took a step forwards. Every word Frank said about his dad was true. But that didn't mean he had to stay here and listen to it.

Frank saw him coming and chuckled with glee. 'A bit of that old violent streak rubbed off on you, has it, son? Your old man certainly dished out plenty of black eyes to your mum, didn't he?'

Raven's fury turned black. His fists burned with a desire to smash Frank's ugly face to pulp. But he stopped himself just in time. He wasn't the same as his father. Hitting Frank Jubb might make him feel better for a moment, but that feeling would quickly turn to shame.

And it would collapse any chance he had of bringing charges against Darren.

He stayed where he was, his hands at his sides. 'The lesson your father never taught you, Frank, is that life's not just about filling your own pockets. It's about doing the decent thing and standing up for what's right. You clearly forgot to teach that lesson to your own son, and that's why Darren turned out the way he did.'

A look of frustrated outrage flooded Frank's face, but before he could say anything, Donna appeared in the hallway behind him.

'Frank? What's going on?' Her arrival brought an end to the altercation, and Frank stepped back, his shoulders hunched like a sullen teenager.

Donna came to the door and smiled. 'Tom! What are you doing here?'

'I came to talk to Darren.'

'He's out. But come on in. Talk to me instead.'

Against his better judgement, Raven followed her inside.

CHAPTER 29

After speaking to Liam, Becca set off along Northway, easing her Honda Jazz through the Saturday morning traffic. It was a nippy little car, ideally suited for getting around – quite unlike Raven's big BMW, which could barely fit down some of the old town's narrow terraced streets – and she made good progress.

She soon left behind the crowded centre of Scarborough and entered the Barrowcliff estate. The area was more open and spacious than the old town, but had a reputation for being rough, with drugs and alcohol in circulation among the kids who lived there, and some of the homes boarded up. Many of the residents were on low incomes, and the estate had been branded one of the most deprived areas in the country in a recent BBC documentary. But Becca knew that the community was close knit, and that local charities did good work, organising day trips to the beach for kids who'd never been, despite growing up a stone's throw from the sea.

She stopped outside a block of flats that had been built sometime in the seventies or eighties and left her car at the roadside, hoping it would be safe. She climbed the staircase up to the third floor and rang the bell to one of the flats. No one answered but from inside the flat she could hear music playing and a young child's high-pitched voice. She rang the bell a second time, leaning on it for longer to cut across the beat of the music.

The door was opened by a woman in her early twenties, her jet-black hair scraped back from a high forehead in a tight ponytail. She didn't seem very happy to have a visitor.

'Leah Briggs?' enquired Becca.

'Who's asking?'

Becca showed her ID.

Leah scowled. 'I were just getting ready to go out.'

'I won't take up much of your time.' Becca had been wanting to call in on Leah ever since visiting her husband, Lewis, in prison. You could say it was curiosity, or you could call it a hunch. She was intrigued by the way that the man who had killed Max Hunt had seemed so resigned to a life behind bars, and the way his eyes had flickered briefly when Becca had asked after his wife and child. There was a story there and Becca wanted to know what it was.

'You'd better come in then,' said Leah grudgingly. 'But I can't hang about. I'm taking Abbie down to the swings.'

It seemed to Becca that Leah was going to an awful lot of trouble with her appearance just for a trip to the playground. She held a mascara wand in one manicured hand, and her eyes were outlined in kohl, the lids shaded in silver and charcoal in the "smoky eye look" that Becca had never mastered. Her skin, with its layers of foundation and concealer, was porcelain smooth. Becca wondered if she was the kind of person who followed Scarlett Jubb on Instagram. Rather than the ubiquitous tracksuit bottoms and hoodie that you tended to see in Barrowcliff, Leah was wearing smart jeans and a cropped, fluffy, pink jumper that showed off her midriff and made Becca think of candyfloss.

A little girl of about three or four dressed in a pink fairy costume was clinging to Leah's leg. 'Ger'off, Abbie,' said Leah. 'Go and play with your princess castle.'

'Is that your castle over there?' said Becca brightly,

pointing at an enormous construction in pink and gold plastic, all turrets and ornate staircases, inhabited by a legion of Disney princesses. The castle dominated one wall of the small living room. Becca couldn't imagine buying such a grotesque thing for a child, but then she couldn't really imagine having a child of her own.

The girl hung on to her mother's leg for a little while longer, sucking her thumb and regarding Becca warily, then brightened and pranced over to her castle to continue playing with her dolls.

The interior of the flat wasn't exactly what Becca had been expecting. With Leah's husband in prison and Leah herself almost certainly having to scrape a living on state benefits, Becca had anticipated a spartan setting. Yet in addition to the elaborate dolls' house, the room boasted a brand-new television and an L-shaped leather sofa arranged around a sheepskin rug. It was Scarborough council estate meets Hollywood glitz.

'What you want to talk about, then?' asked Leah, switching off the music and sitting down on the sofa opposite the TV, which was showing some talk show with the volume turned right down.

Becca took a seat on the other half of the L-shape. 'It's about your husband, Lewis.'

'Yeah. Thought it might be. Gonna let him out, are you?' Leah shot a dismissive look Becca's way. 'No, I thought not.'

'I went to see him this week.'

'Lucky him,' said Leah. 'I don't get no one coming to see me.'

Becca guessed that her current visit didn't count in Leah's mind. She seemed unwavering in her belief that the world was pitted against her.

'It's all right for him,' she continued, 'being waited on hand and foot all day. I'm the one stuck at home on my own with Abbie to look after. Lewis has barely even seen her. She were only just born when he got put away.'

Becca wondered whether Lewis would view things the

same way. Full Sutton wasn't exactly a five-star residence. But perhaps from Leah's perspective as a single mum, her husband had it easy. 'I wondered if Lewis has ever given you a reason why he shot Max Hunt.' Becca kept her voice low so that Abbie wouldn't hear, but the little girl was completely absorbed in the world of princesses.

Leah crinkled her button nose. 'What does it matter? He's dead now, and Lewis is banged up. Makes no difference why he done it.'

Becca could tell she would get nowhere with a direct approach. She tried a different tack. 'A body was washed up on Monday at the North Bay. Did you hear about it?'

'Yeah, I 'eard some of the other mums talking 'bout it.' Leah sounded completely uninterested in the subject. 'What's it got to do with me?'

'The victim was shot in the chest before ending up in the water. There are similarities between that murder and the crime your husband was convicted of.'

'Well it weren't Lewis what killed this guy,' said Leah. ''Ow could he, locked up and that?'

'We know that Lewis wasn't involved in this latest murder,' said Becca, 'but we think he was working for the same person who ordered this hit.'

Leah's eyes were suddenly wary. She crossed her legs and scowled. ''Ow d'ya know Lewis were working for someone?'

'Come on, Leah. It's obvious. Lewis had no reason to kill Max Hunt.' Becca gestured to the sofa, the television, Abbie's castle and princess collection. 'You didn't pay for all this yourself. Someone gave Lewis good money to carry out the murder. And perhaps they're still paying for him to keep his silence? Is that what you want? For your husband to spend the rest of his life in jail?'

Leah refused to meet Becca's eye, suddenly becoming absorbed in examining her painted fingernails. 'Lewis is a fool,' she said, as if speaking of a wayward child. 'He should never have done owt. I told 'im.'

Becca leaned forwards. 'We already have our suspicions

about who ordered the hit. We just need you to confirm them. All you have to do is give us a name.'

Leah looked up but narrowed her eyes, as if searching for a trap. 'What if I tell you? Will it make any difference to Lewis? Will you let him out?'

Becca knew that her hands were tied. A life sentence was mandatory for all convicted murderers, and Lewis's minimum term had been set by the trial judge. Nothing could change that. But there was always a glimmer of hope if Lewis could demonstrate a willingness to assist the police with their investigation. 'I can't make any promises, Leah, but cooperation with the authorities could definitely help Lewis's case. The parole board would consider it when deciding when he can be released.'

'So you can't promise owt?'

Becca could see that Leah was balanced between hope and fear. Hope that she might finally be able to unburden herself of the knowledge she was carrying. Fear that if she gave up the name Becca wanted, she was condemning herself and her daughter to a life of poverty. Becca could only imagine what it must be like to be in that position. 'I promise I'll do my best to help you, Leah. I know it can't be easy being a single mum with a small child. Especially when you know that the person behind all this is walking free while Lewis is locked up in a prison cell.'

A tear appeared in the corner of Leah's eye, and at last Becca caught a glimpse of the vulnerable young woman beneath the angry front and the defensive layers of makeup. 'Lewis said he'd see us all right while he were inside. He said the money would keep coming as long as I kept my mouth shut.' She flashed a defiant look at Becca, daring her to contradict her. 'Don't you think I'd rather have Lewis here with me? He's missing seeing his little girl growing up. And Abbie should have a father. I know it ain't right, me being paid to keep quiet while Lewis is in prison. But what were I supposed to do? I couldn't turn down cash when it's offered, could I? I couldn't say no to him.'

'Who couldn't you say no to, Leah?'

Leah's voice was full of venom, years of resentment finally spilling out. 'Jubb of course. He's the one who brings the money.'

Becca nodded, hardly daring to breathe in case she broke the spell that had finally freed Leah's tongue. 'And did Darren Jubb pay Lewis to carry out the killing too?'

Leah's expression changed to puzzlement. 'Darren? I never said nowt about Darren Jubb. He's never given us owt, the tight-fisted bastard.'

Now it was Becca's turn to be confused. 'Then who, Leah? Who gives you the cash?'

'I thought you said you knew,' said Leah. 'It's his son, Ethan.'

CHAPTER 30

DC Tony Bairstow didn't rate himself as a particularly good-looking guy. He certainly wasn't in the same league as DC Dan Bennett when it came to physical attractiveness. Nor DCI Raven for that matter. But he didn't think he was terribly ugly either. He rated himself as a five out of ten. Maybe five and a half on a good day, but definitely not a six. He wasn't quite as young as he used to be, although that was true of everyone he knew. He lacked a university education, but he felt he was fairly intelligent, and whenever he lacked knowledge in a particular area, he compensated for it with hard work and study. His politics didn't lean hard to the left, nor far to the right, and he tended to see both sides of any argument. In short, he was a middle-of-the-road sort of man, and felt very comfortable occupying that position.

If Tony had been asked to name his one outstanding characteristic, then it would surely be seriousness. Tony was serious about everything he did. After all, life was a weighty business and to get the most out of it you had to approach it with an earnest attitude.

That was why Tony took his job very seriously. And

that was why he had come into work today, even though it was a Saturday, and neither DS Becca Shawcross nor DCI Raven had authorised him to do any paid overtime.

And his diligence was paying off, because he had just made a significant discovery.

After finding out that Patrick's burner phone had been used in the Netherlands on the seventeenth of October, DC Dan Bennett had checked with all the nearest airports to see if Patrick had taken a flight to Holland in the days immediately before. But Patrick hadn't boarded a flight from Newcastle, Leeds Bradford or even Manchester airport, at least not under his own name. Following Tony's suggestion, Dan had widened the search to include the daily ferries from Newcastle to Amsterdam and Hull to Rotterdam, but that had returned nothing either. And since no false passport had been found in Patrick's house, it seemed unlikely that he had travelled using a fake ID.

So Tony had tried a different tack, checking with ports in the Netherlands to see if any private boats had visited them. Now, working through the information that had just arrived, he was gratified to learn that a boat from Scarborough had moored at the Dutch harbour of Vlissingen on the night of the seventeenth of October. The boat in question was *Sea Dreams*, and it had been signed in by Ethan Jubb.

Tony picked up the phone and dialled DS Becca Shawcross. Although it was the weekend, he was sure that Becca would like to hear his news. After all, she was a serious person too.

*

'So what's it like being back in Scarborough?' asked Donna. 'I expect your dad's old house needs a lot of work.'

After getting rid of Frank, Donna had invited Raven through to the lounge where Darren had hosted him on his first visit to the house. Raven inspected the chandeliers, silk curtains and piano. It was very different to the house where Donna had grown up, in a run-down terraced row behind the market. 'Is this your taste in décor, then, Donna? Are you the interior designer around here?'

She took a seat on one of the leather sofas, crossing her legs. Today she was dressed casually, in skin-tight jeans and a baggy jumper. Even so, she managed to effortlessly convey the appearance of a movie star. 'Don't be like that, Tom. There's no need to be mean, just because of what Frank said to you. I know he can be a bastard sometimes.'

'Only sometimes?'

She met his question with a patient expression. 'He's actually quite nice when you get to know him. When the children were growing up, he was always generous with his time. He's just very protective of his family.'

'What about Patrick Lofthouse?' asked Raven. 'Did Frank regard him as one of the family?'

'Well of course he did. We all liked Patrick very much, and Scarlett was devoted to him. It'll take her a long time to get over his death, if she ever does.' She looked directly at him. 'I know what it feels like to lose someone you love, Tom.'

Raven knew exactly what she was referring to. He glared at her. 'Don't use that against me, Donna. It wasn't the same. I didn't die.'

'You might as well have done. You simply vanished. I had no idea what had happened to you. You didn't even phone me or send a postcard.'

Raven knew that he ought to have told her what he intended to do. Why hadn't he? Perhaps because he was afraid she might persuade him to stay. Or because he feared he had already lost her to his best friend and rival. 'And so you turned to Darren for consolation…'

'Oh, come on, Tom. You can't blame me for that. Darren was there for me when you went away. It was your fault that I ended up with him. Everything was your fault.'

The rebuke felt like a slap. But it was no worse than what he'd told himself so often over the years.

Donna softened her tone. 'I'm sorry, I didn't mean

that. You can't blame yourself for your mother's death. But you didn't need to leave town afterwards.'

'Yes,' said Raven. 'I did.'

He wondered if that made him a coward. He had run away at his moment of crisis. If he'd been truly brave, he might have stayed. Then perhaps he and Donna…

He turned away, angry with himself for wallowing in self-pity. The sudden movement caused the previous night's injury to spike in pain.

'What's wrong?' Donna asked, her sea green eyes studying him with concern. 'Are you hurt?' She rose from her seat and came to him, placing a hand against his side. 'You are hurt. What happened?'

'A couple of young hooligans paid me a visit last night. They had a message to give me.'

'I don't understand. What message?'

'Stay away from Darren Jubb.'

She stepped away from him, shaking her head in disbelief. 'What? You think Darren sent someone to intimidate you?'

'They didn't intimidate me, Donna. Not at all. But they did give me a thorough beating.'

Her hand went to her mouth. 'That's awful. But Darren would never do something like that.'

'Wouldn't he?' The Darren Jubb that Raven knew would do anything to get what he wanted. Or more often, he would get someone else to do the dirty work for him.

'Darren's just not like that,' said Donna. She paused, thinking. 'Listen, Tom, I know that you're still bitter about what happened all those years ago. But you have to let it go. The fact is, you went away and I married Darren. I had his children. You can't keep looking for revenge.'

'I'm not after revenge.'

'Then what are you after?' She drew closer to him again, her hand reaching out to take his. 'Why did you really come back, Tom? Was it for me? Did you think I might be waiting for you, still? Because I did wait. I waited for as long as I could. If I'd known you were coming back,

I would have waited forever.' She was just inches from him now. Her red lips parted.

Raven's phone rang in his pocket. He let it ring. Once. Twice. Three times. Donna's gaze didn't leave his.

He reached into his pocket and pulled out the phone. It was Becca.

'Raven here.'

He listened carefully to what she had to say, then ended the call.

'Is Ethan home?' he asked Donna. 'Because I'm afraid that I have to arrest him.'

CHAPTER 31

The case against Ethan Jubb was coming together nicely. Not only had Becca discovered that Ethan was paying Lewis Briggs's wife to keep quiet about the murder of Max Hunt, but Tony had obtained the harbourmaster's records showing that Ethan had sailed to Vlissingen on the same day that one of Patrick's burner phones had been used to make and receive a number of calls in Holland. According to Jess, the CSI team had identified several hair samples that, when analysed, might prove that Patrick had been on board *Sea Dreams*, although disappointingly they had been unable to find any traces of blood on the boat, and the GPS tracking history had been deleted so they couldn't prove where the vessel had been on the day Patrick was murdered.

But to Raven's way of thinking, wiping the GPS records was tantamount to an admission of guilt. Why else would the boat's navigation history have been deleted? It was already clear to him that Ethan and Patrick had travelled to Holland together in order to collect a consignment of drugs. He just needed to build the case.

There was no evidence yet that Darren Jubb was

directly involved, but Raven could sense the man's dirty fingers all over the operation. *Darren's boat. Darren's son. Darren's future son-in-law.* And of course it had been a bouncer at Darren's nightclub who had pulled the trigger of the gun that fired the bullet that killed Max Hunt.

Raven had arrested Ethan himself, despite Donna's frantic screams and protests. He had brought him back to the station and supervised the taking of DNA and fingerprints. Once that was done, Ethan had called his lawyer.

It was little surprise when Harry Hood appeared in the interview room some thirty minutes later. This time the gloves were off and there was no attempt at chummy banter between old friends. 'You'd better have a very good reason for arresting my client, DCI Raven.'

'I have.'

'Would you care to share it with us?'

'Certainly,' said Raven. He waited while Becca started the tape and ran through the introductions. Once all was in order he handed over to her to kick off the interview.

'Mr Hood,' she began. 'We have reason to believe that your client paid Lewis Briggs to murder Max Hunt. We have a signed witness statement saying that he made regular payments to Lewis's wife in return for his continued silence.'

Harry snorted with derision. 'That sounds more like hearsay than evidence. Are you able to disclose the identity of this so-called witness?'

'No.'

'Why not?'

'For their protection.'

'This is ridiculous,' said Harry.

'Perhaps your client would care to answer some questions for himself,' said Raven. He turned to address Ethan Jubb, who was sitting nonchalantly next to Harry. So far he didn't look particularly worried. Perhaps he was under the delusion that a defence lawyer of Harry's calibre could work miracles.

In their brief encounters to date, Raven hadn't taken to the young man. Ethan lacked his father's talent to win people over. Perhaps he didn't think he needed to make the effort.

'So, Ethan,' he said. 'Did you know Max Hunt?'

Ethan seemed to be considering whether or not to favour Raven with a response. He looked to Harry, who nodded his assent.

'Yes,' he said at last.

'How?'

'He was a regular at Vertigo.'

'That's the name of your father's nightclub?'

'Yes.'

'And did you also know Lewis Briggs?'

'Lewis worked as a bouncer at the club.' Ethan leaned back casually in his chair, evidently under the impression that all the questions would be this easy.

'Did you pay him money for any reason?'

'Lewis? No.'

'Did you pay his wife, Leah, any money?'

'No. I've never even met her.'

'Really?' said Raven. 'We have a signed statement by a witness who says you make regular visits to Leah Briggs, and on each occasion you give her money.'

Ethan appeared bored. 'Is that a question?'

'Do you?'

'Of course not.'

Harry was watching the exchange like a hawk. Raven nodded to Becca to take over the questioning.

'Ethan, how well did you know Patrick Lofthouse?' she asked.

Ethan turned to look at her. As Raven had anticipated, a change in the tone of the interview seemed to make him more cooperative. 'Pretty well. He was my sister's fiancé.'

'And did the two of you hang out together? Just the two of you?'

'Sometimes. Pat was a good mate.'

'You got on together?'

'Sure. He was a nice guy.'

'Are you aware that Patrick illegally bought, sold and used controlled drugs?'

The question seemed to wrongfoot Ethan. He sat up straighter in his chair, struggling to find a response until Harry answered for him. 'My client has no comment.'

'Is that right, Ethan?' persisted Becca. 'Were you aware that your friend was a drug dealer?'

'No comment,' mumbled Ethan. His earlier relaxed poise was now gone.

Raven decided to move in. 'Where were you on the seventeenth of October?'

'The seventeenth?' Ethan shook his head. 'I don't remember.'

'Let me jog your memory,' said Raven. 'Did you travel to Holland that day?'

'I… er…'

'The harbourmaster's records from the port of Vlissingen show that a boat called *Sea Dreams*, registered to your father, berthed on the night of the seventeenth of October, and was signed in by you.'

At Ethan's side, Harry frowned. Whether this was news to him or if he was simply surprised that the police had managed to uncover the information, Raven didn't know.

'No comment,' said Ethan.

'It's a simple enough question,' said Raven. 'Did you go to Holland in your dad's boat?'

'All right, yeah, I did.' Ethan gazed back defiantly, but it was obvious that he was beginning to flounder.

Becca picked up the thread. 'Did Patrick go with you?'

Ethan looked to Harry, who offered him little help. 'Pat? Um…'

'We know that a mobile phone in Patrick's possession was used to make calls to a Dutch number on the seventeenth. Those calls were made from Holland.'

'Well, yes,' said Ethan. 'Patrick came with me. It was a lads' night out, you know?'

'Did anyone else go with you for this "lads' night out"?'

'No. It was just the two of us.'

'Did you meet anyone there?'

'I... no comment.' Ethan's earlier languid poise was now completely gone, and he sat hunched in his chair, his hands clasped together, glancing from Becca to Raven like a hunted animal.

Raven leaned forwards. 'Where were you last Sunday, the day that Patrick was killed?'

'I was in a meeting with my dad,' said Ethan.

'This was the meeting with your accountant?' asked Becca.

'That's right,' said Ethan, grateful for some brief respite.

'What time did that meeting finish?'

'I don't really remember.'

'It was twelve noon,' said Raven. 'We checked with your father and your accountant. After the meeting, your father took your mother and your sister out to lunch. Where did you go?'

'I just stayed home,' said Ethan. 'I grabbed a quick bite for myself.'

'And how did you spend the rest of that day?'

'There was a football match on in the afternoon.'

'You watched it alone?'

'Yes.'

'And then what?'

'I... I just stayed home.'

'Alone?'

'Yes!' The single word conveyed a desperate plea to be believed. Ethan Jubb knew he was fighting for his freedom here. As yet, there was no single piece of evidence to convict him, but the accumulation of facts was compelling. The witness statement, his admission that he had gone to Holland with Patrick, plus the fact that he had no alibi for the time of the murder all went a long way. Once the CSI team had finished going over his room, further evidence might well appear.

Raven figured it was worth pushing Ethan further.

'Here's what I think happened on the day of Patrick's murder. You and Patrick had travelled to Holland the previous week. You'd brought back a substantial haul of drugs. But you had a disagreement about how to handle the consignment. Or perhaps you got greedy and figured that if Patrick was out of the way, you could keep the whole lot for yourself.'

'No,' said Ethan.

'You'd already removed one of your competitors. Max Hunt. On that occasion you paid Lewis Briggs to do the job. But that proved to be an expensive mistake. Lewis was an idiot. He got caught. He didn't even have the wit to get rid of the murder weapon. But you'd managed to get away with it, by buying Lewis's silence. Maybe you even bought a police officer to help you cover your tracks.'

'I don't know what you're talking about!'

'This time you decided to do it yourself. Patrick had been on the boat with you to Holland, so you invited him out again, just for a spin around the bay this time. A couple of lads having fun together. But when you were clear of the shore, you shot Patrick and threw his body overboard. Mindful of Lewis's blunder you tossed the gun in after him, and his mobile phone too. Afterwards, you returned the boat to the harbour and deleted the GPS tracking history from the navigation computer. Finally, you took Patrick's car and drove it out of town before walking home along the coastal path. The evidence was all gone and there was nothing to tie you to his murder. You could relax.'

'That's a very nice story, DCI Raven,' said Harry. 'But it seems that you've completely forgotten about the need to back it up with factual evidence.'

'Evidence? Well, for one thing we have tracking data for Patrick's mobile phone, so we know exactly where he was when he was killed. Secondly, after we've talked to all the other boat owners down at the harbour, there's a very good chance we'll find that one of them saw you and Patrick go out on the boat together, and you return alone.' Raven kept his eyes fixed on Ethan. 'But here's the thing,

Ethan. I don't think you were the only one involved in this murder. You've already said that you and Patrick were mates. You liked the guy. You didn't want to kill him. But perhaps someone else told you to get rid of him. Someone who was masterminding the entire operation. Your father, Darren Jubb, for instance.'

'DCI Raven–' began Harry.

But Raven cut him off. 'So you could help yourself, Ethan, by telling me the truth. Tell me what really happened that day, because if you don't, then I'm afraid you're going to be charged with murder and conspiracy to murder, in addition to the supply of class A drugs. And that means you'll be going to prison for the rest of your life.'

Ethan Jubb stared back at him, frightened and bewildered. Raven could almost feel sorry for him. In a short time he'd gone from being confident, thinking himself immune from prosecution, to staring into a bleak future with no prospect of release.

But it seemed that Ethan had nothing to say for himself. Instead, it was Harry who spoke up. There was a flinty look in his narrow eyes. Raven had hauled his client over the coals, and now it was time for him to fight back. 'You've asked my client a lot of questions today, DCI Raven. Now I have some questions for you.'

Raven decided to let him speak. 'Go on.'

'First of all, where were you on the night of the twenty-eighth of October?'

Raven frowned. 'The twenty-eighth?'

'Let me help you,' said Harry. 'It was Thursday this week.'

'I know when the twenty-eighth was,' said Raven. *And I know what happened too.* There was no point trying to deny it. Harry already knew. 'On that evening, after leaving work I first went shopping for some clothes, and then I met an old friend of mine, Donna Craven. I took her out for a drink.'

A look of malice entered Harry's weasel features.

'Donna *Jubb*, I think you mean. The wife of Darren Jubb.'

Raven could feel both Ethan and Becca staring at him, but he kept his face placid, his attention fixed on Harry. 'Donna and I were a couple once. In fact, she was my first girlfriend. But that was a long time ago. I hadn't seen her for more than thirty years. We had a lot of catching up to do.'

'And did you "catch up" nicely?' asked Harry, lacing his question with a hefty dose of innuendo.

'Very nicely, thank you,' said Raven. 'As I said, we went out for a drink together in a public bar. I believe that's how this came to your attention.'

'Indeed,' said Harry. 'And then you drove her home.'

'I can assure you that nothing improper happened.'

'Tell that to the jury.'

So, it had happened. Just as Raven had feared, Donna's trap had now caught him in its jaws.

'So,' said Harry, 'I believe that your case against my client has been thoroughly discredited. Not only is your evidence circumstantial, but your own behaviour is called into question. Ever since the beginning of your investigation you have conducted a campaign of harassment, firstly against Darren Jubb and now against his son. And all because of a personal grudge dating back to when Donna Craven dumped you and chose Darren instead. Is that why you left Scarborough, DCI Raven? And did you return simply to resume your pursuit of Donna?'

Raven stared at his old friend and adversary with loathing. He had no doubt that Harry would deploy this against him if Ethan's case came to trial. Would it keep Ethan out of jail? He couldn't say, but it would certainly damage any chance of conviction. The CPS might even take the decision not to prosecute.

'You can question my motives,' said Raven, 'and cast doubt on my integrity, but the facts don't change. Your client is guilty and we both know it.'

'Do you intend to charge him?' demanded Harry.

'Not yet. We'll keep him in custody for twenty-four hours. Let's wait and see if more evidence appears.'

Raven watched as Becca and a uniformed officer led Ethan away to the cells.

Once again, Harry lingered behind. 'So, Tom,' he said. 'Do you still think this isn't a game?' He slid out through the doorway, leaving a nasty taste in Raven's mouth.

CHAPTER 32

'How could you!' accused Becca. 'You've jeopardised the whole case!'

They were back in Raven's tiny office after the interview with Ethan Jubb. Becca kept her voice down, but through the glass window to the incident room, Raven could see that both Tony and Jess were clearly aware that an altercation was taking place. He didn't know if they could hear the words through the closed office door. There was no sign of Dan. Presumably the young DC had better things to do on his Saturday afternoon than come into work.

Raven met Becca's accusation calmly. 'I did nothing wrong.'

'Did you sleep with Darren Jubb's wife?'

'No.' Although, he had slept with her before she'd been Darren's. He remembered the first time. They'd been sixteen, young and inexperienced, but making up for it with unbridled passion driven on by teenage hormones. His mum had been at work, his dad out on the fishing boat, and they had the house to themselves. He remembered a lot of fumbling around under the bedcovers. *Let's Go To bed* by The Cure had been playing on the stereo in the background, although neither of them had needed any encouragement. It had been the first time for both of them and it had been over before it had barely begun. But the memory had endured. He would never forget it.

Becca glared at him. 'Well, if it comes to court, you'll find it very hard to convince a jury.'

'Maybe.'

'So, what are you going to do now?'

He wondered if she expected him to stand down from the investigation. If she did, she had misjudged him badly. He would keep going until the person responsible was behind bars. 'I'm going to do my job.'

'Fine,' she said. The door slammed behind her as she stormed out.

Raven went out to the incident room, where Tony and Jess were both busy avoiding his gaze. 'Tony?' he asked. 'Did you get those DNA results back from the lab?'

Tony looked up. 'I got them fast-tracked like you asked.'

'And?'

'Here's the report you wanted.' He passed Raven a sealed brown envelope.

*

Becca drove home, still mad after her row with Raven. She wondered how she could ever have thought he was a good boss. He was moody. He was secretive. He was infuriating. He'd managed to severely piss off Holly, who rarely had a bad word for anyone. And even DI Dinsdale didn't go around accusing the Superintendent of corruption. Perhaps Dr Felicity Wainwright had been right with her scathing assessment of him.

Becca still didn't know if she believed what Raven had said about his relationship with Donna Jubb. She'd seen for herself the way Donna had flirted with him when they'd called in at the Jubb's house to bring Darren in for questioning. It wasn't just the way she had touched his arm and called him "Tom". It was the look in her eyes when she said it.

Raven had freely admitted that Donna had once been his girlfriend. In Becca's opinion, that flame was still burning hot.

Opening the front door to the house, she was greeted by the comforting smell of roasting lamb and rosemary. In that moment, she was so grateful for the mere existence of her family that she could have hugged them all, even Liam.

She went up to her room on the top floor and walked to the window that looked over the back of the house. The sun was going down and the North Sands were already in deep shadow. Lights twinkled in the distance from the Old Scalby Mills pub perched on the seafront beside Scalby Beck. Beyond the rocks of Scalby Ness, the sea was a silky black. But it was out there, a few miles offshore, that Patrick Lofthouse had met his violent death. Had Ethan Jubb's finger pulled the trigger? Becca knew that the case against him wasn't yet watertight. And with Raven's careless behaviour, it risked falling apart completely.

Drawing the curtains closed against the night, she changed out of her work clothes into her favourite jeans and jumper, then went downstairs to the kitchen, where Sue was busy preparing vegetables. 'Hello, love. How was your day?'

'Interesting,' said Becca, truthfully. 'We made an arrest.'

'In the murder case?' Sue lifted a saucepan lid to check the carrots, plunging a wicked-looking knife into the bubbling water. Despite being not too many years away from thirty, Becca had never had to fend for herself. Her mum had looked after her too well, spoiling her perhaps. When Becca eventually did leave home, she would need a crash course in cookery.

'Mmm,' said Becca noncommittally. She had probably already said too much, but it was hard always having to keep details of work to herself. After dinner, she would go and visit Sam. Talking to him always helped her to unwind at the end of a long day.

The front door opened and closed with a bang, and Becca recognised the sound of Liam's big feet tramping down the hallway. The kitchen door burst open, and he entered, a cheeky grin on his face. 'Evening, all. Any grub going?'

Sue treated him to an indulgent smile. 'Of course. Have a seat. Would you like a mug of tea?'

He took a seat at the table, putting his feet up on one of the dining chairs. 'Wouldn't say no to a beer.'

Sue scurried over to the fridge and returned with a bottle. Liam opened it and took a swig.

Becca's earlier desire to give him a hug quickly melted away. However much she might take advantage of her mum's hospitality, Liam was even less independent, despite being older and having his own place to live.

'So,' said Becca, 'did you get all your very important work done?'

'Work? Oh yeah. I've been rushed off my feet all day.'

'I can imagine,' she said sarcastically. 'It must be really tough, not having a proper job to do.'

Sue was bustling about, taking the meat out of the oven and giving the gravy a stir. 'Your brother works harder than you give him credit for, Becca. It's not easy running your own business. I should know.'

'Exactly.' Liam pasted a smug look on his face and took another gulp of his beer. 'So why are you giving me such a hard time, sis? I gave you a tip-off, didn't I?'

Becca prodded him under the table with her foot. 'You could have helped me a lot more if you'd told me sooner. What I'd like to know is what else you haven't told me.'

'What makes you think there's more?'

She sighed. 'There's always more, Liam.'

The back door opened, letting in a blast of cold air, and Becca's dad came in. 'Right,' he said, rubbing his hands together. 'That's the gate fixed. It blew off in the wind the other day.' David Shawcross was responsible for all the maintenance in the house, a huge job considering the number of rooms and age of the property. He came over and gave Becca a kiss on the cheek.

Becca helped him to lay the table while Sue served the food. Liam stirred himself to move his beer bottle out of the way.

Over the meal, the conversation centred on Liam's latest business venture. He was in the process of acquiring some rundown properties in Whitby and had grand plans to turn them into luxury holiday lets. According to him, he'd picked them up at a knockdown price, and was going to make a killing on them. Becca could see him developing half the Yorkshire coast given half a chance. Perhaps she was too hard on him. He was clearly a budding entrepreneur.

For once, she was content to let her brother ramble on. Listening to him helped to take her mind off the case. So she was both surprised and irritated when he brought up the topic of Raven.

'Did you give my mate's details to your boss?' he asked.

It took her a moment to realise what he was talking about. 'You mean about repairing his car? Not yet.'

'Oh, I thought it was urgent.' Liam impaled a potato on the end of his fork and popped it into his mouth whole. 'Well, next time you speak to him, find out if he's planning to sell that old fisherman's cottage his dad left him.'

She wondered how Liam had got hold of information about Raven. Not even she knew where her boss lived, although her mum had mentioned a Raven family living near the harbour. 'How do you know about Raven?' she asked.

Liam tapped the side of his nose. 'I have my sources. You know I'm always on the lookout for opportunities. Anyway, if he does want to sell, tell him I'll make him an offer. A direct sale, no need for estate agent's fees.'

'Naturally.' Becca chewed her lamb thoughtfully. 'But why the sudden interest?' Raven had been back in Scarborough for a couple of weeks already, and this was the first time Liam had mentioned any interest in buying his house.

Liam grinned. 'You really are slow for a detective, Becs. Now that Ethan Jubb's out of the way, the field's clear for me. Perhaps for once I'll be able to get in first and grab a bargain.'

She put her knife and fork down and glared at him. 'How did you know that Ethan Jubb's been arrested?'

He shook his head as if she were a slow-witted child. 'The same way I knew about your boss's house. The same way I knew that Patrick and Ethan were dealing drugs together. I ask questions and I listen to what people say.'

'But why didn't you tell me about Patrick and Ethan?' she asked, exasperated. She'd asked him just that morning who Patrick's business partner was, and he'd avoided answering.

'Because they were just rumours. They would never stand up in court. And because I didn't want to reveal my sources.'

'You think you're like a news reporter, do you?'

'Precisely. It's called journalistic integrity.'

'I call it being pig-headed.' Becca began to sift through what he'd just told her. Liam was right that his inside information could never be used as evidence against Ethan. But it would have made a huge difference to the investigation if she'd known from the start that Patrick and Ethan were running a drugs operation together. What was the point of a brother who had access to all kinds of useful intel but kept it to himself?

'Besides,' said Liam. 'I didn't want you to think I was mixed up in anything sketchy.'

A dreadful thought suddenly occurred to Becca. 'Please tell me you're not.'

'Of course I'm not!' Liam shot her a disgusted look. 'How could you even think that!'

'Because I'm your sister,' said Becca. 'And I know what you're like.'

*

Raven boiled the kettle and splashed hot water over his instant coffee granules. If he stayed on in the old house – if he wasn't sent packing back to London once it became known that Donna had put him in a compromising position – he would have to get himself a decent coffee maker. The espresso machine that Lisa had bought him for their twentieth wedding anniversary had been one of the items she'd taken with her when she left him. It seemed an unnecessarily vindictive touch. There were occasions when he missed that machine more than he missed her.

He took the mug of weak black liquid through to the front room and sat down in front of the telly. But he didn't turn it on. His mind was too busy, running over thoughts of Ethan and Darren Jubb.

He didn't doubt any of the facts he'd uncovered, but he couldn't yet see the whole pattern. Why exactly had Ethan killed Patrick? Had Darren known what the two lads were up to? Had he masterminded the entire operation himself? And who was the saboteur within the ranks of the police?

Several things didn't quite fit, but he couldn't put his finger on which pieces of the puzzle were still missing. The tasteless coffee didn't help him think, and before long it grew cold and he set it aside.

When the doorbell rang, he couldn't say he was surprised. Some part of him had been expecting it all along. Perhaps that's what he'd been sitting here waiting for.

He opened the front door, half-expecting to see the red Porsche blocking the street like before, but Donna must have put it in the car park up the road. Her hair, half golden, half copper, seemed to blaze as brightly as the streetlamp that illuminated it from behind. Age hadn't tarnished her looks. She was as beautiful tonight as she had ever been.

'Come on in,' he told her.

She followed him into the small front room. She was wearing an emerald green dress with a plunging neckline. The fabric shimmered softly as she removed her overcoat. The room filled quickly with her scent.

She looked around, her gaze taking in the muted wallpaper, the grubby carpet and the mustard sofa with the cigarette burn on one armrest. 'This place is exactly the same as I remember. Nothing's changed, has it?'

'Nothing,' he agreed. And yet, everything had changed. When Donna had last set foot inside the house, Raven's mum had been alive. Donna's surname had still been Craven. And Raven had been a young lad, full of hope for what the future might bring.

He took her coat and hung it on the back of the door.

Donna stood apart from him, uncertain and wary, as if he were a stranger. The anguish she had poured out when he'd arrested Ethan had all been spent, to be replaced by a strange calm. 'Harry says you haven't yet charged Ethan.'

'Not yet.'

'But you're keeping him in custody.'

'We'll keep him until we have enough evidence to charge him. Either for murder or for supplying drugs, or quite possibly both. We have twenty-four hours before we have to make a decision.'

The room was dark apart from the light bleeding in from the streetlamp outside. Donna's face seemed to glow almost luminously in the shadows. 'And will you find the evidence you need?'

'I think so. Yes.'

She took a step towards him. 'Let him go, Tom. I know that you can. You're in charge of the investigation. Just find a reason to release him.'

'I can't do that, Donna. You know I can't.'

'Just find a way, Tom.' She looked up at him. 'I'll leave Darren tonight and be with you. All you have to do is let Ethan go.'

She pressed herself to him, wrapping her arms behind his back. He felt her soft breasts flattening against him. She was ready to give herself, here and now. He had only to say the word. 'Free my son, Tom,' she pleaded. 'Free our son.'

He hardly dared breathe. 'Our son, Donna?'

The possibility that he was the father of Ethan Jubb had occurred to Raven as soon as he'd seen the date of Ethan's birth. Just eight months after he had fled Scarborough. A month before he had left Donna.

'You know that he's ours, Tom. I was four weeks pregnant when you went away. I was going to tell you.'

'What were you going to tell me, Donna? That you loved me?'

She kissed him gently on the lips and he closed his eyes, letting the moment last. 'I've always loved you, Tom. You know I have. And I still do.'

Her voice flowed like honey, but there was nothing sweet about a lie. The possibility that Ethan might be his son was the reason Raven had asked Tony to fast-track the DNA tests through forensics. If the results had come back positive, there would have been an obvious conflict of interest and he would have stepped down from the investigation immediately.

But the lab report had answered the question definitively. Ethan wasn't his. And that could only mean one thing. Donna had been sleeping with Darren even before Raven had left Scarborough. Everything she'd told him was a lie.

He felt no regret, only sadness and resignation. He'd always known that Donna was a liar. She'd come from nothing, desperate to raise herself out of poverty, willing to do whatever it took to secure a better life. If she hadn't married Darren, she would have found some other rich man to give her the security and comfort she craved. She would never have married Raven. Deep down, he'd known it from the very beginning.

He wondered at her willingness to offer herself to him now. Would she really leave Darren in order to keep her son out of prison? Possibly. But not because she loved Raven. Just like Frank Jubb, Donna would do anything to protect her own.

'It's not too late for us to be together,' she said. 'It's never too late to put things right. You ran away because you blamed yourself for your mother's death. But you have to stop blaming yourself, Tom. You have to stop punishing yourself for what happened. It was no one's fault but the drunk driver. You know what I'm saying is true.'

She'd never looked more alluring than she did in that moment, her green eyes wide, her skin ageless in the half light. And she was right about so many things. Yes, he'd run away from Scarborough like a coward. Yes, he blamed himself for his mother's death. Yes, he knew it wasn't really his fault. And, yes, he'd always desired Donna more than any other woman in the world. That was probably why things ultimately hadn't worked out with Lisa. She simply wasn't the right woman. How could she be, when she wasn't Donna?

'You know how to make an attractive offer,' he said. 'But I have some news for you.'

'Oh?'

'I'm not Ethan's father, and I think you already knew that.'

'No, Tom.' Her lower lip trembled. 'That's not true. How could it be?' Her hair shook from side to side, and even now he could almost believe that she was incapable of lying.

He took her hands and unwrapped them gently but firmly from around his waist, holding her at arm's length. 'It's over, Donna. You and me. It's been over for thirty years. It was over as soon as you slept with Darren behind my back.'

The slap on his face came from nowhere, but again, it wasn't unexpected. 'You bastard, Tom!' she shrieked. 'You knew all along!' She slapped him a second time, harder. 'You fucking bastard!'

He watched her as she spun on her heels, grabbing her coat from the hook. The door slammed loudly behind her, making the whole house quake. Before long he heard the roar of the Porsche's engine as it flashed past the window and was gone.

He breathed out deeply. He'd spent more than half a lifetime opening and reopening the same wound. Now it was time for the hurt and the pain to leave him at last, and for the healing to finally begin.

CHAPTER 33

It's the day of the funeral. A beautiful sunny day, as if all is right with the world. Joan Raven was a much-loved woman, and a large crowd has turned out to bid her farewell. Tom watches as the box that holds his mother's broken remains is lowered slowly into the ground. Donna holds his hand and Darren stands next to him. He won't look at his father. Ashes to ashes, dust to dust. Words that do nothing to help Tom understand what has happened to his mother. Afterwards, when everyone has gone, he returns to the house. He wants to be alone, despite Donna's offer to stay with him. He sits in his darkened room staring at nothing until his father's clumsy movements downstairs announce his return. His dad's been drinking all day, so nothing unusual there. Tom stays in his room, hoping for peace on this day of all days. But before long he hears the heavy tread of boots coming up the stairs and his door bursts open. His father stands there, breathing heavily, his face flushed red by drink. 'You killed her,' he says. 'It was all your bloody fault.' 'Get out,' says Tom. 'Leave me alone.' But when Alan Raven's in this mood, it never ends with words. He pushes his way inside and comes at Tom with fists bunched tight. Lashing out, he catches Tom a glancing blow to the cheek.

It's happened before. And it'll keep on happening unless Tom stands up for himself. He balls his own hand into a fist and throws a punch back, catching his father's lip. 'You little bastard,' Alan cries. But Tom's not little anymore, and suddenly all the grief and anger is channelled through his own two fists. He lands a blow to his father's stomach and follows up with another to the face. His father reels and roars, but Tom is younger, faster, and just as strong. Sixteen years of bottled-up rage pour out of him through hands and feet, and before he knows what's happening, his father is doubled up on the floor, his hands covering his bloody face. Tom staggers back, horrified by his own strength, appalled at the violence he has unleashed. His dad rises up, but his fury is all spent. He lurches away, blood dripping from his broken lip, hands clutching his abdomen. And in that moment, Tom comes to a realisation. He must go, now, and never come back. He must leave the town he's called home his entire life. Because if he doesn't, he's going to kill his father.

He was awake before the gulls. He'd been awake for hours.

It wasn't only his father who'd visited him in his broken dreams as he lay tossing and turning in the narrow bed. Donna had been there too, lovely and treacherous. *I'll leave Darren tonight and be with you. All you have to do is let Ethan go.*

He couldn't deny that he'd been tempted by her brazen offer.

But she had betrayed him, and that was the one thing he could never forgive. If he couldn't have trust in a relationship, he'd rather be alone. Darren was welcome to her, and she was welcome to him.

The first gull of the day screeched outside his window announcing that it was time to get up. Sunday morning, but no rest for Raven. He was so close to solving the case now. Yet before he could finally get to the bottom of it, there was more treachery to be unmasked and another confrontation to be had. It would be easier to stay in bed and avoid it, but Raven knew that shying away from necessary conflict never solved anything. He threw the sheets and blankets aside and got out of bed.

The drive over to Scalby was very pleasant this early on a Sunday. The roads were almost empty and there was room for him to manoeuvre the flowing lines of the M6 through even the tightest junctions. Scarborough really wasn't built for such a large car. But if this next meeting went badly, that would no longer be a problem.

He pulled over on Station Road and took in the view. Broad pavements, mature trees and neatly-clipped hedges. Properties set well back from the road. A long driveway led past smooth lawns to a substantial detached house – red-brick, Edwardian perhaps, with a veranda and a conservatory. Its roof was graced by several tall chimneys. A brand-new car – a Jaguar – stood in front of the double garage.

Her husband is a businessman, Becca had insisted. *So there's no mystery about where she gets her money, and there's no reason to suspect her of doing anything wrong.*

Well, he would soon find out, one way or another. He walked up the drive, his shoes crunching the gravel, and rang the doorbell.

The door opened almost immediately. Detective Superintendent Gillian Ellis was clearly a fellow early riser. But she didn't seem best pleased to see him. 'Tom. You should have phoned.'

'Sorry. Can I come in?'

'Well, there's not much point in standing out here, is there?'

He followed her through a square hallway with parquet flooring and a polished wooden staircase. The interior of the house was finished in a minimalist style, with large frameless canvases fixed to the white walls. Raven paused to examine one, but was unable to tell what the bright splashes of paint were supposed to represent.

'My husband collects them,' remarked Gillian. 'Come on through to the drawing room. Can I offer you something to drink?'

'Nothing, thank you,' said Raven.

The drawing room was a large space with a triple aspect, looking out onto green lawns and shrubs. It was largely empty, with just a few leather chairs placed strategically beneath tall floor-standing lamps that resembled metal insects. A single bookcase contained a collection of hardbacks, and some kind of modern orchestral music was playing from the integrated speakers fitted into the ceiling. Gillian turned the music off and sat down. She gestured for Raven to take the seat opposite.

'So, how can I help you, Tom? Is it about Ethan Jubb?'

Raven had called the previous day to fill her in on the progress that had been made. She had sounded pleased by the arrest. But had that been an act? Someone within the department had stolen the old case files. Someone determined to sabotage the current investigation.

'I wanted to show you something.' He produced the newspaper article that he'd clipped out of *The Scarborough News* and passed it to her.

Gillian slipped on a pair of reading glasses and inspected it briefly. 'Well, Tom, my husband and I attend regular charity events. It's no secret, but it isn't something I boast about. Why are you bringing it to my attention?'

'Because Darren Jubb also attended that particular event. Perhaps you spoke with him? Perhaps you've spoken to him before, at other events?'

Gillian's steely expression gave nothing away. 'Perhaps I have. What of it?'

'Darren Jubb has someone working to help him. Someone within the department.'

She stared silently at him for a moment. 'That's one hell of an accusation to make, Tom. I hope you know what you're talking about.'

Raven hoped so too. If not, he was making a career-limiting mistake and would soon be heading down the M1 to London. 'The case files from the Max Hunt investigation have been removed from the archives.'

'Is there no record of who took them?'

'None.'

Gillian turned to gaze out of the nearest window. Outside, a squirrel scampered quickly across the lawn. 'There could be an entirely innocent explanation for that. It might simply be an administrative error. Such things can happen.'

'They can.'

She turned back and fixed her eyes on him. 'This is a very serious allegation you're making. Do you have any more evidence of sabotage?'

He shrugged. 'Two men followed me down to the harbour and gave me a beating. They didn't try to steal anything. They were simply delivering a warning – for me to stay away.'

'From Darren Jubb?'

'I think so.'

'And yet you arrested his son.'

'I'm not easily warned off.'

'I can see that, Tom.' Gillian brushed a stray hair away from her face. She was wearing black trousers and a cream, cashmere sweater. Like the house itself, her clothing was immaculate.

'So, what precisely are you saying, Tom? That someone within the police is being paid by Darren Jubb to protect him and his family? That they stole case files to hold back the investigation? And that the person in question is me?' She raised her eyebrows, challenging him to confirm it.

'Is it you?'

She leaned forward, the chair tilting as she shifted her weight. 'You've got a bloody nerve, Tom. I could kick you out just for suggesting that I'm corrupt. I've already given you two warnings. This time you've really overstepped the mark.'

'I need to know I can trust you.'

'You're not scared of anything, are you?' A faint hint of a smile appeared on her lips. 'That's why I took you on. I had a gut feeling about you.' She nodded with satisfaction.

'Well, you could be right. Someone in the department might be in the pay of Darren Jubb. But I can assure you that it's not me.'

'Can you prove it?'

She gave a short deep-throated laugh. 'You're like a ferret, aren't you? Relentless. You don't stop until you catch your prey. I like that. Well, here's your proof, if you're willing to believe it.' She passed the newspaper article back to him. 'I didn't speak to Darren Jubb at this dinner. I didn't speak to him because he wasn't there.'

'Wasn't there? With respect ma'am, how can you be so certain of that?'

'Because my husband is the secretary of Scarborough Rotary Club, which organised the event. He sent out the invitations and kept a record of everyone who attended. And I can assure you that Darren Jubb was invited but didn't show up.'

'But that was Jubb's alibi for the time of the murder,' said Raven. 'One of my team checked it out.'

'In that case,' said Gillian, 'I suggest that you go and find that person right away, and ask them the same questions you asked me.'

CHAPTER 34

DC Dan Bennett left the newsagents, clutching his pint of milk and a copy of the Sunday paper. As usual, he turned straight to the back pages and the racing results. A horse he'd quite fancied had come in first in the 2.15 at Doncaster the previous day and he could have kicked himself for not putting a few quid on it. Still, there was another race coming up that afternoon at Ripon, and he might risk a bob or two on that.

It was his grandpa who'd first got him interested in horses. Dan hadn't been a copper then, just a kid, ten years old and growing up in a post-industrial city in the north of England. Bradford. Population half a million. Unemployment rate 10%. The city was still reeling following the closure of the textile mills and not quite certain what to turn to next. Just like Dan, knowing that he wanted to do something with his life, just not sure what.

'Never mind all that,' his grandpa had told him. 'A boy of your age shouldn't be worrying about the future. Come with me to the horses. Have a little fun. There's no harm in it. Just don't tell your mum.'

Although Dan wasn't legally old enough to gamble, his

grandpa had given him a pound to bet on the Grand National, and offered to place the money for him. It would be their little secret. All Dan had to do was choose the name of the horse. He chose *Lucky Star,* because it sounded like a winner. Grandpa tried to explain to him that "high odds" meant it was less likely to win than "low odds", but Dan had a good feeling about the horse and stuck with his choice. That afternoon they'd sat on Grandpa's old and shabby sofa eating crisps and watching with bated breath while the horses galloped around the course at Aintree. It was, quite simply, the most exciting thrill that Dan had ever experienced. The sheer power of the animals, the stomping of their hooves on the ground, the impossibly high hedges, and the spectacular falls when horse and rider tumbled head over heels in a tangle of legs and dust. And just as Dan had expected, *Lucky Star* romped home to victory, taking the commentator by surprise just as much as his grandpa.

'You've got a talent for spotting winners,' the old man told him, and Dan knew that he'd found his passion at last. They went straight down to the bookies to collect his winnings. Fifty quid. It was more money than he'd ever had in his life.

But over the years the horses weren't kind to Dan. His initial luck seemed to desert him, and he followed it up with a string of losses. By the time he reached eighteen, he'd lost much of his interest in racing. It was too much like hard work. Studying form, keeping abreast of all the runners, then hoping and praying that the one you'd picked wouldn't have an off day. When he moved to Scarborough, he found a much better way to spend his time and money.

Slot machines. The town was packed with them.

Now it wasn't just the chance to win big that lured him in and kept him coming back. It was the glitter, the sounds, the flashing lights. Even the names of the arcades along the seafront gave him a buzz. Silver Dollar. Coney Island. Casino Royale. Scarborough wasn't exactly Las Vegas, but it was the closest thing this side of the Pennines.

Dan loved to play the machines. There were so many different ways to win. He studied all the tactics and learned which games and strategies gave him the best chance of coming out on top. He wasn't like one of those daft punters you saw, blindly feeding money into the slot and trusting to luck. Dan knew the average return rate and volatility of each type of machine, and understood the bonus game features like the back of his hand. He was primed to win, and win big.

Yet somehow, his luck let him down again.

At first the losses were modest. He was surprised when his bank contacted him to say that his account was overdrawn. But then the credit card balances started piling up too.

It was surprising how quickly you could lose money when fortune turned against you.

Soon he was struggling to pay the interest on his debts. And that was when Frank Jubb came to his rescue.

Dan had noticed the old man hanging around behind the counter at the arcade, but had never paid much attention to him. But it seemed that Frank had been studying him.

'Hello, son. Not your lucky day? That's how it goes sometimes. Maybe I can do something to help.'

'Like what?' asked Dan. He'd been so naïve back then.

'Come into my office and we'll have a little chat,' said Frank.

Soon Dan's debts were sorted, and he had a new side hustle. It was easy enough, keeping a watch for any police matters that might affect Frank's family. Frank's son, Darren, owned a nightclub in town. Vertigo. It was a place that Dan knew very well. There were sometimes complaints from the clientele or from nearby residents. Low level stuff. Noise. Fights. Alleged breaches of licensing. Dan helped to make those problems go away, or at least give Frank a heads-up if trouble was brewing.

It had all seemed harmless, until Patrick Lofthouse

showed up dead.

Now Dan was in far too deep, but there was no way to keep his head above water other than to keep swimming.

All he'd ever really wanted was to win a few quid so he could pay for his lifestyle. He liked his clothes. Designer labels, expensive suits, smart shoes, a huge collection of ties, a nice watch that looked almost like a genuine Rolex… a guy had to take care of his appearance if he wanted to impress the ladies. And Dan knew how to make a good first impression. Usually he had no problem attracting women, or "chasing skirt" as his grandpa would have called it, but despite his best efforts, the girl he really wanted remained tantalisingly aloof. For some reason, no matter how hard he tried with DC Jess Barraclough, she just didn't seem interested. Well, it was her loss. He had plenty of other takers.

Perhaps he would put a couple of quid on that horse that afternoon. Heaven knows, he was long overdue a change in his luck.

*

Raven considered phoning Becca and asking her to join him at Dan's house, but in light of their previous disagreements he decided to call Jess instead. Thankfully, she had no problem coming out, despite it being a Sunday.

She met him outside the property that Dan rented on Cromwell Terrace. A row of three-storey terraced houses, some with rooftop loft conversions. Judging by the number of wheelie bins outside, the houses had all been converted into apartments.

Raven was hoping to find Dan at home, but a long ring on the doorbell produced no response.

'Dan? I just saw him popping out ten minutes ago,' said a young woman coming out through the front door. 'Is he in trouble?'

'Perhaps we'll just come inside and wait for him,' said Raven, holding the door open. He and Jess made their way up to the top floor, where they waited on the landing outside the door to Dan's flat.

Jess appeared anxious. 'Do you really think Dan would sabotage the investigation, sir? I know he can be a bit of a creep at times, but...'

'Let's see what he has to say,' said Raven.

A few minutes later the front door of the building opened and they heard footsteps climbing the stairs. Before long the footsteps reached the top landing and Dan's familiar well-dressed form came into view. He stared at Raven and Jess open-mouthed.

'Hello, Dan. Nothing to worry about,' said Raven. 'We'd just like to ask you a few questions. And we'd like to have a look around your flat, if you don't mind. That isn't going to be a problem, is it?'

The newspaper and carton of milk that Dan was carrying fell to the floor and he turned on his heel and ran.

'Shit,' said Raven. He set off down the stairs in pursuit, but the steps played hell with his leg and he soon began to struggle.

'Let me, sir.' Jess slipped past him and began to run downstairs at speed. Raven was surprised at how fast she was on her feet.

By the time he reached the ground floor and emerged from the building, Jess had almost caught up with Dan. He watched in admiration as she sprinted after him then dragged him to the ground, before snapping a pair of cuffs onto his wrists behind his back.

'Ow! Bloody hell!' cried Dan. 'That hurts!'

Raven went over to her. 'Well done, Jess. Good work.'

'Thank you, sir.'

He turned then to the fallen man, who lay sprawled in the middle of the pavement. 'Quit moaning, Dan. It's time for you to start talking. Darren Jubb's alibi – did you cover for him?'

Dan's face was pressed to the ground, his cheek grazed from the fall. Jess rolled him onto his side so that he could speak more easily.

'Darren was invited to the dinner,' he said sullenly, glancing up at Raven. 'He should have been there.'

'But he wasn't, was he? And you knew that.'

'Yes, I'm sorry, sir.' Dan had obviously decided that it was time to come clean. In fact, he sounded almost relieved to talk about what he'd done. 'I didn't think it was important. I just figured it would be easier all round if Jubb had a solid alibi. I never imagined he would turn out to be a suspect in the murder of his future son-in-law.'

Raven felt only disgust for the young constable. 'You're a disgrace, Dan. Do you know that? I hope Darren Jubb was paying you a lot of money for your services, because you're going to pay a hefty price. You've ruined your own future, and you've let everyone down.'

'I'm really sorry,' Dan said. 'But it wasn't Darren Jubb I was working for. It was his father.'

'Frank?' Raven couldn't say he was too surprised at the revelation. Frank Jubb had never been afraid to break the rules. People like Frank didn't even think the rules applied to them. 'Was it you who scratched my car?' he asked.

Dan nodded. 'I'm sorry about that too, sir. It was after you went to Full Sutton to interview Lewis Briggs. I just thought I would send a message. You know… to back off. I didn't want you reopening that old case. I was afraid of what you might find.'

'And so you stole the case files.'

'I just took them for safe keeping. They're in my flat.'

'I thought they might be. And it was you at the harbour too, wasn't it?' Raven had known there was something familiar about the voice of one of his attackers. Dan had tried to disguise it, but that West Yorkshire accent was hard to hide.

'I didn't mean for you to get hurt,' said Dan. 'The plan was just to scare you. Shake you up a bit. But that guy Frank sent along with me…'

'Save it,' said Raven. 'I don't want to hear your excuses. You betrayed your own kind, Dan. Even Frank Jubb didn't stoop that low. Dan Bennett, I am arresting you on suspicion of conspiracy to commit misconduct in public office and attempting to pervert the course of justice.' Raven read Dan his rights, a formality given that Dan was a serving police officer and knew exactly what his rights were. But he had known his duty too, and had failed to perform it.

Raven nodded to Jess. 'Get him out of my sight. I don't want to see him again.'

CHAPTER 35

Dan's unveiling and his subsequent arrest had cleared the air between Raven and Becca.

'You were right about Detective Superintendent Ellis,' he told her when she arrived later that morning. 'She wasn't to blame for the missing files.'

'I'm glad,' said Becca.

'So am I.'

She glanced awkwardly around his office, unable to meet his eyes. 'I'm sorry if I was a little… abrasive about the way I spoke to you.'

'Not at all,' said Raven. 'I need a sergeant who's not afraid to challenge me. And you did well persuading Leah Briggs to admit that Ethan was paying her to keep quiet.'

'Thanks. How are your bruises?'

'Developing nicely.' He grinned. 'But thanks to Jess I didn't need to give chase to Dan this morning.'

He looked through the window into the incident room beyond and was pleased by what he saw. All his team had come into work now, despite it being a Sunday. Becca, Jess and Tony. Finally, he knew he could depend on them all.

'By the way,' said Becca, 'I've got a recommendation

for a guy who can fix your car.' She passed him a name and number that she'd written down.

'Cheers. I owe you one.'

'Just be careful. My brother's recommendations don't always turn out to be reliable.'

'I'll bear that in mind.'

The investigation was moving at a pace now. A key found when Ethan's room was searched had led to the discovery of a stash of drugs in an empty holiday property. The haul was considerable and Ethan had been charged with a variety of drug-related offences. Frank Jubb had also been arrested on suspicion of bribing another person and attempting to pervert the course of justice. Harry Hood's services were in high demand, but he'd looked defeated when Raven had faced him across the interview room. If this was a game, then he had played and lost.

But there was still no direct evidence to link Ethan Jubb to Patrick's murder. In fact, Ethan continued to protest his innocence, denying that he had ever owned a gun. According to him, it was Patrick who had arranged the murder of Max Hunt, sourcing the weapon and paying Lewis Briggs to carry out the shooting, but Ethan who'd had the job of cleaning up afterwards and buying Lewis's silence. If what Ethan said was true, and he had never owned a firearm, then Patrick may well have been murdered with his own gun. But who had pulled the trigger, and why?

There was no indication that Darren Jubb was involved in any way, but Raven was keeping an open mind.

'All right,' he called to his team, 'Let's have a brainstorming session.'

With DC Dan Bennett gone, it was much quieter in the incident room. Raven had stopped off on the way back to load up with croissants and energy drinks in the hope that a boost would help them come up with ideas. They needed a breakthrough and they needed one quickly.

There were a good number of suspects on the whiteboard now. Raven reviewed them in turn. 'All right, first up is Ethan Jubb. We now know that Ethan and Patrick were business partners, bringing in drugs from Holland and selling them here. If Ethan is to be believed, it was Patrick who planned and arranged the murder of Max Hunt, paying Lewis Briggs to carry out the killing. Ethan and Patrick sailed to Vlissingen on the seventeenth of October, precisely one week before he was murdered. It's quite possible that Ethan decided to kill Patrick so that he could profit from the shipment himself, or because they had some kind of falling out. Ethan had access to his father's boat, *Sea Dreams*, and we know that Patrick was killed at sea and his body thrown overboard.'

'Most likely with the murder weapon and his mobile phone too,' said Becca.

'Right, which brings us to the question of why Patrick sent a message to his fiancée, Scarlett Jubb, telling her that he was going to visit his friend, Shane Denton, in Redcar.'

'Because he didn't want her to know that he was going out on the boat with Ethan?' suggested Jess.

'Perhaps,' said Raven. 'Or did he in fact intend to go and see Shane Denton, but was killed before he could go?'

'Sir,' said Tony, 'do you think that Shane might be involved in the killing in some way?'

'We can't rule it out,' said Raven. 'Shane was close to Patrick and was also involved in drugs. In fact, it's quite probable that it was Shane who first introduced Patrick to cocaine. And he's been unable to provide an alibi for the time of the shooting.'

'But there's nothing specifically to tie him in,' said Becca. 'What about Darren Jubb?'

Raven turned his attention to the photograph of his long-term rival. Whatever his personal feelings about Darren, it was crucial to set them aside now and examine the evidence dispassionately. 'Darren is quite clearly linked with all the players in the case. He's Ethan's father and was going to become Patrick's father-in-law. Also, it was his boat that was used to import the drugs. Thirdly, although we initially ruled out the possibility of Darren having any direct role in the shooting because of his comprehensive alibi, with Dan Bennett's arrest all that has been tossed aside. We just can't say where Darren was at the time of Patrick's death.'

Raven studied the whiteboard. 'And then there's Frank Jubb. It was Frank who bought Dan's services, paying him to remove evidence and trying to intimidate me. It's easy to picture Frank as a "godfather" figure ruling over a criminal family. Frank claims that he was working at the amusement arcade on the evening of the murder, but we still have to verify that.'

There was one final photograph on the board, and although it seemed unlikely, Raven couldn't ignore it. 'Patrick's father, Gordon Lofthouse, was aware of his son's involvement in drugs, and strongly disapproved. He had also caught Patrick stealing money from the family firm. We know that Gordon confronted Patrick on the morning of his death, challenging him over his illegal activities and making a threat.'

'But sir,' said Jess, 'could he really have killed his own son?'

'Perhaps not intentionally,' said Raven, 'But the man has a temper that he struggles to control. I've seen it for myself.'

'And he owns a boat, too,' added Tony. '*Kittiwake.* We might be completely wrong about *Sea Dreams* being the vessel in which Patrick was killed.'

'It's possible,' agreed Jess. 'CSI didn't find any traces of blood on board Darren's boat.'

'So, where do we go from here?' asked Becca, voicing the question they were all thinking.

Raven hated to admit it, but he just didn't know.

'There is one thing,' said Jess. 'I looked again at the dates when Patrick stayed at Gisborough Hall. And I cross-checked them with Scarlett Jubb's Instagram.'

Raven looked at her blankly. 'I don't see the connection.'

'It's just that in the months leading up to Patrick's

death, Scarlett was busy with wedding preparations. She visited bridal fairs, wedding dress shops, cake bakers and nearby hotels, with a view to choosing a venue. Everywhere she went she posted it online. I think that was probably the main purpose of her visits, to be honest.'

Becca nodded. 'Scarlett breathes self-promotion the way the rest of us breathe oxygen. She never does anything without documenting it for her fans to "like" and "comment".'

'Anyway,' continued Jess, 'in September she visited Gisborough Hall. It's a popular venue for weddings. Fabulous for photos.'

'I can imagine,' said Raven.

'And it just happens that Patrick was booked into the hotel on the same date.'

Raven pondered the information. 'Did they go together?'

'It's possible, I suppose. But take a look at Scarlett's Instagram from the visit.'

Raven watched as Jess thumbed her phone with a dexterity that he could never hope to master. She found what she was looking for and passed the phone for him to see.

The screen was filled by a photograph of Scarlett beaming in front of the hotel. The place looked like a stunning venue for a wedding. The country house made a fine backdrop and the grounds were clearly magnificent. But its relevance still escaped him. 'What am I looking at?'

'Well, for one thing, Patrick isn't in the photo.'

'That doesn't prove anything. He might have taken it.'

'Yes, except look at the car parked next to Scarlett.'

Raven's eyes homed in on the black Range Rover at her side. 'It's Darren Jubb's car.'

'Right,' said Jess. 'So I'm thinking that Darren took her there, not Patrick. Instead, Patrick was there separately, staying with–'

Raven completed the sentence for her, his synapses finally making the necessary connection. 'His Iseult. His forbidden lover.'

'Exactly.'

Raven snapped his fingers. 'Let's go round to Jubb's house right now.'

CHAPTER 36

It was a very subdued Darren Jubb who met Raven at the door to his home. He seemed hardly able to summon up the will even to sneer. 'What is it now?' he asked. 'Haven't you done enough damage already?'

'Can we come in?' asked Raven.

Darren shrugged and led the way along the hall into the lounge. Even the bling decoration of the house seemed to have lost its sparkle. Darren slumped on the sofa after pouring himself a large whisky. He didn't offer Raven a drink this time.

Raven remained standing, with Becca and Jess at his side. Tony had stayed behind at the station in case any matters needed seeing to.

'When are you going to release Ethan and Frank?' asked Darren.

'Frank can probably come home tomorrow,' said Raven. 'But we'll be keeping Ethan in custody. He might not be free again for a very long time.'

'So you got your revenge at last, then,' said Darren. 'You're a real bastard, Tom.'

Raven shook his head. 'I never wanted revenge, only

justice.'

'Well, I hope you're happy.'

Raven waited while Darren took a sip of his whisky before beginning his questions. 'You took Scarlett to Gisborough Hall on September the twenty-eighth. Is that correct?'

'I took her there,' confirmed Darren. 'Since I was footing the bill for the wedding, I wanted to see where my money was going. But I don't remember the date. If you say it was the twenty-eighth, I'll take your word for it. Are you going to arrest me for that, now?'

Raven ignored the snide remark. 'Did Patrick go with you?'

'No, it was just me and Scarlett.'

'I see. But while you were at the hotel, did you happen to see Patrick?'

Darren seemed annoyed by the question. 'I don't know what you're talking about.'

'I think you do, Darren.' Raven paused. 'Was that when you first found out that Patrick was sleeping with your wife?'

Darren threw a furious look in Raven's direction. 'What? Is this your idea of a sick joke?'

'It's no joke. Patrick was booked into the hotel that same night. He was staying there with his mistress. When his body was recovered, he was wearing a ring with the names Tristan and Iseult engraved on it. Does that sound familiar? Does Donna own a similar ring?'

Darren shook his head. 'No!' But a dread fear had entered his eyes. His gaze didn't waver from Raven's for an instant.

'Perhaps we can ask Donna herself,' suggested Raven. 'Is she at home now?'

'No. She's gone out.'

'Then do you know where she keeps her jewellery?'

'Of course I do.'

'Do you mind if we take a look at it?'

Darren's mind seemed to be churning furiously, but

after a moment he came to a decision. 'If it will put an end to this ridiculous notion, then no, I don't mind. I'll show you where it is.'

He put his whisky on a side table and led the way upstairs. Feeling slightly awkward, Raven followed him into the master bedroom. It was hard to keep from looking at the bed Darren shared with Donna.

'This is where she keeps her jewellery,' said Darren, marching over to a dressing table in an adjoining room. The table was arranged with several boxes, a matching set, all inlaid with mother-of-pearl. He stood back. 'Take a look if you want.'

Raven nodded to Becca and Jess, and they began to search through the boxes, removing each item for inspection. Donna's collection of earrings, necklaces and other items was extensive, but it didn't take long before Becca found what they were looking for. She held a gold ring carefully in her gloved hand.

'*Tristan & Iseult*,' she read. 'It's identical to the ring that Patrick was wearing.'

Darren sat down on the bed, a stunned expression on his face. 'I've never seen it before. She never wears it.'

'Perhaps she was ashamed of her relationship with Patrick,' suggested Becca. 'Or afraid of being caught out. Perhaps she only wore it when she was alone with him.'

Raven studied Darren carefully. The man's face was ashen, just as it had been when he'd first learned about Patrick's death.

'You didn't know Donna was sleeping with Patrick, did you?' said Raven quietly.

'I had absolutely no idea.'

'Where is Donna now?'

'She went out with Scarlett.'

'Scarlett?' A fresh idea was taking form in Raven's mind. 'Darren, where were you on the evening Patrick was killed? You claimed that you were at the charity dinner in town, but we know that you weren't.'

Darren looked set to refuse to answer, but then his last

resistance seemed to crumble. 'I was with Scarlett. She phoned me up just as I was getting ready to go out. She needed a lift, so I drove over to her where she said to meet her, and I brought her home. By the time I got back here, it was too late to go to the dinner. In truth, I wasn't bothered. Events like that bore me.'

'Where did you go to collect Scarlett?'

'It was over on the other side of town.'

'Near Cloughton?'

'Yes. How did you know?'

Raven exchanged a glance with Becca and Jess. They had clearly guessed the same as him. 'Darren, did Scarlett explain what she was doing there? Without her car?'

'She told me Patrick had dropped her there. He'd gone dashing off to meet some friend of his in Redcar. I was really angry with him, to be honest.'

'And you didn't think that it was worth mentioning any of this to the police?'

'Why would it have been? What's Scarlett got to do with any of this?'

'Darren,' said Raven. 'I need you to tell me exactly where Scarlett and Donna have gone. I need you to tell me now.'

CHAPTER 37

'I can come with you, if you like, sir,' said Jess.

Raven considered her offer briefly before dismissing it. Although he had no doubt whatsoever about Jess's fitness and bravery, he wasn't willing to put her at risk. This was a job he had to do by himself. 'Thanks, but I'll handle it. You stay here and help coordinate operations on the ground.'

While Becca liaised with the coastguard, Raven prepared himself to leave. Darren's revelation that Donna and Scarlett had gone down to the harbour changed everything. The harbourmaster had confirmed that *Sea Dreams* had already left its mooring, heading out to sea. Raven was in no doubt that Scarlett was on board, and that she had taken Donna as her hostage.

Darren was sitting in a daze on the leather sofa. 'But Scarlett couldn't possibly have killed Patrick,' he murmured. 'She loved him. Why would she want to hurt him?'

'Because she found out that he was having a secret affair with Donna,' said Raven.

Darren shook his head. 'But even so, why kill him?'

'Scarlett's perfect world was shattered,' explained Raven patiently. 'After making such a big deal of her wedding, how could she face her millions of followers with the news that her fiancé had cheated on her with her own mother?'

But Darren seemed incapable of absorbing this latest shock. Raven left him and headed outside. The coastguard was sending a helicopter to meet him, and it was scheduled to land on the open field at the top of Oliver's Mount. Raven climbed into his car and set off.

He had already returned briefly to the police station to collect a gun – A Glock 17, familiar to him during his time in the Met. As an Authorised Firearms Officer, he was permitted, unlike most British police officers, to carry and use a weapon when the situation required it. Scarlett had used a gun to kill Patrick, and the murder weapon had not yet been recovered. It was possible that she still had it in her possession, and it would be folly to go into a hostage situation unarmed.

His last few questions about Patrick's death had now all been answered. It hadn't been Ethan who deleted the GPS records from the boat, but Scarlett. She was the real brains of the Jubb family, and had obviously inherited the ability of both her parents to manipulate and deceive. Raven recalled how convincingly she'd appeared to mourn Patrick's death, playing the part of the innocent victim.

Even Donna had been taken in by her act, apparently believing that it was Ethan who had carried out the killing. And Donna didn't seem to have taken long to decide where her loyalty lay, choosing to side unconditionally with her son and to forget about her dead lover. Just as she had once picked Darren instead of him. No one could accuse Donna of being indecisive. But in this case her unwavering support for her family had come back to haunt her. Scarlett had taken her, and if Raven didn't succeed in stopping her, Donna would become her daughter's next victim.

It was only a short drive to the top of the mount, following the curve of Weaponness Park as it sloped upward. The car's powerful engine roared as Raven accelerated uphill. This was where he had come as a teenager to watch the motorcycle street races that were held on the steep, twisting roads that covered the sides of the hill leading up to the summit. The road soon became a single lane track lined by woodland to either side, before breaking out in a hairpin bend onto the flat peak of the hill. The views through Raven's side window gave onto miles of green countryside, but he kept his eyes firmly in front. Ahead stood the metal frame tower of the television and radio mast, and next to it the town's war memorial, a stone obelisk bearing the names of service personnel and civilians killed in two world wars and the Korean War. Raven left his car by the small café named Olivers on the Mount and walked the short distance to the open expanse of grass that covered most of the hilltop.

A distant thudding heralded the approach of the helicopter. It was coming from the south, following the line of the coast. Raven looked up at the sky. Although the day had begun fine, dark clouds were piling up on the horizon and the wind was picking up. The grass on the mount stirred in the breeze.

He watched as the helicopter drew closer. A Sikorsky S-92, scrambled from the nearby base at Humberside. The search and rescue helicopter was painted in red, white and blue livery. Raven waited for it to land, standing well back from the spinning rotor blades. The door of the copter opened and the co-pilot ran across the grass to meet him.

'DCI Raven?'

'That's me.'

'I need to warn you that a storm is forecast. We can't fly under storm conditions. If the wind gets too strong we'll have to turn back.'

'Then let's bloody well get this bird in the air before it arrives.'

The man helped him get suited up. Raven climbed on board and into one of the side-facing seats bolted to the fuselage. Inside the aircraft, the noise from the whirling rotors was deafening. Speech was possible only with the aid of headphones and a mic.

The chief pilot turned back to greet him. Raven was slightly surprised to hear a woman's voice over his headphones. 'Captain Lauren Booth. Have you ever flown in a helicopter before, Chief Inspector?'

Raven nodded. 'In Bosnia, 1994. We used Royal Navy Sea Kings for transport and evacuation.' An image flashed through his mind. Shouts, men running, loading him onto a stretcher. He was taken from the battlefield and flown by copter to the field hospital in Vitez before being airlifted back to the UK. Farewell, Bosnia.

She acknowledged him with a tilt of her head. 'I flew Merlins in Iraq until 2009. All four of us are ex-RAF. Welcome aboard, Raven.'

The S-92 was bigger than a Sea King. A twin-engine medium capacity craft with room for around twenty passengers as well as a crew of four. In addition to the pilot and co-pilot, a paramedic winchman and a winch operator completed the team.

Raven strapped himself in and a minute later they were airborne. The Sikorsky lifted upward, dipped its nose and turned out towards the sea. Already he could feel the wind buffeting its side.

From this height, the view over the coast was spectacular. Both North and South bays were laid out before him, the ruined stump of the castle on the central headland above the harbour and pier. His own tiny cottage was down there somewhere, but he hardly had time to look before they were out over open water.

'The coastguard is tracking the vessel by radar,' explained Captain Booth. 'Its present position is approximately six nautical miles northeast. It's heading in the direction of Whitby.'

Raven had no idea what Scarlett was planning. He was sure of only one thing – that escape wasn't on her mind.

'Wind speed twenty knots,' said the co-pilot. 'Wave height 2.5 metres. It's going to be a bumpy ride. I hope you've got sea legs, Raven.'

Raven rubbed his right thigh. It still hurt a little from the beating Dan and his mate had given him, not to mention his old war wound. But now wasn't the time to mention that. 'I don't mind a few bumps,' he said.

*

The helicopter made good progress, flying out over the sea away from the coast. Already a dark speck was in view, slowly resolving itself into the form of a boat. But the wind was rising all the time and they were heading directly into rolling storm clouds.

The voice of the co-pilot in Raven's ear gave a running commentary. 'Wind speed increasing to thirty knots. Visibility one nautical mile. Descend to 500 feet.'

The helicopter dropped to a lower altitude, beneath the darkening clouds. The gusts eased off, but now the waves on the sea seemed to grow higher. At Raven's side, the winch operator looked out nervously across the watery expanse of the North Sea.

Raven pushed aside all thoughts of bad weather. He needed to focus on the objective of his mission – to get himself onto the boat and diffuse the hostage situation. He would need all his wits to negotiate with Scarlett and rescue Donna. He checked the Glock once more before securing it in his holster. Hopefully Scarlett wouldn't be armed and he wouldn't need the weapon, but he had to be prepared for anything.

The helicopter closed in steadily on the boat until it was almost directly overhead. The captain manoeuvred the Sikorsky into position, hovering some thirty feet above the surface of the water. Close up, the condition of the sea was made frighteningly clear. Waves of up to ten feet raced across the surface, their white caps driven on by the strengthening wind.

There was no sign of either Scarlett or Donna onboard *Sea Dreams*. They would be in the safety of the cabin, no doubt. To stand on deck in these conditions would be suicidal.

A fresh gust blasted the helicopter, shifting it to the side, and the voice of the co-pilot cut across Raven's headphones. 'The wind's getting too strong. We'll have to turn back.'

'No!' shouted Raven. 'A woman's life is at stake. Now get me down there!'

Once again, the captain moved the helicopter back into place, directly above the boat, and held it there.

Raven left his seat and peered out through the open door of the helicopter. Down below, the sea was a boiling mass. A wave broke across the bow of the boat, spraying white foam over the deck. Scarlett had sailed into the heart of the storm, whether by intention or accident, doubling the challenge that Raven now faced. He had never carried out a sea rescue before, let alone during a storm, and certainly not in a hostage situation. Then again, he thought with a wry grin, Donna had never made his life easy.

It was time to go. The winchman made one final check of his harness before giving him a thumbs-up and beginning the procedure of lowering him down.

A cold gust blasted Raven as he left the safety of the helicopter and began his descent. The cable that held him wound slowly down as he dangled helplessly in his harness. He looked back up briefly as the open door of the helicopter receded. There was no time for second thoughts now. Beneath his feet the sea was alive, and *Sea Dreams* rode it like a cork, bobbing helplessly up and down.

Rain pelted his face and the cable twisted as the wind swung him from side to side. Lightning forked in the darkened sky, freezing a monochrome image of the yacht on the back of his retina. But inch by inch he was descending, drawing closer to the deck of the boat. There was still no sign of anyone on board.

As he drew close, he became aware of a new problem. The deck was dropping down and rising up by as much as twelve feet as each new wave coursed beneath the boat's hull. At some point, he was going to have to release the harness and drop the last few feet.

The Sikorsky was drifting in the high winds, despite the captain's best efforts to hold it steady, and *Sea Dreams* was being pounded by the waves. Raven waited until he was sure the deck was beneath him, and then released the harness.

He fell, perhaps six feet, and landed.

Sharp pain lanced through his right leg and he rolled, sliding and tumbling along the wet decking as the boat dipped on the downside of a wave. He grabbed hold of a handrail just at the edge of the deck, and held himself steady while he regained his poise. The boat rose and fell, taking his stomach with it each time it went, and cold seawater washed against his face.

Slowly, not relaxing his grip on the rail for an instant, he began to haul himself towards the cabin. His leg was injured, he was certain of that, but just how badly it was impossible to tell. Even if he'd been fully fit, he doubted he'd be able to stand upright for more than a few seconds in these conditions.

The boat had turned sideways to the oncoming waves and was being battered hard. Waiting for the deck to tilt in the right direction, he released his grip on the handrail and staggered to the door at the rear of the cabin. Then he unholstered his gun, gripping it in two hands, before kicking open the door and half-tumbling into the cabin as the boat lurched once again.

'Tom!' shouted Donna as he regained his balance. She was seated at the front of the boat, her hands on the steering wheel, her eyes wide with terror.

Scarlett stood next to her, one hand gripping a hand rail, the other holding a gun. As Tom stumbled inside, she turned the weapon in his direction. 'Drop it!' she screamed. 'Or I'll shoot both of you!'

Raven had just moments in which to judge the situation.

For a tense few seconds, he and Scarlett pointed their weapons at one another. But then his military training kicked in automatically. He was the professional ex-soldier and she was a scared young woman whose perfect life had careened out of control. She was liable to make a rash decision at any second. It was up to him to try and defuse the situation. And, besides, he was here to arrest her, not kill her. He preferred to bring his suspects to trial alive and well. And there was Donna to think of. Donna who had lied to him, but who nevertheless didn't deserve to die like this. He really had no choice.

'All right,' he said. Slowly raising one arm, he held the gun out to the side. Then, struggling to keep his balance, he lowered it carefully to the floor and pushed it aside.

'Sit over there!' commanded Scarlett, gesturing to a leather seat at the side of the cabin. 'Don't say a word, and don't move a muscle!'

*

The boat was out of control, each wave pummelling it like a sledgehammer and threatening to turn it onto its side. Through the window opposite, an enormous wave came into view, surging towards them and towering above the boat. For a second Raven thought it would engulf the yacht entirely, swallowing it whole like a whale devouring a mouthful of fish, but *Sea Dreams* rose up to meet it, and the oncoming wave crashed against its side, tilting it forty-five degrees before it passed beneath the hull and the boat plunged down the other side.

'We have to turn the boat into the wind,' he said. 'The waves will flip us over if we carry on like this.'

'I told you to shut up!' yelled Scarlett, but then she turned the gun back on Donna. 'Do as he says! Turn the boat into the waves.'

In her dress and heels, Donna looked ill-equipped to sail a boat in any weather, let alone a storm, but she struggled with the wheel, trying to drive the boat around. It started to turn, but then the next wave arrived and pushed it right back to where it had been before. Water sloshed across the deck, spattering foam against the window.

Donna gritted her teeth and tried again. Each oncoming wave did its best to force the boat back into place, but slowly it began to turn until it was riding the sea, up the face and down the backs of the huge swelling waves.

Scarlett drew out her phone, snapped a photo of her mother at the helm, and one of Raven in his seat, and slipped it back inside her bag. The gun didn't leave her hand for a second.

'Is that Patrick's gun?' asked Raven.

She said nothing, just turned it in his direction.

'It must be either Patrick's or Ethan's,' he continued, 'and Ethan told me he didn't own a gun.'

'It's Patrick's,' she said. 'Now be quiet!'

Raven shifted his leg, testing to see if it was capable of holding his weight if he tried to stand. Now that the boat had turned, the vessel had become a lot more stable. It was still rising and falling alarmingly with every fresh wave, but the side-to-side rolling motion was less and it was no longer at risk of flipping over completely. He thought he might be able to stand and even walk if he had to, but for now he was content to sit.

'So,' he said, 'was it Patrick who ordered the killing of Max Hunt?'

'Stop asking questions,' snapped Scarlett.

'I'm sorry,' said Raven. 'But I'm a policeman. Asking questions is what I do. And you might as well talk to me now that I'm here.'

Scarlett stood sullenly for a minute, but Raven knew that few people had the self-control to keep silent for long. 'Pat was an idiot,' she said at last. 'Once he and Ethan got this mad idea of getting into the drugs trade, he thought he could do anything. He thought he was some kind of mafia boss. So he paid that jerk, Lewis, to carry out a hit.'

'You didn't approve of what he did.'

'Of course not! I never wanted any of that. But what could I do? I loved him, so I stood by him.'

At the wheel, Donna turned to face her daughter. 'You should have come to me, darling. If you'd told me what was going on, I could have helped. I could have spoken to Ethan, and Pat too.'

The barrel of the gun swung back to face Donna. 'Shut up, you whore! I could never talk to you! And you were sleeping with Pat! What were you thinking?'

Perhaps it was the storm that put terror into Donna's heart, or perhaps it was the possibility of a bullet in her own chest that forced her to consider the consequences of her own behaviour. Or maybe it was just years of practice at lying. Whatever the reason, she somehow managed to look contrite. 'I'm so sorry, Scarlett. Please forgive me.'

'Never!'

Raven slid along the seat, bringing himself closer to Scarlett. 'Put the gun down, Scarlett. Let's turn the boat around and get safely back to shore. We can discuss this on dry land.'

Scarlett shook her head. 'There's nothing to discuss.'

'There's plenty to discuss. Patrick's parents are desperate to find out what happened to their son. You could speak to them and explain why you killed him. They hated the fact that he was into drugs. Perhaps they would understand that you're a victim too.'

'I don't care about Pat's parents. They never liked me. They thought I was trash.'

'Well, there are other people who do care for you. Your brother, your father and your grandfather. They don't want you to come to any harm.'

The change in Scarlett's expression told him that he'd found his mark. But after a moment she shook her head. 'It's too late for that. I've gone too far already.'

'No,' insisted Raven. 'You can still stop. There's no need for anyone else to suffer.'

Scarlett's eyes clouded over with tears. She looked to Raven as if hoping he might yet save her from herself. She lowered the gun a fraction.

'That's right, sweetie,' said Donna. 'Just do what Tom

says and put the gun down.'

'No!' Donna's words reversed the work that Raven had done, and seemed to fill Scarlett with new resolve. 'I brought the gun with me for a reason, and I brought you here for a reason too.'

'Scarlett,' warned Raven.

But she took no notice of him now. Instead she clutched the pistol tightly, both hands on the grip. 'This is how I killed Patrick,' she said. 'At close range, so that I wouldn't miss and he could see me do it. And it's how I'm going to finish you.'

Raven lurched to his feet just as the next wave struck the boat. The vessel rode up high on the surge, then plunged back down like a rock rolling into a canyon. A sharp pain jolted through his right thigh and he began to fall. He staggered forwards, reaching for the gun and succeeding in locking his hands around the grip just as Scarlett's finger curled around the trigger. He tumbled sideways, pushing the gun as he went.

The weapon went off, firing wide of its target, and Raven toppled to the floor, dragging Scarlett with him. Donna screamed and released the wheel. The boat began to spin. Raven wrestled with the gun, pulling it out of Scarlett's grasp before she could fire another shot. The floor dipped beneath him as another wave rolled in, and he had a sudden vision of the boat capsizing and dragging them all to a watery grave just as he had managed to disarm Scarlett and save Donna.

'Bloody hell, Donna!' he bellowed in frustration. 'Grab a hold of that wheel and don't let go again!'

Some families were simply more trouble than they were worth.

CHAPTER 38

A gull shrieked, stirring Raven from his slumber at last. Daylight filtered through the threadbare curtains, and the time on his phone told him that he had slept like a dead man. For once, he had enjoyed the dreamless sleep of an untroubled mind.

His leg still ached, however, and he was stiff all over. He was getting too old for the kind of stunt he had pulled off the previous day. And he sincerely hoped that next time he took to the air, it would be in a comfortable seat, jetting off somewhere sunny. Not that Raven had ever enjoyed summer holidays. He couldn't see the point in lying on the beach or sitting beside a pool. Taking time off work wasn't really a skill he had ever mastered.

He swung his legs out of bed and went downstairs to wash and shave. His hair was still stiff with salt and he massaged it thoroughly with shampoo, sitting in the tub and rinsing himself with the shower hose for as long as the small hot water tank permitted. Then, after briefly surveying the limited contents of his fridge, he decided to treat himself to breakfast out.

St Nicholas' café was possibly the finest location in

Scarborough to enjoy a morning snack. Situated on the clifftop just a few yards from the Grand Hotel, it enjoyed a commanding view over the South Bay and spa. The café building was comprised of two cars from the old funicular cliff railway that had once operated here, taking tourists from the clifftop down to the beach and back up. Now the cars were fixed in place, no longer providing transport for visitors, but instead offering a fine choice of light refreshments.

Raven ordered black coffee with a Danish pastry and took a window seat.

Below him the old rail track led down to the beach. The previous day's storm had eased off, but white breakers were spilling onto the shore, throwing spindrift into the air. Gulls took to the sky, swooping and rising on the wind as they searched for unsuspecting victims to harass. This morning, Raven found that he didn't mind their aggressive behaviour half as much as usual. Their raucous cries were as much a part of the seaside experience as sandcastles, candy floss and bingo.

He took a bite out of his pastry and considered the way events had turned out. After Scarlett had been disarmed, a lifeboat had been sent out to pilot *Sea Dreams* safely back to the harbour and to return the boat's occupants to shore. Scarlett had been led away into custody, while Donna had been delivered back home to her waiting husband. It was hard to read Darren's reaction. Too much had happened too quickly for him to process. His daughter was under arrest on suspicion of murder. His son had been charged on a variety of drugs offences. His wife's sordid secrets were exposed for all the world to see. Darren had said nothing to Raven, neither thanks for saving Donna's life, nor anger for arresting Scarlett and Ethan.

Frank Jubb, however, had not been so reticent.

'You're a bastard, Raven,' he'd shouted. 'You've destroyed my family.'

Uniformed officers had restrained the old man, holding him by the arms as he ranted and raved.

'No,' said Raven. 'It wasn't me who destroyed your family, Frank. They did it all by themselves, but you're to blame. You built a house of cards and now it's all come crashing down. The dice were cast when you taught your son to cheat and lie his way through life. Once you'd done that, the rest was inevitable. Like you said, Frank, there's no such thing as luck.'

Raven hoped he would never see Frank, Darren or Donna again. He drained the last of his coffee and headed out of the café. He had a man to see about his car.

*

After all the overtime that Becca had worked during the investigation, Raven had told her to take some time off. She allowed herself to lie in for an hour, then went downstairs for breakfast. As always, her mum was busy in the kitchen, frying up sausages, bacon and scrambled eggs. Her dad was busy carrying plates through to the guests in the dining toom and Liam was sitting at the breakfast table, a mountain of food in front of him and a mug of tea in his hand.

'Morning, love,' said Sue. 'How are you feeling today?'

'Good,' said Becca.

'You caught your villains, then,' said Liam. For once, she sensed a hint of grudging respect beneath his flippant remark. Perhaps arresting a murderer and breaking up a drugs ring actually counted for something in his mind.

Becca took a seat at the table with him. 'Raven did the heroics. I just helped.' Although, she reflected, she had played a key part in the investigation. If it hadn't been for her, they might never have discovered that Ethan Jubb was paying off Leah Briggs. Jess's insight had been key too, making the connection between Scarlett's Instagram photo and Patrick's illicit visit to Gisborough Hall with Donna. And Tony had played his part, diligently following up leads and providing them with the evidence they'd needed to untangle the twisted trail of facts and follow it to its conclusion. And she couldn't forget the hardworking Holly from CSI and Dr Felicity Wainwright the pathologist either. They had all done their bit, working together as a team. Apart from Dan, that is. He would never work as a police officer again.

'So what will happen to Ethan, now?' asked Liam.

'I expect that he'll be going to prison for a long stretch,' said Becca.

'So he'll be off my back, then,' said Liam with a grin. 'I can't say I'm sorry. It'll make my life easier, although perhaps less of a challenge.' He speared a sausage on the end of his fork and began to chew.

Sue deposited a plate of food in front of her, together with a hot mug of tea, before bustling away to continue her work. Becca eyed the steaming hot breakfast thoughtfully. 'You could really have helped me out, you know, Liam,' she said.

'Yeah,' he mumbled, his mouth full of food, 'but–'

'You wanted to protect your sources,' she said. 'I get that, I think. But even an anonymous tip could have been really useful.'

'Sure.'

'And about that,' she continued. 'I've been thinking. Back when we were investigating the Max Hunt killing, we received an anonymous phone call.'

'Really?' Liam piled scrambled egg onto his fork and stuffed it into his mouth.

'Yes,' said Becca. 'It's what made us carry out the search of Lewis Briggs's house, which led to the discovery of the murder weapon. It was key to his arrest. The tip-off came from a phone box and was made by a young man who refused to identify himself.'

Liam was looking anywhere but at her. 'Oh, yeah?'

'It was you, wasn't it? Why didn't you come to me directly?'

He reached for the tomato ketchup and squeezed a healthy dollop onto the remainder of his sausage and egg. 'Really, Becs? It's not so hard to understand. I heard a rumour, and I called it in. I didn't want to answer any awkward questions. I didn't want to tell the police where I picked up my gossip. And I certainly didn't want you thinking I was mixed up with the kind of people who knew more than they ought to about gangland killings.'

She considered his explanation, trying to see it from his point of view, but she couldn't be happy about his attitude. 'The thing is, Liam, you're my brother. I need to know I can trust you.'

He wiped his plate with a slice of toast and took a slurp of tea. 'You can trust me, sis. You should know that. Anyway, my tip-off led to the guilty man being arrested, so what's the problem?'

A belligerent tone had entered his voice and Becca decided not to push it. In a way he was right. His information had helped the police arrest the guilty man. And although he obviously hung out with a lot of shady characters, there was no reason for her to suspect that he was involved in anything illegal himself. Or at least, not very illegal. She gave him a wry grin. 'All right, bro. Just make sure that in future I'm the first to be informed if you hear any more tips from your dodgy friends.'

*

'So you're sure you can get it back to me in two days?'

Raven had called the number Becca had given him, and explained his problem to the man who answered the phone. The bloke had seemed keen, but a tad unprofessional in his telephone manner. It didn't sound like he ran a proper vehicle repair shop. Now that Raven was with him in person, his worst fears were confirmed. The guy seemed to be operating out of his own home, the garage to the front of his house stuffed with oily tools and old car parts. His "workshop" was tacked onto the side of his house, in what appeared to be a flagrant breach of all known health and safety regulations. Raven was reluctant to leave the BMW in the man's care.

The bloke ran a lax eye over the scratch on the car and wiped his hands on a dirty rag. 'No problem, mate. You leave it with me. I'll take good care of it.'

'I hope so,' said Raven.

'You don't see many of these around, do you?' said the man, stepping back to admire the sleek lines of the M6. 'It's a right shame to see it so badly treated.' He gave Raven an accusing glance.

'I can assure you that it wasn't me who put that scratch there.'

'Of course it wasn't, mate. Some kid did it, eh?' The man winked conspiratorially. 'Don't worry, when I'm finished with it, it'll be as good as new. A hundred per cent. I don't do shoddy workmanship.'

Raven had half a mind to reclaim the car and take his business elsewhere, but resisted the urge. If Becca had recommended this man, he must be okay.

As he walked away, his phone rang. For a moment he wondered if it was his daughter. Hannah had eventually replied to his email the previous evening, apologising for the delay in getting back to him. Coursework at uni was keeping her busy, or at least that was her excuse. She'd sounded upbeat in her email, telling him a little news and asking after him. She'd promised to give him a call sometime.

But it wasn't Hannah calling now, it was the estate agent who'd visited the house over a week ago to give him a valuation. 'Mr Raven, I was just calling back to review options and see if you're ready to put your house on the market yet? I'd recommend moving quickly – it'll be Christmas before we know, and the market goes very quiet at that time of year.'

Raven listened patiently to the man's sales patter before giving his reply. 'Thanks for your call,' he said, 'but I've decided not to sell after all.'

*

Becca took the chair nearest to Sam and sat down, nursing a cup of hot coffee in her hands. She was glad the case was over. Now she could finally spend more time with her boyfriend. There was certainly a lot to tell him. She knew that she wasn't supposed to discuss details of the investigation with anyone, but in Sam's case it was different.

'So, Scarlett was taking pictures on her phone the whole time, even when Raven was lowered from the helicopter! She had photos of Patrick's murder too, all recorded for posterity. Apparently, she was planning to post them to Instagram, but fortunately she wasn't able to get a signal that far out from the coast. She'd lived her entire life online and she intended to die that way.'

Becca had friends who seemed to document their lives on social media, posting photos of food, pets, friends and clothes, but Scarlett Jubb really had taken it to a new level. Only the lack of a phone signal had prevented her millions of fans from being subjected to gruesome images of a real-life murder.

'It was Scarlett who sent the message to herself from Patrick's phone saying that he was going to visit Shane in Redcar,' she explained. 'It was her alibi, as well as being a distraction to send the police on a false trail. I think she knew that with Shane's record, he was likely to be arrested for Patrick's murder, or at the very least for possession of drugs. So I suppose there was an element of revenge too. She blamed Shane for getting Patrick hooked on cocaine in the first place. And I think she deliberately copied the murder of Max Hunt in order to throw suspicion on her own brother, Ethan, who was Patrick's partner in the drugs business. Everything was about revenge – her life was ruined and she wanted to take down as many others as possible. She planned it all meticulously.

'But if there's one good thing to come out of all this, it's that Gordon and Janet Lofthouse have offered to give some money to help Leah Briggs. They feel bad that Patrick persuaded Lewis to carry out a murder, and they want to use their money to make amends. So that means Leah and her daughter should be okay now that Ethan won't be paying them anymore.'

Sam said nothing in reply. His eyes remained closed, his chest slowly rising and falling as the ventilator did its work. Beside the hospital bed, his life support monitor blinked like a metronome. Heart rate. Blood pressure. Oxygen levels. All steady. There was nothing to indicate that he had heard a single word she said. But the doctors had told her there was still hope. She had to believe that by talking to him she could make a difference.

Like Raven's mother, Sam had been the victim in a hit and run accident, but unlike her, he hadn't been killed. There were times when Becca almost wished that he had. Then it would all have been over in an instant, instead of this slow-motion agony that might never end. But she felt that way only on the blackest days. On days like today, she didn't know what she'd do without him. Some of her friends thought that it was weird to carry on a relationship with a boyfriend in a coma, but Becca didn't see it that way. Sam needed her more than ever now, and the thought of abandoning him made her sick. How would Sam feel if he regained consciousness only to discover that she had ditched him? And how could she forget about him when there was still a chance he might recover?

It had been almost a year since the accident, but Becca hadn't given up on Sam.

After all, love was forever.

Her mum had started dropping hints that it was time to move on, and Liam had even tried to fix her up with a date with one of his friends. But Becca was going nowhere. Her father was the only one who really understood. David Shawcross might not say much, but his passions ran deep. 'If anything happened to your mum, I'd stand by her side,' he'd told Becca. 'No matter what.'

Becca took Sam's hand in hers, feeling the warmth and knowing that however he might appear on the outside, he was still a living human being, with hopes, dreams and memories just the same as everyone else. She didn't know how long it might take until he regained consciousness, or even if he would. The doctors had warned her that although there was hope, it was slim. But she knew that when, or if, he awoke, she was determined to be by his side.

She gripped his hand hard. There was no response and his fingers remained limp in hers. But that didn't matter. She held onto them just the same. She wasn't ever letting go.

*

Raven turned right out of Quay Street and climbed the hill. He wasn't sure where he was going, but somehow his feet seemed to have their own plan. A flight of stone steps led up to a grassy path and he followed the familiar, well-worn route that he had walked a thousand times in his youth. The muddy track led steeply upward, past the castle walls, then dipped again as he crested the headland. He passed the church of St Mary's and the grave of Anne Brontë and carried on into the town itself.

He stopped on the way and called in at a small florist, picking up a bunch of chrysanthemums – his mother's favourite. He set off again, knowing now exactly where he was headed. A long walk with another hill still to come, and no doubt his leg would be complaining by the end of it, but there was nowhere else he would rather go.

He was puffing and panting by the time he reached his destination. Two tar-black birds were perched on top of the headstone. *The eyes and ears of Odin.* They flew away with an angry *quork* as he approached.

He cleared away some old, dry flower stalks and placed the chrysanthemums in the holder. Then he stood back to admire his handiwork. Not bad. His mum would have arranged them better, but she would have appreciated the thought.

Joan Raven, born 1946, died 1991. Beloved mother and wife.

'I'm home, Mum,' he said.

It had been a long time coming, although when he'd left the town all those years ago, he'd vowed never to return. Now he was back, and it seemed that he was here for good. His path through life had been almost as twisty as the path he'd just taken to reach the cemetery. In the complex matter of human life it was often hard to pin down cause and effect, but in his own case he was pretty clear in his mind about why he'd gone and why he'd returned. Both decisions had been forced on him by events beyond his control. First his mother's death, then his father's. A broken family, twice over. But on each occasion the choice to stay or go had been his, and his alone. He didn't regret either.

He lifted his face towards the pale fleeting sun as it slid towards the horizon, casting long autumnal shadows across the grass. It would be winter soon, Raven's favourite time of year. Hot drinks, cold mornings, cosy lights indoors. It was a season for bracing walks and comfort food. Not to mention curling up in front of a real fire afterwards. There was only a gas fire in Raven's house, and it would be unlikely to pass a safety inspection, but perhaps he could get it replaced with a log burner or even an open fireplace. Already he was starting to think of it as "his" house, and to consider a future living in it. And that was something he had never expected to find in this place.

He turned and began walking back down the hill, hoping that this walk would become a regular one for him. From harbour to castle to graveyard, and back again. As long as his leg held up he would do it as often as he could.

Like those first tourists coming to the spa in search of a cure, Raven had arrived in Scarborough a broken man. And he had found healing of a kind. A painful treatment, to be sure. But an effective one. Now the cancer that had been slowly eating him from inside for so long had been excised and he was free again. Free to do what, he didn't yet know. But here, amid the stones and the trees, looking down at the town and the sea beyond, while the wind battered him and the gulls shrieked their mournful cries, he could taste freedom. And the taste was good.

BENEATH COLD EARTH (TOM RAVEN #2)

A buried skeleton. A dark conspiracy. A ruthless killer.

When flash floods unearth a human skeleton at a local beauty spot, DCI Tom Raven is called to investigate. Who is the dead man, and how did he end up there?

Help is on hand from forensic anthropologist Dr Chandice Jones who enjoys the challenge of working with old bones. But is Raven one challenge too many for her?

Meanwhile, Detective Sergeant Becca Shawcross is called to a local nursing home where an elderly resident has taken his own life. The death appears to be a routine case of suicide, but Becca has her suspicions. Could foul play be involved?

As the two investigations widen, Raven and Becca begin to find common threads. And when things take a sinister turn, they must work together to untangle the connections between the two deaths.

Because some secrets are best left buried.

Set on the North Yorkshire coast, the Tom Raven series is perfect for fans of LJ Ross, JD Kirk, Simon McCleave, and British crime fiction.

THANK YOU FOR READING

We hope you enjoyed this book. If you did, then we would be very grateful if you would please take a moment to leave a review online. Thank you.

THE TOM RAVEN SERIES

The Landscape of Death (Tom Raven #1)
Beneath Cold Earth (Tom Raven #2)

THE BRIDGET HART SERIES

Aspire to Die (Bridget Hart #1)
Killing by Numbers (Bridget Hart #2)
Do No Evil (Bridget Hart #3)
In Love and Murder (Bridget Hart #4)
A Darkly Shining Star (Bridget Hart #5)
Preface to Murder (Bridget Hart #6)
Toll for the Dead (Bridget Hart #7)

PSYCHOLOGICAL THRILLERS

The Red Room

ABOUT THE AUTHOR

M S Morris is the pseudonym for the writing partnership of Margarita and Steve Morris. They both studied at Oxford University, where they first met in 1990. Together they write psychological thrillers and crime novels. They are married and live in Oxfordshire.

Find out more at msmorrisbooks.com where you can join our mailing list.

Made in the USA
Las Vegas, NV
18 March 2023

69294927R00173